ON THIS DAY

ON THIS DAY

A NOVEL

Nathaniel Bellows

HarperCollins*Publishers*

HarperCollins books may be purchased for educational, business, or sales promotional use. For information, please write: Special Markets Department, HarperCollins Publishers Inc., 10 East 53rd Street, New York, NY 10022.

FIRST EDITION

Designed by Nancy Singer Olaguera

Printed on acid-free paper

Library of Congress Cataloging-in-Publication Data
Bellows, Nathaniel.
    On this day : a novel / Nathaniel Bellows.— 1st ed.
      p. cm.
    ISBN 0-06-051211-3 (acid-free paper)
      1. Brothers and sisters—Fiction. 2. Parents—Death—Fiction.
    3. Grief—Fiction. I. Title.
    PS3602.E65 O5 2003
    813'.6—dc21

                                    2002027272

03 04 05 06 07 ❖/RRD 10 9 8 7 6 5 4 3 2 1

ON THIS DAY

1

Some Pilgrims named these islands after animals—hogs and rats and dogs. The smallest islands are the size of small houses and have names like Breadbox and Wagon. People live on Diamond Island and Mule Island, and a boat goes between them in the morning to pick up children and take them to the bus stop on the mainland near the town launch. Monk Island has a lighthouse on its point. The light comes in my window, because our house sits on the granite cliff of Pigeon Cove. We face east toward the outstretched ocean and a chain of islands called the Seven Sisters. Joan went on a field trip for school when she was in fifth grade to one of the Sisters. Her class was supposed to collect plants in plastic bags and draw pictures of flowers and leaves on the lined pages of their notebooks. Soon after they arrived, Joan was hit in the face by a bird. A huge white seabird flew up from its nest as she was walking in the marsh. "It was being protective," their Nature Reserve guide told her.

The Nature Reserve shares Pardon Island with the Coast Guard station. The buildings stand among the ruins of an old fort, whose turrets and thick stone facades still bravely face the sea. It was a lookout station for enemy ships. I don't know when this was, or if it's true. But a stone tower does remain intact on a high hill, and a few winnowed stone walls snake along the ground toward the bluff. Pardon Island sits on the other side of the harbor; I can't see it from my window. I see the Seven Sisters, Dog Island, Monk Island, and Rattlesnake

Island. I see the rocky edge of Quahog Island through the trees. To the northeast there is Misery Island and Little Misery Island, barely in view beyond the clutter of chimneys puncturing the roof of The Chimneys, a mansion whose lawns I used to cut and whose garden topiary I used to trim, sharpening the shapes of deer and birds and bears.

Once, a classmate of mine had a birthday party on Misery Island. His father drove all of us out in his boat for an afternoon picnic. When we arrived, a group of teenagers were on the beach pouring boat fuel on a pile of trash in a sandpit. The whole place smelled like sewage. There were a few teenagers standing around a couple who lay on an army blanket. As they thrashed on top of each other, kissing and groping, the others looked on in a disinterested way. My classmate started to whimper because he was afraid of them. We all were. A few of the teenagers came toward us; they didn't care that my friend's father was our chaperon. They swore at him and laughed and threw on more driftwood, until the fire was gigantic. My classmate cried because his birthday was ruined. Back in the boat, his father yelled at him and said he was acting spoiled. All the guests—we were five seventh-graders—ate birthday cake off red plastic plates as the boat slapped against the high waves, speeding back through the channel toward the marina. We sat on flotation pillows with our backs against the sides of the boat as the bilge soaked our shorts and shoes.

Joan picked me up at the park gazebo near the marina, and when I told her what had happened she said, "It figures," because everyone knew Misery Island was where people did drugs and had sex or got raped.

I can hear Joan downstairs in the kitchen. A brown paper bag is being loudly crumpled, and I know she is tearing the top of a muffin off to heat in the toaster oven. We always fight about this because no one will eat the leftover half, the part that's still in the paper cup, and most times we're left with an oil-stained brown paper bag filled with crumbs and all these stale bottom halves. Our mother used to throw them out the window for the birds, who'd pick each muffin's paper cup clean and leave it somewhere in the yard, where it would turn up in a wad, clogging the teeth of the rake. Once, I saw one flattened, stuck like a patch to the rear tire of my father's truck. Joan brings everything home that doesn't sell at the bakery, even the things that are days beyond the half-priced or free day-old stuff. I know Joan is downstairs ripping apart a muffin—it's Sunday morning, and I hear her making coffee and unwrapping the newspaper from its plastic bag.

We're going to lunch with Aunt Yvonne this afternoon. We call her Auntie E and have since we were kids, even though it sounds strange to us now and requires some dexterity to say. She called us yesterday and told us she'd pick us up at one o'clock. Joan and I stood over the answering machine and exchanged expressions that meant *No way* and *I'm not going*.

Once, when I was twelve and Joan was fourteen, Auntie E took us out to lunch at Peking Garden on Route 1. We sat in a booth near the darkened lounge where a television was blaring a violent movie and the wait staff sat at banquet tables snapping the ends off string beans and throwing them into an industrial-sized metal bowl on the floor. Auntie E had four Mai Tais by the time we'd returned from our second trip to the buffet. She picked at the food we brought her and ashed her cigarette into her teacup. Our waiter disappeared into the lounge and ignored us for forty minutes. Auntie E became annoyed at this and banged on our glasses with her chopsticks. She really got into it—drumming on all the glasses and plates and bottles with an intensity we couldn't account for. When he finally came back to ask her to stop, she took the opportunity to act imperious and ordered another drink, a plate of fortune cookies, and four small colored paper umbrellas for us to take home as souvenirs.

At the end of the meal, Auntie E crushed the fortune cookies with the base of her water glass and read our fortunes out loud; she slurred and wept and dabbed her eyes with a napkin's corner that she had twisted into a point just for the task. She said she loved us and loved taking us out to lunch. These are *our lunches,* she'd say. We were getting so big and she knew us when we were babies and how her boys, our cousins, were men now but still her boys. Joan and I knew that her boys had moved out of the house; Nick was working in a package store and Chip was on the lam because he had just been kicked out of the police academy for possession.

Auntie E paid the check. On the way home we went through a drive-through, where she got coffee and a box of doughnuts. She told us the doughnuts were for us but we should keep them hidden from our mother. In those days, our mother did not like us eating junk.

Auntie E wants to take us to The Surf. Peking Garden closed years ago; now it's a steakhouse with a patriotic motif and a massive steer on the sign. The Surf is a seafood restaurant near our house where fishing nets filled with buoys and plastic lobsters are suspended from the rafters. An old ship's lantern with a yellow bulb hangs from a rope above the receptionist's podium and gives Auntie E, newly tanned from a trip to Palm Beach, an eerie shellacked glow. Her hair is the color of a peach—all the colors of a peach; it has the look and texture of cotton candy, a series of intricate wisps combed into place. When she leans into the lantern's beam, I can see through her hair right to her scalp, which looks polished and wet.

At our table Auntie E removes crackers from their clear plastic envelopes and arranges them around a large glob of port-wine cheese in the center of her bread plate. She pushes the plate into the middle of our table, looks at it proudly, and peers up at us, smiling, her large teeth a bank of yellow, white, cream-colored, and gray—all in a row like corn. Auntie E signals the waitress, a girl Joan and I both knew from school, by raising and tinkling the ice in her empty glass.

We enter into a conversation about Auntie E's hair because Joan has complimented her on its luster. Her friend dyes and then conditions it with a hot oil treatment, she tells us joyfully. Joan knows just how to have a conversation with Auntie E.

"Is that Grandma's ring?" she asks, in a girlish way.

"You don't know this one? It's silver, and look how it goes." Auntie E stretches out her fingers, holds up her hand, and rotates it in a small staggered circle. "It's entirely crafted from a spoon."

Auntie E's voice is gruff, like a man's, but gentle, like a man speaking to a child in a whisper. Except Auntie E rarely whispers—in fact, she's loud and laughs in quick, unexpected blasts. Her voice is rough because she smokes, but whenever she speaks to us, it is with tenderness. "It was my mother's," she explains.

She takes off the ring and slides it along the table for Joan to look at. It's a baby's spoon shaped into a ring. The bowl has been stretched backward so it overlaps with the base, adorned with a spray of engraved flowers.

"It's silver," she says, inspecting a reddish groove on her finger where the ring was.

At the funerals last winter, Auntie E gave Joan a few pieces of jewelry that were our grandmother's. Joan keeps them in a box on her desk and never wears them. She wears the spoon ring throughout lunch, however, and gets to keep it when Auntie E insists. "I have no use for it, Joan!" she moans, and she begins to cry just as the waitress—Jenny Trippit, who used to be in Joan's class and whom I knew as the girl who picked fights with other girls—comes by with Auntie E's third Manhattan. Jenny looks at Joan and me, ignoring the fact that we all know one another but seeking confirmation that the older woman we are sitting with is actually crying and wiping her face with a cocktail napkin.

Joan says plainly, "She's fine," and Jenny turns her mean, tight expression toward the other side of the dining room and walks away. Auntie E dabs her eyes and says she's sorry that she doesn't come to see us more often. She says she feels terrible. We take her hands in ours and try to comfort her; we've practiced this gesture. Her hands are soft, flecked with spots, and the nails are the color and shape of red cough drops. She peers up at us while sipping from the two thin red straws of her Manhattan. We sit this way for a while, like we're in prayer, until Jenny Trippit comes back and asks in an impatient voice if we'd like to make a selection from the Dessert Rotunda.

After lunch at The Surf, Auntie E, Joan, and I go to Marshland Nursery, the greenhouse our father owned. Everyone there knows us because, growing up, we were always hanging around, and today we're taking Auntie E in to meet Richard, Dad's oldest friend and the new owner. Auntie E is tipsy and tells him in a loud voice how healthy the place smells. Richard smiles politely and barely manages to keep from laughing in her face. I lead Auntie E into one of the walk-in freezers, and we wait as Joan picks out cut flowers from the plastic buckets on the floor. I watch a few customers on the other side of the glass doors looking at the bouquets on display. We are behind the display racks, behind a wall of flowers, where the cut flowers are stored. Joan hands the flowers she selects to Auntie E, who holds them securely against her chest like a pageant winner. Water from the flowers' stems streaks down the front of her dark red blazer. Richard offers to help Joan sort them into two separate bouquets but Joan refuses and goes about separating them on her own. I manage a vague conversation with Richard about the business, which he assures me is better than ever. We say goodbye to everyone, and Auntie E accidentally kicks over a large jade plant on the way out.

We drive back through town, telling Auntie E which way to go, past the library and the series of shingled historic houses lined up like plastic replicas against the backdrop of the ocean. We reach the town cemetery gates, and the Buick slides beneath the arched iron portico; there is no attendant in the guardhouse, so we tell Auntie E not to stop.

As we drive along the cemetery's winding paved roads, the perfectly lined rows of stones and tombs and statues pass by us like waves, a flickering rush of white and gray. All the statues are of angels or children or children with lambs or children with birds. A bald saint looks up into the trees with extended arms and upturned hands; as we pass by, his expression seems to change from beseeching to bawling. Three stone fish below him spray thin streams of water from tiny pipes hidden between their lips.

The cemetery trees are lush and full, their leaves waving high above the car; I watch them admit the flickering light through the tinted glass of the Buick's sunroof. A willow drops its leaves and seeds as we pass beneath it, and they clatter softly on the hood and windshield of Auntie E's car. She sighs loudly and puts on her wipers. Joan is sitting in front and I am in back. Her dark brown hair is pulled back in a clip and I notice, as she turns to Auntie E to direct her toward the plot where our parents are buried, a few pale yellow petals, like ash or confetti, lodged in the grooves of her thick hair.

2

Our house is falling apart without my father here to work on it. I should have paid more attention to what he was doing when he got out his tools every weekend. Joan and I manage to keep the inside clean, because our mother used to be so good about straightening up. She was good at making us straighten up the house. She wrote a schedule and put it on the refrigerator. It was a chart; I remember the day she sat down at the kitchen table and drew it up. I was eight and Joan was ten. She used a pencil from Joan's bookbag. It was funny to see her writing out the chores with a Day-Glo pencil adorned with a purple-haired plastic troll.

"I'm not getting into the *This is man's work, this is woman's work* thing with you two," she said, as she drew a rough graph. "You're old enough to decide between yourselves who does what."

"Mom!" Joan cried, in an exasperated huff. "Why do you have to say things like that?"

"Things like what?"

"The man-and-woman thing," Joan said. "We're kids!"

"Joanie, I've studied these things, the dynamics between the sexes."

We both squirmed at the word *sexes*.

"Look," she said dryly. "Just look on this list, see what needs to get done, and then do it." She wasn't angry with us; she seemed slightly defeated, as if the task of explaining housework was a difficult and disappointing thing to have to do.

Joan was pissed off. When it came to chores she usually made herself scarce; she was the type of child to step carefully, on her way out the door, over a pile of dust that had been swept up. She was the type to throw a fit when she was yelled at for her unwillingness to help, the type to whine and say that she didn't know she was expected to volunteer. I usually didn't mind helping, especially if it involved being outside and never if it involved going up on the roof—cleaning out the gutters, for instance. Because of this, I was thought to be more considerate and willing than Joan was—though I was rarely held up as an example. I had been known on a few occasions to pretend not to hear my father yelling up the stairs for someone to come down and help unload the groceries from the car. I was probably listening to the radio; I was probably engrossed in some comic book. It's not that I didn't want to help, it's just that I didn't want to go downstairs and unload groceries.

It was clear that the purpose of the chart was to bring us closer to what our parents believed was a sense of responsibility and pride of ownership. My father said to us as he explained the function of various vacuum cleaner attachments, "You'll know what it means to own and take care of something so that it lasts."

"What do we own?" I asked Joan later that day. I had my comics. I pictured my assortment of replica ships on my bookshelf, the sails torn and all the rigging frayed or missing. I thought of my clothes, but that didn't seem quite right.

"Nothing," she said, her brow pinched in a way that expressed injustice, "but they own us and we have to do what they say."

What, in fact, the chart accomplished was to bring Joan and me closer together, with toilet brushes, Top Job, and my mother's assortment of hard-to-find oil soaps. We divvied up the chores, creating a system that made sense only to us. Vacuuming the downstairs equaled taking the trash out of the shed and downhill to the side of the street; washing the windows with glass cleaner and wiping them streak-free with newspaper matched weeding the front flower beds plus raking the grass clippings. We worked it out but fought about it constantly.

The other day I came downstairs and noticed the curtains in the living room were getting brown along their lace borders. And the house smelled weird, like mold and wet dog, and all the furniture felt damp and clammy, like skin sweating. When Joan got home I told her about it, and she looked at me suspiciously. She recommended that I try to get out of the house more often; make it a goal, she said. I walked her around the house, making her inhale deeply through the nose. Finally she agreed with me that something smelled gross and unclean, so she vacuumed the couch. It didn't help. We got down on our hands and knees and lifted the couch's skirt to see if something had died under it. There was nothing but large wisps of dust and hair, which we sucked up with the vacuum's extra-long pipe extension.

Today, I notice that the smell is stronger and I'm upset that Joan is out because she would really have to agree with me; it seems to dominate the entire first floor. And now the piano seems unwell. It sounds eerie and cheap; the keys scrape together when I press them and produce a tortured, muted sound. The piano was my mother's grandmother's, and I worry that whatever force of odor and dampness has invaded the house will seep into the piano and ruin it.

My father used to sit at the piano and play. He played everything in the same minor keys, with his shoulders slumped, his feet pressing and releasing the pedals for what appeared to be no predetermined effect. I would watch him, standing at the side of the bench like a page-turner even though there was no need for one, since there were no books or sheet music. He couldn't read a note.

But he was amazing. He could play anything by ear. We would hear something on the radio or on television, and he could sit down at the piano and begin to play it. It was never exactly right, but it was close enough. It was his own way of playing it, which at first made it foreign and then gradually familiar, the way the most recognizable song can be made different, but still known, when deliberately changed in an intelligent way. His were not the most intelligent transpositions, but they were instantaneous, and in that way, in the immediacy of his creation, he astounded me.

That is, until I began my own lessons, when suddenly everything he played started to sound the same, elementary. "He's much better than I am," I told my teacher, when I imitated something my father often played.

"Hardly!" said Mr. Trego, my teacher, with a sniff. "Certainly not based on that."

Mr. Trego taught a handful of students at the Community College Music School, and I began lessons with him after my fifth-grade music teacher, Mrs. Levinson, told me to find someone outside of school. "You'll need someone with experience and patience," she said.

Mr. Trego was an older man with thick-framed glasses and sparse white hair. He scuffed around the drafty church auditorium where our lessons were held. There were two pianos in the auditorium hall; both were grand, one black, one brown. His was the black piano, though he only sat at it to demonstrate something or correct me; otherwise he sat leisurely in a folding wooden chair beside his bench. There were two small lamps with flexible necks and metal shades, one on each piano, which provided pockets of light when the sun went down beyond the pine trees on the other side of the high church windows. The lamps plugged into an orange extension cord, which ran across the large empty room and into the dark area behind the stage, where the heavy velvet curtains always remained sullen and closed.

Since Joan and I grew up in this house, we felt it was ours before it officially—legally, as of a few months ago—became so. We live on the second floor and our rooms are side by side, with views of the water and an alcove with two interior doors that join them. The house has three stories but is small, built into the cliff, covered in worn gray shingles the color of stones. On a boat, from the water, our house looks like a birdhouse caught in the upper branches of the trees that surround it. In the late autumn and in the winter the house looks bleak and sad, as if snagged like a piece of trash in the trees' bare limbs.

These trees are full now because it is summer; it is mid-August, and the shade beneath them is cold. I am walking through the yard to the mailbox; the ocean wind stirs the heavy boughs above me and their shadows move around the lawn as if they are alive. The flag on the pole near the shed is frayed and snaps loudly in the wind. "We have to take that down," Joan said the other day. "It's basically a rag."

I walk down our sloping front yard to get the mail, following a familiar yet invisible path we trudge along every winter, packing the snow into a narrow walkway down the steep field of white. I remember watching Joan amble down the path every night last December, steadying herself with her outstretched arms, as if she were in the circus.

I watched her from the window in the kitchen. There was always a truck parked on the street with its headlights turned off waiting for her. It was Mike Mitchell. She used to go with him on his late-night shifts to plow and salt the roads around town. They would drive around from twelve to three in the morning; then he'd drop her off at the bakery when she had to start work. Last winter she used to sleep for the entire day, wander around the house, and go back to bed. Then she'd get up around the time Mike's truck honked for her at the front of the house.

The mail hasn't come yet, which makes me annoyed, since it's something I live for—an unhealthy anticipation. But the trip down the lawn is worthwhile, as the weather outside is amazing. The sun is still hot and the air is heavy, textured with salt and the tacky whiffs of foam. In the open, raw air, my hands sting from the bleach I used to fix the living room curtains. I took them down to remove the brown streaks that had mysteriously appeared along their lace edges. I laid the curtains one on top of the other in the bathtub. I filled the tub and poured the bleach in. The entire downstairs of the house started to smell like bleach because I kept the bathroom door open. I was afraid the fumes would knock me out, and I didn't want Joan to find me facedown in the bathtub filled with bleach and the curtains our mother made from the lace she'd bought when she and my father went to Sweden years ago.

When I thought I'd done enough, I took the curtains out and held them up into the light. They were ruined, marked with streaks of gray and streaks of white. I don't know how this happened. I rinsed them under the faucet and wrung them into ropes. I was tempted to throw them out, but they would be too obviously missing; without them the living room looked brash and harshly lit. Joan would notice and I'd have to explain. I'd tell her before she noticed. I'd tell her that in my attempt to clean the curtains, I'd ruined them.

Our front yard has a steep pitch and a granite boulder at its center, so it's tricky to move quickly down the snow path. Mike would honk, but usually Joan knew when he was coming, and she would wait in the kitchen with her jacket on and her hood pulled over her head. If you happened to be in the kitchen with her while she was waiting for Mike, it would be silent; she wouldn't speak. It was like sharing a room with an object—a large doll keeping constant watch at the window. You could rest something on her shoulder, a utensil or an unopened envelope, and she wouldn't even notice.

Mike was afraid to come in the house because once, when he and Joan first started going out, my mother bitched him out because she had seen him in his truck on the side of the road, pulled over by the police.

"I have one daughter and one son," she said to him sternly over dinner. "I have very few things!" Joan was mortified. So was I. When was I going to ride in the truck with Mike Mitchell? What did I have to do with it?

But Mike had been uncomfortable from the moment he'd arrived at our house; he was unprepared for the scene. My mother was cooking and drinking her wine and shimmying around the room to a bebop musical interlude the public radio station used as a segue between stories. I was sitting at the kitchen table reading the newspaper and laughing at her. My mother gave Mike and Joan a flirty little wave and smile; no words just yet, because she was deep into her performance. I looked over in time to see Mike's face blanch.

At dinner I sat across from Mike and took notice of how nervous he seemed—a silence I chose to interpret as rudeness. I also noticed his strong resemblance to the elves in our favorite storybook, the one my mother had read to us every day of our childhood. His eyes were large, round, and wet-looking. His nose was thin and slightly upturned; it moved up and down when he talked, which was hardly ever. But it was distracting—that his nose moved when he talked and that he looked like these elves, only huge, more than six feet tall, and thin. He didn't smile as often as the elves in the book did (which was almost always, because they had every reason to; it was the point of the book, detailing the joyful lives of elf communities), but when he would, he certainly had an elfin grin. And over the next few weeks, as his hair grew longer, falling in many hooks around his face, it was as if he were deliberately trying to emulate the elves, because all their hair was unkempt and wild like his began to be. The first time I saw him wearing his favorite yellow felt hat with the floppy brim I blurted out, "Oh, my God!" I couldn't help myself. The elves wore hats exactly like this.

After the time with my mother, and the time when my father hung up on him because he'd called too late at night (nine o'clock), Joan didn't invite Mike to socialize with us anymore. She liked Mike and didn't want him to dump her. Joan was eighteen and had never had a serious boyfriend before.

"Are we that awful?" our mother asked, every time she suggested that Joan invite him back for dinner. "Joan, bring him around—we'll go out on the boat."

But Joan usually went out on Mike's boat, because his father had a small fishing fleet that Mike worked on. On their second or third date he'd taken her on a ride around the harbor. I saw them from my window. I watched as the boat chugged slowly along, the sun low over the Seven Sisters. I could just make out Joan's white sweater and Mike's red long-sleeved sweatshirt; I imagined he must be cold out there in just a sweatshirt, but I was intent on not caring about his comfort. Someone else was driving the boat so Mike could stand with Joan at the railing and point things out. They veered between Mouse Island and the shore. I could see Mike pointing up toward our house; I could see Joan nodding in an interested way; I could see that they were standing next to each other without much space between them. It was late in the day and the sun kept getting caught in a bank of clouds, so the light was mostly flat against the water. I could see the vague reflection of my own eyes and face in my window and a slight mist forming where my mouth was pressed almost completely against the pane.

3

I have spent my entire life waiting for Joan to come and pick me up or get ready to leave the house to go somewhere or do something. Joan is slow, and it's easy to believe, if you don't know her, that she only looks out for number one. I am waiting for her on the front lawn so we can go to the boatyard to talk to the harbormaster about our father's mooring. He called the other day to say he wants to buy it back from us and also wants to buy our father's boat. Joan is out driving around somewhere trying to find something.

I am lying on the grass of the front lawn looking up at the heavy boughs of leaves. It's five-thirty in the afternoon, so the sun is coming in at a slant through the bank of fir trees on the far side of the yard. I lie and listen to the sound of bells from buoys ringing behind me. One of the neighbors is calling their dog: *Taffy, Taffy, Taffy*. Stretched out in the cool grass beneath the trees, I notice a thin green vine climbing up and across the boulder in the center of the yard. It is almost invisible because it is a new vine, but I look closer and recognize what kind it is: trumpet, a slender version of the wild tangled trumpet vine that clogs the arbor beside the back door of the house. Every year when it came into bloom my father would praise it. "Look at it!" he'd yell, and point. He'd planted it when they first moved into the house years ago; he'd stolen the clipping from a friend of my mother's whose vine had overgrown into a dense mass, sparked with bright blossoms on the roof of her porch.

The flowers are red-orange, fluted and curled into miniature horns. My father was pleased when the vine prospered, because so many of his other projects involving stolen clippings had rebelled against him and would not grow.

＊ So now, I conclude, there will be more hummingbirds. The vine and its blooms near the house have always attracted hummingbirds, which hover in the air with a dim mechanical sound. They are luminous and weird, fast and afraid of us. "Where are their nests?" my mother asked, every time one would dart from a flower and vanish. She wanted to catch one and keep it in the house. "They're like jewels," she'd say, in a dreamy way, "and I want one."

I lift my head from the grass because I hear the train. Across the street, behind the neighbor's house, halfway up the hill, a train is slowly passing on the tracks. The train used to carry granite from our town's quarries to other towns, places where libraries and banks were in need of carved facades and decorative pillars.

I'd taken the train into the city last fall to see my father in the hospital.

I found my father sleeping in his bed. I sat in a chair beside him. Above where he lay and where I sat, a white paper bellows heaved, rose, and fell inside its glass chamber. I looked at my father's neck; the tendons resembled the roots of a tree or the webbing of a net; his gown was opened and his chest was bandaged and taped.

A nurse came in and said, "Hello, it's time to change your dressings," and my father's eyes fluttered open. He opened his mouth and wheezed, small ropes of saliva stretched between his lips and teeth. "Get out of here while she does this," he said to me. I hesitated, and he said, "Go. Seriously. You don't want to watch this." And I got up and left the room. I waited in a chair in the hallway and watched the nurses in their station talk and pin their hair back. The nurse came out of my father's room and said, "He's asleep again. I had to give him his meds early because he had a lot of pain. He'll sleep through the night, so you can just come back tomorrow." The sheets she had bundled in her hands were stained brown and gray; she clutched them to her chest with gloved hands.

Joan said, "Warren, you have to deal with those curtains. You have to put them back up." The car is in the driveway; I am still lying in the yard. Joan jumps over me and runs up the lawn into the house to get something before we leave for the boatyard. "Seriously, Warren, they're going to fly away," she calls back.

"I know." The curtains that I bleached are still hanging on the clothesline, some by only one or two pins. "But they're ruined," I say, when I hear her come down the hill toward me.

"They're not ruined. You should have left them the way they were, but they're not ruined. Just hang them back up in the living room, it's fine."

Joan would have done the same thing—maybe not ruined the curtains, but she would have tried to fix them, too. After she'd agreed with me about the stench in the house, she'd taken it upon herself to vacuum all the downstairs furniture. And she looked insane while she was doing it too, making use of all the attachments, going at the chairs and the couch like a surgeon.

It's funny that we rarely talk about these things, these improvements. Only afterward when we realize that we've failed in making anything better do we become reproachful of each other for making an effort. I had ruined the curtains, Joan had tried to remedy the strange effect the salt air had on the living room by vacuuming and cleaning with solvents and rags. We both had intended for the last six months to clear out our parents' room on the top floor of the house. But we just put it off. We failed. This is the status of the house—falling apart in ways we didn't know how to repair. For instance, the wallpaper in the kitchen has begun to buckle and peel and we walk by it every day as it sags closer and closer to the floor. We say to each other, "Look at this shit!" and laugh, as if the situation is completely out of our hands.

*   *   *

At the boatyard the harbormaster gives us a regretful look that means he's sorry for our loss, but it's disingenuous, like the smile of a drunken person. I should have paid more attention when my father took us out on his boat. This way, I would have a reason to refuse the harbormaster's generous offer.

My father had given us some lessons on how to drive and dock the boat and instructed us on the rules of buoys, running lights, and general harbor protocol. But neither of us felt any ownership over the boat—even though both of us were pretty good at driving it. Joan showed more interest than I did, and at times she was allowed to take it out with her friend Grace, because Grace's father owned a boatyard in the next town over and she'd had her own Whaler since she was ten years old. I think Joan learned to drive the boat from Grace, not from the few lessons our father provided. I think my father let Joan take the boat out because he knew Grace had experience. He'd told Joan as much, which resulted in a fight, Joan accusing him of not trusting her and him saying nothing at all and walking out of the room.

We grew up with the boat; it was part of our lives, I realize, as we sit in the harbormaster's office signing over the rights to my father's mooring and the purchase and sale agreement for the boat. We grew up going out with my father around the harbor and into the narrow canals and estuaries. How many evenings had we spent motoring through the salt marshes at high tide, my father steering and Joan and me at the stern watching for deer or egrets, our fingers trailing in the brackish water? In the fall we would go out in sweaters and scarves and he would drop us off to pick cranberries in the bogs near the Sanctuary. Sometimes my mother would come, with a basket to collect things in to take back to the house, where we would lay our findings out like a museum display on the window ledges of the sun porch. I remember going there, the rich green marsh set against the gray sky, the dilapidated piers and ruined houses we would explore as my father fished off the prow, smoking a cigarette as the boat drifted from side to side in the marsh's dark gutter.

Those images are in my head as I sit with Joan in the harbormaster's office, which is clogged with papers, cheap sailor figurines on plastic plinths, and nautical posters tacked recklessly on the wall. I have the image of our father balanced on the bench of the boat. I see him from where we played in razor grass or tide pools or on the jetty by the landing near where the marsh spilled out into the sea; he is standing like a totem, like a column, a mast of a man with his sail of smoke.

When I took the train last November to see him in the hospital room where he would remain for two or three more months, off and on, before coming home to die, the train stopped along a stretch of track that borders a familiar marsh near the Sanctuary. I was staring out the window. I was annoyed at the train because it had been stopping for no reason throughout the trip. But I was relieved, too. On the other side of the window a couple sped by in a boat, their wake a green plume. It was hard to see who they were or if they were old or young. From where I sat I could see that they both had white hair, and from that I determined that they were old. The white hair beneath their hats and the fact that they waved at us; they were probably retired, out on the boat for the afternoon. Who are they waving at? I remember thinking. I could see they were smiling; they were far away from the train but I could see they were smiling. Smiling and waving at the black reflective windows of the train, which was stopped and useless on its track. I remembered being on my father's boat with Joan, waving at the other boaters in the harbor because boating is a friendly culture. But sitting in the train watching the old couple speed off toward the ocean, I felt sad for them. Who were they waving at? At that moment there was nothing sadder to me than what they were doing, waving at a group of strangers they couldn't even see, people trapped on a train, people who couldn't care less that the couple were enjoying themselves and feeling friendly toward their fellowman.

Joan and I sell the mooring and boat to the harbormaster and leave his office, step into the cool air of the boatyard, and shake his hand. He turns from us and gives the key to a guy my age to go bring the boat out, so we can get anything that might have been left in it.

"Don't worry about it," I am surprised to hear Joan say. "There's nothing in the boat except some cushions, and you can have those or throw them out. We don't need them."

The harbormaster squints and the deep grooves around his eyes contract and release. He looks surprised at Joan's bluntness; he probably thinks she's a bitch. In his reaction to her, I realize he is sincere in his sympathy. He probably liked my father; they probably knew each other. For a second I feel angry with Joan for making the harbormaster upset or confused, for making a delicate situation harder and more awkward for us all. This was an example of something I was always having to remind myself; this loss was other people's loss, too. I don't know why Joan doesn't understand that.

Joan and I walk to the car and lean against the hood and wait. The boat, driven by the boy my age, who is small and handles the boat capably, arrives at the dock. Joan and I watch as they throw the cushions out of the boat onto the wooden dock, where they land with a hiss. The boy hauls up a rusted gas tank, a Clorox bleach bottle with its base cut off, the top of a Styrofoam cooler, and an old straw hat, wide-brimmed and bashed in on the side. It was our father's fishing hat. The harbormaster grabs it and holds it up to us, his eyes wide with meaning. He waves us over. We open our doors and wave back. There is no gesture that feels right, so we just wave and get in the car. The car is hot because the windows had been rolled up while we were in the harbormaster's office. The vinyl seats burn the backs of our legs and we both say, "Shit!" and look at each other. We are crying, facing forward in the front seat of the car, staring out over the masts of the boatyard with their snapping flags and ropes and bells, with their tightly rolled sails zipped into slim canvas sheaths.

4

Last summer was when we got the news. Actually, when *I* got the news—I got it before Joan, but I immediately told her because I didn't want to be alone with the knowledge and didn't want her to be in the dark, even though she might have preferred it. My reasoning was this: If I know, we both have to know.

I came home from being out at night with my friend John and his sister, Cindy. The house was quiet. The foghorn was sounding and, as always, the bells were ringing off the water, but otherwise the house was quiet and I thought no one was home. Where was Joan? I remember wondering.

A light was lit on the sun porch and a strange noise was coming from where it sat on a table, reflecting itself on the three windowed walls of the room. I went out to the porch. It was a nice night; the warm summer air had not yet been replaced by autumn's metallic scent. My mother was sitting on the sun porch with all the windows open, wailing—that is the perfect word for the sounds she made. The wind was coming in through the windows and was blowing the sheer white curtains around; their rings were softly clicking as they slid along the wooden curtain rods.

I was glad Joan was not with me. My mother sat drunk in the wicker rocker. She could barely speak; she gurgled like a blocked sink. I had been out for three hours, and while I was out she got completely hammered. How did this happen? Where was Joan? I wished I knew, so I could call her and tell her to stay out until I got my mother up to bed. My father was at the nursery and would probably not come home for hours. No, he was probably fishing or working on the boat. It turned out that he was at the nursery.

"OK, Mom, let's go upstairs. I'll get you some water and aspirin. You have to sleep now so you won't feel like crap tomorrow."

"Sit down, sit down," she slurred, and she wagged her hand toward a metal-framed patio chair across from her. Four moths circled and slapped against the lamp's white shade. It was strange for these moths to be here, I thought. How have they survived?

I stood over my mother and told her, "No. Let's go upstairs." I didn't know what else to do. I started to order her around; I was sounding mean. "Come on, Mom," I said sternly.

"No. You sit there," she said slowly, raising her head toward me, her eyes firmly shut. Then she suddenly opened her eyes up wide and said, "Pop!" and laughed in an unsettling way. It was something a child would do to act cute. It was something Shirley Temple would do, and it freaked me out.

"Jesus, Mom. Come upstairs. Now."

But she wouldn't go upstairs with me; she shook her head and told me again and again, no.

I couldn't help thinking of our old dog, Peanut. She used to act this way because she hated to go in the car. I'd try to pull her by her collar but she wouldn't budge. She would plant her hind legs on the ground and try to dig her claws into the driveway. "Come on, Peanut!" I would yell at her. She had the worst look on her face when I tried to get her in the car, like she was afraid of me and I was going to hurt her. My mother looked up at me with the same expression, except in place of fear I could see that she was angry. And I was afraid of her. Her head lolled back and forth; her mouth was slack. With Peanut it would eventually take two of us to pick her up and haul her into the back, where she would cower against the seat and whimper. Or she would hide on the floor.

My mother was staring at the floor and had started to cry. I sat down in the metal-framed chair across from her.

"You can't. . . . oh, shit . . . I hate this." She tried, but she was so drunk she couldn't speak. She couldn't make any words. I thought to myself, This is what she will be like when she is old and losing her mind.

"You've poisoned yourself, Mom. The only thing you can do is go to bed. Let's go." I was afraid she would accuse me of acting like my father, even though I was making more of an effort to sound kind.

She shook her head; her hair was matted on one side of her face. The skin on that same side was indented with the wicker pattern from the chair. She would not get up. In my helplessness I wondered if I could really carry her upstairs on my own.

Later, I tried to. My fingers dug into the soft folds of her back and got caught in the wide band of her bra. She couldn't stand, so I held her hand and wrapped one arm around her waist. I could feel her skin punching out over the top of her jeans. It was cool from her being out on the porch all night. She didn't know what was going on, but she was aware enough to resist and try to fight her way out of my grip. I walked her out of the sun porch and into the living room. When she caught sight of the staircase she braced herself against the wall and forcefully pushed me away. She bent down low from the waist and stayed hunched over for ten minutes.

"There's so much pain in my legs," she moaned. I stood beside her, completely confused. I could barely make out what she was saying, because she was speaking into the floor.

"Did you take some kind of medication, Mom?" The idea suddenly occurred to me. I figured a mixture of alcohol and pills had ruined her. I had only been gone for three hours.

She swayed beside me, bent over at the waist and tottering. I tried to pull her up, but she swatted me away. "My legs are locked up and there's so much pain."

I didn't know what to think. I thought she was lying. While I was gone, how had she gotten so drunk and developed leg pain? I'd never heard this complaint from her before. Where was Joan? Did she know that Mom had leg pain?

My mother straightened up and looked at me. Her eyes were flat, no dimension to speak of. They were like a doll's, and so was the rest of her face, slack and white as lard. She fluttered her hands at me and moved away from the staircase where I had led her. She slammed into the wall next to the bathroom and rolled into the door to push it open. "Mom, please!" I heard myself whine. She shut the door in my face.

She wouldn't come out of the bathroom, and I wouldn't open the door even though she had not locked it. She turned on the fan and I could hear her jewelry clinking against the porcelain of the toilet. She was coughing and spitting into the bowl. The shadow under the door was large, so I knew she was lying on the floor. I knew that she would pass out on the tiled floor of the bathroom. I was afraid to open the door and find her naked or covered in vomit. Regardless of what was happening, I could not go in. I waited patiently on the other side of the door. This was a rule. She used to take baths all the time. She would lie for hours in the tub and we were not allowed in, even as children. We spoke to her from behind the door.

"Mom, you can use the bathroom upstairs." I was whining again. I felt embarrassed because I knew I was sounding like a child; I felt ashamed that I was not managing to act like an adult.

Before I led her to the staircase, before she had shut herself in the bathroom, she was crying on the wicker rocking chair and I was sitting across from her. She was crying and dragging her fingers across the bottom ridge of her eyes to wipe them. "I want to talk to you," she stammered, trying to focus on me sitting three feet away.

"What do you want to talk about, Mom?" I said bitterly.

Her mouth was opening and closing like a fish's, no sounds.

"Shit, I hate this." Her head fell back and she snapped it up. "I hate this."

"Mom, you're hammered, let's just go upstairs and get you in bed. I would feel much better if I knew you were up there, safe in bed." This was more pleading than whining. My tone was measured but desperate.

"No. I have to talk." This took two minutes to say. "About things I can't normally say." This took four minutes.

My heart sank. She did this a lot, divulged horrible details of her life to us when she was drunk: her childhood living on a large estate with lots of money, and then no money and cruel alcoholic parents who abused her and her siblings and made them feel worthless. I knew many stories about these people and had a hard time, when they were alive, being around them when we went to their houses for holidays.

"About what? To whom?" I said quietly.

She looked over at me, her mouth in a tight frown designed to keep herself from crying. "To you," she mewed.

I couldn't help it. I leapt up. "No, Mom, no. I can't hear this. I can't help you with this! There's nothing I can say about any of it!" I was on my feet and pulling at her arm to get her out of the chair. She started to cry again, holding on to the arm of the chair to keep me from yanking her to her feet. I was pulling at her hard.

"No!" she shrieked and held on tighter; her hand was red against the white wicker. "No! Let go of me!" she screamed, and she looked at me through the net of sweaty hair that had spread itself across her face. "You, let me go!"

"Mom, please!" This is when I started crying. I had become a baby, unabated.

"No!" she wailed, tears rolling down her face. It was like I was attacking her. She was shouting, "Please! Please!"

I didn't want to listen to her. I let go of her arm; my hands were wet and red.

I sat back down in the chair and cried.

I looked up at her and her eyes were closed. I thought she had fallen asleep. I thought about whose bed I would strip to make a place for her to sleep here on the floor or the couch.

"I'm so worried about your father," she said, with sudden frightening clarity. "He won't tell you two." Her voice trailed off and she started to heave.

"What?" Shut up, I thought to myself.

"He knows he's sick and knows his situation—" She raised her palms to her face.

"What are you talking about? Mom, can we please go upstairs?" My face was hot and I caught my reflection in the window across from where I sat; it was grotesque, distorted in the antique, swirled panes of glass. My eyes filled with tears again and my throat was raw. "What are you talking about?"

"Soon."

John and Cindy were going down to the beach because Cindy's friend worked at Twin Lights, and she was known to give out free ice cream. John had called and told me to meet them at the flagpole in the center of town near the wharf. I had planned to be gone for three hours, so that I could be home before nine to watch a television show about how cathedrals were built in the Middle Ages.

Cindy had just gotten their mother's old car as a graduation present. Cindy had a bad reputation.

When I got to the flagpole, Cindy was sitting on the hood of the green car in cut-off jean shorts and a child-size T-shirt with a glittery pink kitten on it. She was smoking and making flapping noises with her sandals against the hard skin on the soles of her feet. John was in the passenger seat playing the radio, flipping around the stations.

Walking up to the car, I noticed that Cindy looked pretty; her hair was bleached from the sun and tied back in a ponytail. She was tan in the way that high school girls tan, a smooth transitionless brown, a summer project. The sun was starting to go down behind the shops, and the late-summer light came through the spaces between the buildings in bands of orange and gold. All around the square, the shops, benches, porches, and flower beds glowed richly, as if it were sunrise, or as if somewhere close by a fire blazed.

"Hi," I said.

Cindy held out a stick of gum toward me and John looked up out of the passenger seat with an amazed expression, as if he were surprised to see me. His eyes glowed like pilot lights because he was looking at me, unflinchingly, and directly into the sun.

"Hey!" he said, in an excited way.

"Come for the free ice cream?" Cindy said to me. "Free ride, free ice cream. Nice life." She smirked. "What else did you come for, Warren?" She smiled at me and stuck out her tongue. "Hah!" She laughed. "I can give you shit if I want."

"There was the best thing on the radio, Warren, and now I can't find it—it's this thing." John always used the word *thing,* ending his sentences in an unfinished way. He turned the knob of the radio slowly, listening closely to the speaker in the door. "It was awesome, the best thing from—"

"Can we go now?" Cindy said impatiently.

"Let me just find it. Warren, you'll love it. It's on the science show."

John was a good friend of mine. Actually, I didn't have many friends besides him. Of course I had Joan, and maybe Mrs. Caldwell from my job at the library, but John was, I suppose, my best friend. But I didn't want Cindy to associate me too closely with how much he irritated her, so I tried to get him to drop it.

"It's OK, John, let's just go," I told him.

"Wait a sec," he urged. "Let me just find it again."

Cindy rolled her eyes and vaulted herself off the hood. "Forget it, Johnny, we're listening to my mixes."

We all got in the car.

"What's on them? What's on your mixes, Cindy?" I was shouting because by then I was in the backseat of the car and felt far away from the action up front. The car was as wide and long as a boat. The fabric that covered the interior was coming loose all over the place; it sagged from the ceiling, hung down like a tent children put up in the yard to spend the night in.

John and Cindy lived on the "Site," a shabby inland military base on top of the hill off Route 1. Their father was in the air force, except he didn't fly planes; he repaired them. Their house was one of hundreds of identical houses—a single-story ranch with a slanted corrugated tin roof that extended out over the driveway, creating a makeshift garage. In back there was a wide field of rough yellow grass and a broken-up landing strip where planes would land in the late afternoon. We would go through a tear in the backyard fence and along a tamped-down path of grass and weeds to watch the planes come in.

We got our ice cream, and John, Cindy, and I sat for a while on the hood of the car near the beach, listening to songs Cindy spent her afternoons taping off the radio. We drove around, and I listened to John and Cindy fighting in the front seat. John teased her about how crappy the recording was and she just told him to shut up, over and over again. Anita, Cindy's friend, was going to come with us, but she had to stay and close the store. Cindy teased me. "Are you sad that Anita couldn't come with us, Warren? Keep you company in the backseat?"

"Not really," I said. "I think there are some rats back here that are keeping me company."

"Shut up, Warren!" Cindy said.

"Hah!" John laughed and turned around and gave me a look of admiration. "Clean your car, Cindy."

"You can't have a ride home now," Cindy announced, and she

smiled at me wickedly through the rearview mirror. I knew what she was doing. "You can walk home—you've done that before. We're going home and when we get there, you can walk home on your own. How about that?"

John looked at her, confused but not bothered. He didn't know what she was talking about.

"Fine with me," I said cheerfully.

"Good," she said.

I wanted to stay out with them; I wanted to do something; I didn't want to go home. I knew what lay in store for me there—my mother listening to records in the living room, the lights low, drinking wine and eating tasteless crackers from the health food store, waiting for my father to come home from wherever he was. Maybe Joan would be there, up in her room doing her hair in an endless variety of hairdos—always on the phone. I was thinking we could go to the quarries or the wharf. It was a nice night; we had all the windows open because it still felt like summer. We weren't doing anything, we were just driving around, but I was having a good time—it had been awhile since I had been out like that. I said, "Let's go to the quarries. Let's go to the wharf." But they were just going to go home; they would drop me off; they didn't want to stay out and do anything, find anything to do.

"Come on, you guys," I pleaded.

"Sorry, but she wants to go home," John said regretfully, looking at Cindy as if she was the cause of all misery.

"Shut up," Cindy said.

They dropped me off at the end of the driveway and left, bickering. Walking up to the house, I noticed no lights were on in front, so I figured no one was home. I looked at my watch. I was in time to see the show I wanted to see about cathedrals. I began to feel happy that I would be able to watch TV alone in the house. Then, as I walked into the kitchen, I heard a strange sound and saw the sun porch light was on.

5

In October our town has a parade, and every year I wake up to the sound of a marching band coming across the water. The horns and flutes and muffled beats of the drums seem to be in perfect time with the bells and boats and quiet slapping of the waves against the granite cliffs below our house. The first time I heard the music I looked out my window and saw the flat-bedded ferry, the one that takes cars and trucks up the coast, circling the harbor at a steady crawl. A fully uniformed marching band with shining buttons and white plumes in their hats was marching in tight formations around the deck of the boat. At the front of the band were three girls in yellow leotards twirling batons and two boys waving triangular-shaped flags. They had no space to perform, so they just snaked in and out or went around and around in a circle.

This morning I heard the marching band and saw the ferry motoring around the harbor. It was windy and the batons that the girls spun flew into the water and disappeared. The girls ran to the side of the boat and peered helplessly into the green water where feathers from the caps of the musicians and sheet music floated, gathering like trash in the boat's wide wake. The song the band was playing was upbeat; it had a lot of drumming and horns, so it was nice to wake up to. Joan had come into my room and asked if I wanted to go into town to see the parade.

*   *   *

"My memory doesn't go that far back," Joan says, as we cross the bridge that arches over the train tracks.

I was asking her if she remembered the time when we were young and our parents took us down to the fall parade. We were so small we both fit in the wheelbarrow together. Thinking about it now, I can't imagine that it happened—the idea seems absurd and not something my parents would participate in: the two of them walking along the road with a wheelbarrow filled with their children. On second thought, it makes sense if it was my mother's idea. My father would be against it. But if she won the argument, there's a chance it might have happened; it could have. That was an aspect of the memory that I thought could be speculated upon with Joan's help.

We were small and wearing knit sweaters our mother had made, and our father pushed us down the sidewalk. Our mother walked behind or beside us and held our hands or rewrapped our scarves. We went down to where the parade was and everyone loved that we were in a wheelbarrow, and our parents laughed in a surprised way, as if noticing for the first time what a strange sight we all were. I remember not understanding why people laughed at us. In my memory there was snow on the ground, which couldn't be true because it was fall. Then I thought I was confusing it with a cookie tin Auntie E had brought to our house one Christmas. The picture on the tin was of a family huddled together in a sled, and the sled's blades dug deep rifts in the snow. For some reason I imagined the wheelbarrow leaving a trail behind us, a trail in the snow as we were wheeled into town.

That's why I asked Joan if she remembered it the way I did, but she wouldn't answer.

We walk slowly toward town. From the highest point of the concrete bridge, we can see the town common and all the floats lined up along the boulevard. The band that was out on the boat is now safely crammed into the common's gazebo, twenty or more uniformed band members, some of them sitting on the railings and steps, wearily playing the last of their numbers for the day. There is a large crowd on the lawn, picnicking on blankets or sitting in beach chairs with thermoses, children, and umbrellas.

There are probably more than a hundred people down there—more than *two* hundred people, I think to myself. We're going to have to deal. I look at Joan as she stares down on the scene. "We're going to have to deal," I say.

"I know," she says in a distant way, looking out beyond the parade through the trees to where the water is a brilliant blue between the spaces of changing leaves.

I think Joan is lying when she says her memory doesn't go back that far. We both remember everything. We've had contests to see who could remember what, when. We've re-created entire holiday gatherings, down to people's outfits and food. Car-ride conversations. We used to sit around and talk about things that had happened. But she's not willing to talk about these things anymore. Instead of telling me that she's not willing to talk about these things, she lies to me and says she doesn't remember them.

"Think about it, you have to remember. We were little and they put us in the wheelbarrow? We had on our sweaters." I say this clearly, walking her carefully through the image.

"Warren, please," Joan moans.

The sound of the crowd gets louder as we near the bottom of the hill. Someone is on the PA system announcing the results of a raffle. The announcer is a man who works at the church. He was at both funerals; he read the same two psalms at both services in his large booming voice. Today, with the aid of the microphone, he sounds even mightier, except there is feedback, so his effort is undermined.

Joan is tense—from the corner of my eye I see that her jaw is clenched. Our eyes are in sync, darting around. People are moving about at different speeds, children on the run and parents lurching behind them. A few old people are being wheeled around in their wheelchairs.

We turn as a unit, like Rockettes, to watch as the winner of a gift certificate for dinner at the yacht club is announced. It's the easiest thing to do—participate in the occasion, just stand and watch.

"The winner is Mike Mitchell! Mike Mitchell is the winner! Come on up and get your prize, Mike!" The man's voice blares over the speakers and he waves his hands around, showing impressive sweat circles beneath his arms.

Joan's mouth falls open. We both see Mike appear out of nowhere in the crowd and watch him angle his way up the gazebo steps to the podium. He has cut his hair short and his face is tanned. I think about Joan bawling in her room last winter when he left, how she would come into my room and sleep in my bed with me because she didn't want to be alone. She would cry and cry and cry. And I'd say, Don't cry, Joan, it will be OK. And she'd wail, What do you know, Warren? How would you know?

Joan grabs my hand, digs her nails in. "No way," she says. "Fuck. No the fuck way."

We stand holding hands in the crowd.

I realize that people have begun to recognize us. They are looking and making sympathetic frowns in our direction. We stand like one statue, fused. A woman I work with at the library comes up with two paper cups of cider, which I manage to fit into one palm, and says, "Hi, Warren. Have some."

"Thank you," I say.

Joan is in shock because Mike Mitchell has won the raffle. Because Mike Mitchell is not in Washington state, where he said he'd be, indefinitely, last January when he left Joan in the driveway in front of our house. I remember seeing her from the kitchen window, standing between the snowbanks in the streetlamp's light, flurries swirling around them. Mike had taken her hood down to kiss her, and the whole time she just stood in front of him in shock. Then he got in his truck and drove off. I watched as she ambled up the snow path, banged the snow from her boots on the porch steps, took off her coat and boots in the mud-room, and went up to her bedroom for what seemed like forever.

I search my memory to see if there really was snow on the ground when we rode in the wheelbarrow. The image is getting vague. Some other people come up to us to say a few kind words. We are holding hands. People must wonder things about us, I think.

I'd thought the whole town came to the funerals. But now I realize that the people near the cannons were not there. The children by the picnic tables did not attend. The band was not there, in full regalia, playing a mournful song with plangent horns and a flute solo that would have risen high and reassuring, like a bird's song over our heads. That would have been nice. That might have helped. Mike Mitchell was not there. He had left, indefinitely. Joan and I were there. Both times, we sat in the same pew. We walked out to the hearse with our arms linked, carrying the lace throw that had covered the box of ashes and the casket, respectively. I remember because it was not even a year ago. Joan remembers too; we've talked about it. Together we could re-create the entire scene, every minute detail, down to the flowers floating, stemless, in the fonts.

Joan always got so worked up because Mike would make plans with her and then blow her off. This was in the beginning of their relationship, around the time when my father was going into the city for tests and my mother was carving out her custom-fitted place at his side. I remember being annoyed at Joan, because given the choice between feeling worried about our father and nervous about whatever upcoming date she had with Mike Mitchell, she was nervous.

Both our parents encouraged us not to worry. They both worked overtime to make us feel that everything was going to be OK. In hindsight, I realize they did this by withholding key bits of information. My mother said to me back then, "If there's a problem, we'll deal with it."

And I said, "I know we will, but what kind of problem could it be?"

And she said, "We don't know yet, but it's going to be our problem—your father's and mine."

"Can't it be my problem, too, and Joan's?" I asked, thinking that she'd laugh gently in a comforting way and say, "Of course, of course!"

"You have enough problems!" my mother barked, and then she chuckled.

"Mom!"

My feelings weren't hurt; it was funny. She did things like this all the time; this was her sense of humor, astute and sudden, a wiseass. She knew I could handle it; it's how she'd attempted to raise us— with a tougher skin than she had. It was her way of not having me worry; it was also her way of not telling me anything.

Joan lets go of my hand and grabs it again. I sense that she is getting riled up, looking around frantically, searching the crowd. Mike has disappeared; she is panicked. Oh, God, I thought, let the games begin.

In the past, sometimes Mike wouldn't even show up for plans he'd made with Joan. And it was not because he was doing something with someone else. He was usually doing nothing, all alone. This drove her crazy. One time I was riding my bike back from the library when I saw him turn his truck up one of the roads that goes through the woods to the quarries. I followed him because I was convinced he was going to shoot up heroin or do something equally illegal and disturbing.

He parked his truck in a clearing where there were a few other cars. Mike was wearing jeans and a faded green T-shirt that had a dark line of sweat down his back, from being pressed against the driver's seat of his truck. He had a glass bottle in a paper bag, which looked like it was whiskey. But it was juice. He placed the crumpled bag carefully on a pile of garbage that was spilling over from inside an old oil drum. I sat on a rock fifty feet from Mike, who faced the wide misshapen mouth of the quarry. He couldn't see me because I was behind him, camouflaged by some low branches. Before long I grew bored with watching him. He wasn't doing anything bad that I could report or keep secret. He just sat there, looking out at the quarry, occasionally throwing an acorn in the water.

When I got home Joan was upstairs in her room playing the radio. I came in and dove onto her bed, which she'd just made in her perfectly taut way.

"Warren, don't ruin it!" she yelled, and rushed over to smooth the blankets.

"What's wrong with you?" I asked.

"Mike and I had plans to go swimming at the quarries," she huffed. She was wearing a pair of jean shorts over her bathing suit. Her toenails looked wet but had actually been polished with clear lacquer.

"Really," I said.

"But he totally blew me off," she said in a teary chirp, her eyes immediately releasing two large tears that seemed to spring from her face like a cartoon character's.

"When?" I suddenly felt weird because I, in a way, had spent the afternoon with Mike at the quarries.

"Like, three hours ago," she mewed. "He said he'd pick me up at one o'clock." Her clock radio said four fifteen. "But the fucker never showed up," she said, putting on her sweatshirt and zipping it up.

"What an ass," I said. It was a bit after one o'clock when I'd cagily taken my place behind the branches to observe his uneventful afternoon.

Joan and I escape the fall parade in a few quick maneuvers through the crowd and go back to the house, where we sit in the kitchen and snack. There's nothing of substance in the cabinets or refrigerator, so we end up eating strange things: saltines, Tootsie Rolls, and cheese, and we drink tonic water with lime. Joan is glum.

"What are you thinking about?" I ask.

"What do you mean, what am I thinking about?"

"What do you think about seeing him?"

"I can't believe he's back, is what I think."

"Me neither," I say. She's miserable all over again. "It's a major surprise for each and every one of us."

Joan looks at me bitterly. I look back at her, shrug, and pop another piece of cheese in my mouth.

"Did you know he was back, Warren—had you seen him around?" she finally asks, desperately.

"No."

"No one told you?"

"How would I know? Who'd tell me?"

"I don't know, I'm just asking. It's so weird." Joan settles against the back of her chair and sulks.

"Are you mad because he didn't call you?" I ask, knowing how idiotic it sounds but feeling justified, for some reason, in torturing her with ridiculous questions.

"No! Warren, think about it! Yes! Jesus, I haven't seen him in months. I thought he was gone for good! " Joan looks at me with her mouth open, sneering, and shifts around in her chair.

"How long has he been back?" I have to control myself to keep from smiling. What she doesn't realize is that she hates him. Or at least she did the last time I checked. Where was he in your time of need? Where was he for us? Washington state, lady. I don't care. She's acting stupid.

"Shut up! I just saw him for the first time! You were with me!"

"Oh, OK. I didn't know if you'd seen him before."

"Why are you being such a fucker?" Joan cries out.

"I'm not!"

6

On Halloween, it was always my mother's tradition to hand out fruit or some other healthful snack to trick-or-treaters instead of candy, which we always found embarrassing and lame. This year Joan and I decide not to hand anything out to the children who come to our house. We keep the lights turned off to make the house look unwelcoming. But they still come. We watch them amble up the driveway in their different costumes. We ignore their knocks. Some of their parents urge them to knock again, to give us a chance to get to the door in case the TV is on. One child, hidden inside an appliance box, which is spray-painted black with green numbers and an antenna protruding from his shoulder, walks around the house and peers in the windows. From where we crouch behind the window on the second-floor landing, we cannot tell what his costume is. Is he a cell phone? Next come two small girls in white leotards with wings made of coat hangers and plastic wrap. They open the mail slot with their small fingers and call out, "Joan? Joan?"

"This is weird," Joan says, as we hunch in the dark. "This is something perverts would do."

"No it's not. We didn't get any candy to give to them," I say factually.

"You know what I mean."

We sit on the landing for a while in silence. There is a lull in activity outside, no feet on the porch. What we are doing is not perverted, it is stealthy, fascinating, and educational. This allows us to see how people are living in the world, which is what we have to learn. Why doesn't Joan see the usefulness in that?

"About time! Look at her!" Joan says with elation. "She's a frickin' flapper!" The girl is seven or eight, wobbling precariously up the driveway in high heels. "Wow, a real flapper," Joan says with admiration.

"Or a hooker," I add.

"Warren!"

"What. She could be."

"OK. Actually, you're right. She does kind of look like a little hooker."

"A little hooker!" I raise my arms up in triumph.

"Shhhhh! Jesus, Warren!"

As the little girl comes up the driveway, we notice that her dress is not like a flapper's, because it has too many sequins and not enough fringes. She looks more like the kind of singer who performs on a cruise ship. Still, we can tell that she is supposed to be a flapper—she wears a tight pleated hat and the curl of her hair flips out from under it. Someone has put makeup on her in a 1920s style: miniature red lips painted over her mouth, black fluted lines framing her eyes, a heavy dot for a mole on her cheek. The girl is with a young boy who is dressed, less ambitiously, as a cowboy; he has a felt cowboy hat, a handkerchief tied around the neck, and a plastic holster.

"Don't they see the lights are off?" I whisper. "There's no one home!"

"They're greedy." Joan says. "They want their candy."

After a few minutes of knocking, the flapper and cowboy give up and walk back down the driveway to a car that waits for them by the mailbox. I feel bad for them. The boy's pillowcase appears to be only half full. I imagine the girl stows her loot in the evening bag she hangs in the crook of her arm. It shimmers under the streetlight because it is covered in beads. Up close the pattern of the beads forms the intricate shape of a bird perched on a branch surrounded by leaves and clusters of fruit. The handles of the bag are made of lacquer, which click together with a tiny hidden clasp. Joan and I recognize it from where we peer down on to the scene. The bag had been our mother's. A few months ago, in our latest-ditch effort to clean out the house, we had given it to the Salvation Army along with the rest of her clothes.

7

When my father was not doing well—that was the phrase for it, the term for his condition: *not doing well*—my mother was not doing well either. One night last fall we were having dinner together and she was telling us about her day at the hospital.

"He's mean as a snake. His meds make him that way." Her voice expressed an exhausted pride. She had just gotten home and changed into her favorite pink robe.

"Mom, when can Dad come home?" Joan asked. We were eating on the sun porch and the windows were open. It was a mild night, even though it was at the end of November. The warm weather worried everyone because they thought it was a symptom of a larger environmental problem. This is what they were saying on the news. We had been watching it on television in the kitchen while we heated up dinner and my mother sat at the table and had her wine. "Don't talk to me about symptoms," she told the female meteorologist, who was gesturing toward a computerized map of the world.

We ate leftovers from Thanksgiving. Auntie E had wrapped them in dozens of tinfoil packages and sent them back with us. She'd hosted the holiday because my mother wasn't up to it.

"Daddy had turkey on his plate for Thanksgiving," my mother said in a baby voice, which was the voice of three glasses of white wine. We knew he'd had turkey, because we went to see him with our mother before we went to Auntie E's.

At the hospital, the orderly came in with a tray. On the tray was a large plate, a small plate, and a plastic cup with a bendable straw. In the center of the large plate was a piece of turkey, pulverized and gray, with brittle orange skin. On the edge of the plate a mound of cranberry sauce bled a bright red stream of juice into the mashed potatoes, sullen and sturdy in a whipped yellow blob. Some mysterious greens fanned out at the bottom of the plate, boiled to the point of near invisibility. On the small plate sat five or six candy corns.

At this point in my father's illness, he needed someone to cut his food, load the fork, and put the fork in his mouth. My mother did this with eager promptness as Joan and I sat in chairs on the opposite side of the bed. Joan held the plastic cup and handed it every now and then to our mother, who would hold it up to our father's face and angle the straw into his mouth.

At Auntie E's house the dining room table was crammed with dishes, a few different pieces from a few different sets. Auntie E was in the kitchen scrutinizing a Pyrex dish of yams as it spun in the microwave. Her best friend Linda was washing out an ashtray in the sink. Both of them were wearing leather pants.

My cousin Chip was in the TV room watching football with his friend Mark. Auntie E's boyfriend, Terry, sat on a couch and clutched a pale orange drink in a stout glass. He chewed ice loudly and said "Hey, kids!" when Joan and I walked in the room.

The odors in the house were of the cooking food, cigarettes, cologne, and sweat. I noticed that the hallway bathroom door was wide open and the fan was running loudly. It was frightening to think about what had gone on in there. An aerosol can of air freshener stood on the toilet tank and was visible from where I stood in the TV room. That piney-flowery scent was another smell in the myriad odors I was cataloging in my first ten minutes at Auntie E's.

The good part about this, I thought, is that Joan is here; we're together. Because no sooner had we arrived than our mother was wearing oven mitts and mixing it up with Auntie E in the kitchen, giving her a hard time for using iceberg lettuce (no nutritional content) in the salad and aerosol-whipped cream on the store-bought pies. Linda kept coming into the TV room with various snacks. "Who's winnin'?" she asked every time she came in. Chip and Mark told her each time, "It's just the pre-game show."

During a commercial Chip asked us about our father, and Joan said, "He's OK. We think he'll be home for Christmas."

She looked at me for support.

"Yes," I said. "Home for the holidays."

The screaming electric guitar solo from a truck commercial filled the otherwise silent room.

Chip said distractedly, "So, probably Christmas? He'll be out, we'll see him then?"

"Who's he?" asked Mark, who hadn't been listening.

"Their father. He's been in the hospital for a couple months."

"Only one and a half," Joan said, but they had turned back to the TV. The pre-game show was back on and a dance number had started up. Someone in a red furry eagle suit was running around riling up the crowd; every so often he came up behind one of the cheerleaders and wrapped his wings around her waist.

"Thank you, Lord, for everything you've given us," Auntie E intoned at dinner, her round tinted glasses reflecting the ten-bulb chandelier so she looked like a fly with faceted eyes. "Thank you for this food and our time here with each other." She looked around at us with her fixed, toothy grin. "Thank you for all our good fortune. And hopefully the Pats will pull it out for another win this year!"

"Yeah!" Chip and Mark exclaimed loudly.

After dinner everyone crowded into the TV room to watch the game. I asked my mother if Joan and I could go for a walk to get some air. "Don't be snobs, you two," she said, with a disappointed smile.

We went down the street, through the entrance of the state park, into the woods. It was twilight; the sky was gray and it was windy. We walked along the path toward the marsh. We used to come here when we were children, when my cousins were younger and liked to show us around their town. As we walked, we talked about Thanksgiving. Joan talked about Auntie E's weird hair and the unfortunate flattening effect Linda's leather pants had on her ass. I pointed out how Chip had no neck and how his left eye wandered uncontrollably all around the room when he talked. I briefly mentioned how the plumbing system in the house must be in peril. Joan said something about BO. By then we had reached the end of the trail and the marsh opened up before us.

The wide flat land was carved with gullies where thin streams of water barely flowed. The marsh grasses were red and brown and every shade of yellow, shifting around us. Mud sucked at our shoes; it had the rich smell of dirt, roots, and nests. Dead trees stood in staggered ghostly stands, leafless and branchless, white as bone. We walked up to one tree, a white spire surrounded by ochre grass, and touched its skin. The tree was cold, and the whorls in our fingers took away the minute dust that covered the white wood.

The grasses in the marshes where our father took us were deep green, yellow where they were pressed down—"where deer lie," he had told us, when we'd found a spot where the grass was imprinted with the vague shape of an animal. He explained the names and types of trees and how a meadow can become a forest in thirty years if left untouched.

That morning at the hospital, our father had looked angry. But he was not angry; it was just the way the sickness made his face look. But it was a familiar look all the same. From where Joan and I sat at his bedside, he still possessed his noble features, his profile like the portrait on a coin.

Our mother presented our father with the bread Joan had made for him. He was only allowed to eat certain things, so Joan made the bread to be decorative. It was an egg-washed bread in the shape of a harbor seal with clumps of poppy seeds for its large black eyes and a cherry for a nose. The significance of the bread was that our father used to take us out in the boat to watch the seals bark and flop along the rocky shores of the Seven Sisters.

"Joan made you this bread. Isn't it sweet?" my mother chirped. She held it up for him to see, rocking it back and forth the way someone might move a model ship in a puppet show.

He blinked his eyes.

"It's like the seals we'd see off the islands," Joan said in a loud voice, as if he were a child.

"Just like the seals, except made out of bread," I said, in a voice like Joan's.

"Warren!" my mother scolded. She stood up and propped the seal against a shelf, where a few baskets of flowers sat withering. "I'll put him here so you can watch each other."

"Don't be an ass," Joan said to me. "Here's your coat, Mom. We should go soon. Auntie E is waiting."

"Why don't you leave Daddy and me alone for a while? Go find something in the gift shop. I'll be ready in fifteen minutes, and then we'll go to Auntie E's."

"We just got here, Mom," I said, in an effort to redeem myself.

"I know, Warren, but, please, I need to be with him," she said, and she started to cry.

8

It's not easy like it was in the beginning," Joan says, after announcing that she and Mike are back together—barely a month after we saw him at the fall parade.

"How could it be easy?" I say in a neutral way. "You said you hate him."

We're sitting in the kitchen talking about what we're going to do about the upstairs part of the house—when we're going to clean. Before the intrusion of Mike into the conversation, I was making the point that however unpleasant the selling of our father's boat at the end of the summer was, once it was over and done with it felt like a kind of resolution. Joan agreed but then immediately started talking about Mike. She made no sense; she thought of one thing only. She's like my mother in that way.

After our father died, Joan, my mother, and I took his ashes—they were more like a fine gray powder with mysterious white shavings and hard white pebbles in it—out on the ferry with us. We held the plastic bag over the water. We stood at the railing of the boat with the bag in our hands and tried to sprinkle the ashes gently into the water. We were not praying, though we were silent, thinking kindly of our father and crying for him and ourselves. But the wind coming off the water blew the ashes back at us; I heard each tiny grain hiss as they pelted our rain jackets. We got the ashes in our eyes, in our mouths. We reeled back; we were in shock; we were spitting to get the grit out of our mouths, but we did not want to spit him out. In a panic, we dumped him in the water. We threw the plastic bag in too. What were we going to do with it? We couldn't use it again!

It was a terrible moment, barely any ceremony to it, especially since we knew he would have been upset with us for littering. We knew we had done him wrong, though in the end, he ended up in the ocean, where he'd wanted to be. Except it was not all of him. Our mother had divided him in half. The day we received the ashes, we'd found her in the kitchen pouring half the contents of the thick plastic bag into a jam jar.

We said to her, "I thought he wanted to be thrown in the ocean."

She said, "We'll do half. And don't say 'thrown,' say 'placed.' 'Thrown' sounds crude and disrespectful, like you're talking about a football."

"I thought we were going to *place* him in the ocean, Mom," I said. "That's what he said he wanted."

"He said so, Mom," Joan added.

"It's my decision now, kids, and my choice, and the other half will be buried beside me when I die."

"Well, that's a cheery thought," I said.

She gazed at me coldly.

Joan and I stood looking at each other; we were losing her.

"Mom, that's so grim," Joan said.

"Seriously," I said. "You don't want to be placed in the ocean too?"

She stopped what she was doing. She looked up at us. I felt Joan move slightly against me.

"Of course not!" my mother wailed.

9

The phone rings. It's Joan. She's alone at a pay phone in town near the wharf. Mike had to go to work. She wants to know whether I want to come and meet her at the diner for coffee. "I know you've got nothing better to do," she says.

"That's the truth," I tell her.

The phone rings again. It's Uncle Steve. I immediately wish I had let the machine get it, because he's called sporadically over the last few months and we haven't called him back.

"Hi," I say.

"Warren, did I wake you up?" he asks, in his odd nasal voice. He sounds far away. I hope he's not on a car phone, in some nearby car.

"I was taking a nap," I lie.

"A nap in the middle of the day? Life of leisure. Nice." Uncle Steve's voice registers a note of derision, which is characteristic. He can be funny; he's perfected a sort of comic intolerance to almost everything. He lives in Canada.

One summer Uncle Steve turned up unexpectedly at our house when my parents were away. We hadn't seen him in years. He showed Joan and me a bunch of paintings he had stowed under a blanket in the back of his station wagon. He said he was taking them to a friend in the city. They were really ugly, done in a style that involved applying paint to the canvas in dense blobs and smearing it around. We talked to him in the driveway; we were weary of him even at a young age and we kept him out of the house.

I look out the window while Uncle Steve talks on and on. It's cloudy outside but the sun is trying to burn through. Uncle Steve is talking about his life in Canada and how he's writing a book of witty comebacks.

"This is going to secure me a small fortune," he says, in a way that makes me wonder if he's drunk. I try to calculate the time difference between where I am and Canada, but I give up. Are there time zones in Canada?

"Are you in Canada?" I ask.

"I love it up here. Lots of artists. Community. Creativity. Yes," he says.

"Are you actually there right now, as we speak?"

"I'm with my people," he says. "Where else could I be?"

"I don't know."

"That's the thing, Warren, you got to find where you've got to be, you know? You find your home, man."

"Right," I say.

"Lucky day." He sighs deeply.

I put on a sweater, putting the phone down for a minute.

"So, what's your book about? Comebacks? What is that?" I ask, to sound interested.

"Oh, Warren, come on! You know. They're great. They're the things you wish you'd said, you know, at the time when you wish you could have said them. Real zingers to put people in their place." Upon hearing this I realize Uncle Steve's main purpose in life is to put people in their place.

"Oh, I see. Have you organized these comebacks by chapters?" Why has he called? I wonder.

"Each chapter is a specific instance. For example, 'Things you say to people at your high school reunion when they point out how poorly you've aged.' Things like that."

"Is that a long chapter?"

"It's getting to be."

He chuckles for about a minute, and I hear some clanging and banging of objects coming from his end of the phone.

"Well, that sounds good," I say. "But, Uncle Steve, I've actually got to go. I told Joan I'd meet her in town."

"Oh, you're meeting Joan? How's Joan doing?"

"Good. You know, she's Joan." I cram the phone between my ear and shoulder and begin to lace up my boots when I notice that the sole on the left boot is beginning to come off. I scuff over to the linen closet to find the epoxy.

"Well, Warren, no, I really don't know what she's like. Either of you, really. It's funny—how long have I known you? Awhile, now, right?"

"I suppose it's been awhile since we were born."

"Yeah, but we've never spent all that much time together, have we?"

"Not really, I guess."

"I'm thinking I may come down there, spend some time with you guys. Motor around, show some people in the city my manuscript. I have a lot of movie ideas too. I'm full of ideas, Warren. My creative juices are really flowing."

The idea of Uncle Steve's juices makes me nauseated, and I have to take the phone away from my face for a moment. The image in my mind is of the time Uncle Steve was visiting and we all went swimming at Small Quarry. Once we'd put down our towels, he took off his shorts and began to stride back and forth on the rocks in a tiny red bikini bathing suit. "Oh, my God!" Joan gasped. The suit was almost made of string, bright red. It reminded me of the rubber bands used to keep lobsters' claws together, only as if stretched around an apple—digging into the soft pocked skin of an old apple.

My mother yelled, "Stephen, put your shorts on, for God's sake!"

At first he was embarrassed and looked frantically around for his towel. But then he fixed an imperious gaze on my mother, became brazen, and began to prance around, giggling and singing some weird song in a falsetto voice.

My mother was beside herself. "Please, Stephen. Please! Jesus, we *know* people in this town!" She was covering her eyes, bent over, hysterically laughing. He was doing the cancan, picking up and waving an imaginary skirt. Joan and I wanted to die. "You are a diseased man!" my mother screamed. Tears ran down her face.

"When were you thinking of coming?" I ask in shock.

"I don't know, it won't take me long to pack. I could be there in a month, a week. I don't know. I figure you guys could use some company."

Long stretch of silence.

"How's your aunt?" he asks.

"I don't know. We haven't seen her in a while. She was doing well when we saw her, though."

"When was that?"

"A few weeks ago, maybe."

"Really?"

"Uh-huh."

"Oh, that's interesting."

"Do you talk to her?"

"Nah, not so much. Sometimes, though."

Long stretch of silence.

"Well, Uncle Steve, I have to go and meet Joan, I guess we'll talk . . . soon." I decide that the idea of him coming to visit is not possible. "Good luck with your book."

"Warren, let me ask you something," he says hurriedly.

"I really have to go and meet Joan."

"Hold on for just one second. Let me ask you one more thing."

"What?"

"Is it weird? Are you guys lonely?"

"No. We're OK."

"Good. I'm glad to hear it's not too weird."

"It's not. It's nice of you to ask, though. Thanks. So, we'll talk soon. OK?"

"Wait, Warren, wait."

"What?"

"Did your parents leave you with enough?"

"What?"

"Enough to live on, to survive."

"Um." The truth was that our parents had. We were fine. At times it felt like a joke—our parents left us with enough to live a life that no longer included them. "I suppose," I said.

"Would you say you live pretty comfortably? You'd say that you live pretty comfortably, right? Since your parents passed away? You would say?"

10

Joan's sitting in a booth by the window in the diner. She's reading the paper, scratching her scalp neurotically. She gives me the *What the hell?* face when I tap on the glass and wave. "What's wrong with you?" I hear her yell through the window. The people sitting at the counter behind her turn around.

"Just wait!" I yell back. The people passing by look at me.

The diner is small and somewhat junky. Nothing much has changed since I was a child, which is comforting and odd. My father brought us here on Sunday mornings when my mother was sleeping in. They always treated Joan and me in a friendly way, used our names when we walked in, when we ordered.

"She's been waiting for you," said Monique from behind the counter, replacing a pie beneath a plastic cake bell.

"I know," I say. "I was on the phone."

"That'll do it." She smiled.

The diner is empty except for two fisherman types at the counter, their yellow rain gear folded over empty stools. Monique wipes down the counter while Tina, an older waitress with peroxide-dyed hair and faint traces of acne, sits at a booth in the back filling the sugar bowls from a large industrial-sized bag of sugar. It's three in the afternoon, and a sweaty-looking chef appears every now and then through the kitchen's narrow window. A radio in back is playing oldies.

Joan's eaten a grilled cheese sandwich. "Why" she asks, peering up at me, "are you soooooooooo late?"

"Guess who called when I was walking out the door?"

"Mike?" She perks up.

"Yeah, he called to ask me for your hand in marriage."

"Shut up. Was it Mike?"

"No. You were with Mike. Why would he call the house?"

"Because he had to weave me."

"Joan! No baby voice!"

"What are you talking about? I didn't!" she says, guiltily.

"Anyway, it was Uncle Steve. He called."

"Red banana hammock?" She gasps. "Why did you pick it up?"

"He called right after you did. It rang and I answered. I was still holding the phone. I thought it might be you again."

"What did he say? Was he completely out of his mind?"

"Totally crazy. At first I wasn't paying attention. I was just trying to get off the phone. I was trying to fix my boot." I pick up my foot to show her the smear of glue along the sole. Joan nods in appreciation and tests the bond with a pull. "But then he got that bitchy tone in his voice. And then he got new-age. He was telling me about some book he's writing, then about Canada. He was crazy."

"Was he calling from Canada?"

"I'm pretty sure he was. But listen."

"I am listening. But did he *say* he was in Canada? Remember when he showed up in the driveway with all those books he'd stolen and was going to sell in the city? Remember Mom and Dad were away?"

"They were paintings. They were in the back of that crappy station wagon. Yes, so clearly stolen."

"They weren't paintings, they were books."

"I know they were paintings. I remember how ugly they were."

"Warren, I know they were books. I remember."

"Joan, paintings."

"Whatever, Mr. Memory. All I know is he is such a freak. I remember looking out the window and seeing him lurking around the house, trying to get in."

"We were the only ones home. Where were Mom and Dad? Were they in Sweden?"

"And remember, we wouldn't let him inside?"

"And we basically made him take a leak behind the shed? Because we wouldn't let him come in and use the bathroom?"

"That's right, we told him the water had been turned off." Joan reflected. "He's such a freak. What did he want? Why was he calling?"

"I couldn't tell for sure, but I think he wants to come and visit."

"What? No. No way." Joan throws out her hands.

"That's basically what he was saying. I'm sure that was the point of the call."

"Did you tell him no?"

"I was just trying to get off the phone. There's no real way to talk to him."

"Warren, he *can't* come."

"I know, I know, I know. I don't want him to come either."

"But do you think he will? Did you get the idea that he would, that he would just come anyway?"

"I don't know. I just told him I had to go. And then he was all, like, 'I was thinking about coming to visit. See some agents.'"

"Agents? I'm serious. We cannot deal with him on our own. He's crazy."

"I know, I know, I know."

"Seriously. He's been arrested. He went to jail—something really illegal. He's totally shady."

"OK," I say. "Maybe we should get a guard dog."

"And we should dig a moat."

"Something for protection. From him and from all people."

"We don't need protection from people in general."

"You say that now."

"You sound like Dad. Mr. Fortress-on-a-Hill."

We sit in the diner for two more hours, recovering from the intrusion of Uncle Steve, which requires companionship and food. Plus, Joan and I had fought after we'd returned from Auntie E's house for Thanksgiving. This time together feels like we're making amends. Though frankly, she should be the one making amends with me, since she was the jerk.

Joan has two more cups of coffee and dabs up the crumbs from her sandwich with her fingertip. I order a plate of french fries and douse them with A-1 Sauce.

I say, "Will you eat half?"

"I'll eat half. But, Warren, no one's going to accuse you of being unhealthy just for eating a few fries."

"What did you call them?" I ask.

"*Fries.* I said *fries.* What did you think I said?"

"Fwies."

"What?"

"You said *fwies.*"

"No, I didn't!" she says. "I said *fries,* as in *French.*"

"You didn't! You weren't doing a baby voice. You just said it that way." I've caught her. "Now, take your half of the fwies so your arteries will be just as hard as mine."

"You're not going to keel over from eating a few fwies." Joan shovels a mass of fries onto her plate.

"I know," I say, holding up a single fry and thoughtfully considering it as if it were a fine piece of crystal. "Though they are forbidden, I just love them. I love fwies."

"Me too," Joan says, examining one in her hand like a jeweler.

And like swords, or champagne flutes, we toast each other, tap the french fries together across the table, and say, "Fwies."

By the time we've scraped up the sauce with the crunchy overcooked bits of potato, it's almost eight o'clock. We've occupied the booth by the window for most of the afternoon. But the waitresses don't seem to care. We feel wanted here, if only for not being asked to leave.

The windows of the diner face a cobblestone square. The greatest asset to this otherwise oversized traffic island is a granite rock with a plaque commemorating various lost sailors and ships. It sits stout and immobile, protected by a tiny fence of foot-high poles and nautical rope. Spotlights shine on it and on the withering wreath that adorns its crown. Tonight a flurry of activity surrounds the commemorative spot. Some workmen are struggling to install an unwieldy Christmas tree. They all look frustrated and annoyed at one another. Some other guys stand close by, untangling large-bulb spools of Christmas lights. Another group tapes down scraps of outdoor carpet to cover orange extension cords snaking around the scene.

Behind a sawhorse is a group of young children, probably first-graders or kindergartners. They're confused and cold, clutching ornaments made from dowels, construction paper, pipe cleaners, glitter, and gimp. Each time one of their teachers' faces is illuminated in a spotlight's beam, it is a mask of supreme displeasure. And there is a group of parents, none of whom are speaking; they are chaperons, and they are fed up. I notice a tall youngish-looking woman standing awkwardly with some perturbed older mothers. She is wearing a knit hat and has long red hair that flashes in the light. It's Valerie. I should tell Joan, but I'm afraid she'd say something mean about her. Or she might get in a bad mood at the sight of her. It's not worth it. And I want to watch Valerie without any distraction; she stands demurely, watching the men and the tree.

The scene could look like the site of an accident. Everyone waits for the men to put the tree up, but they have stopped acknowledging the teachers, who periodically wave their hands at them trying to get some answers—since these children cannot be kept waiting all night out in the cold. Joan and I watch from behind the window. She accepts a refill on her coffee. We order and share a slice of key lime pie.

11

Last year at Christmas, we did the right thing. We threw our tree into the river. I had heard on the radio that the fish use the tree as a habitat. I couldn't imagine it. How many fish can live in one tree? I wondered.

I'd gotten stabbed in the eye with a pine bough's needles while walking in the woods near the quarries—it was an uncommon amount of pain. The fish couldn't sleep in the drowned boughs of the tree; they might lose their eyes. Why was this recommended on the radio? The river would be clogged with trees and the fish would be eyeless. I remembered seeing people's old Christmas trees lying out on the curb, tinsel hanging from the needles. Had those trees been thrown in the river, the tinsel would have wound up in the mouths of fish or been strewn across the mud of the banks and caught in the branches of the trees that had fallen over and lay half drowned in the river.

But, at least in that respect we were ecologically in the clear, because my mother never allowed tinsel on our trees. So, a week after Christmas, Joan and I took the undecorated tree and put it in the back of our father's truck. We held it from the stone bridge, where we could see the river moving swiftly beneath us, dropped it, and watched it vanish immediately into the black water. We ran to the other side of the bridge to see if it would bob up. It was under the ice, we knew, shuttled to some remote part of the river.

When we got home our mother was in the living room sweeping the tree's fallen needles into a pile.

"Why don't you use the vacuum?" I asked.

"Shhhhhhh!" She frowned. "It makes too much noise."

My father was asleep on the couch, a brightly colored afghan pulled up under his chin.

"Try to be quiet. Let him sleep," my mother said.

"Why doesn't he go up to bed?" Joan asked. "Shouldn't he be in bed?"

"He didn't want to miss anything," my mother said, without looking up. "But don't wake him. It's been an eventful morning for him."

We had been up at seven. Joan was baking special digestive bread, a recipe she'd cleared with the nurses at the hospital; I was making coffee and keeping her company. At nine-thirty our mother helped our father down the stairs. Then we did our usual thing: stockings, carol singing, present-opening, eating.

"What's there to miss?" I asked.

"He doesn't want to miss out on the action. Where were you two?"

"We threw the tree in the river," Joan reported.

"That was some serious action," I added.

"You didn't!" She gasped. She glanced over at my father. "Shhhh." Her finger pushed up against her lips, she glared at us. "Tell me you didn't throw our tree in the river!"

"I heard that that's what you should do. I heard it on the radio!" I said to her, smiling, uncertain if she was angry or playing.

"Oh, please, Warren! It's a waste!"

"We talked about this, Mom! Ecologically speaking, it's the right thing to do. It makes a home for the fish. The fish live in the tree." I was laughing.

"A home for the fish! The river *is* a home for the fish!" said my mother with impatience and fatigue. "No more talking! Ecologically speaking! I can't believe you two."

"Dad agreed to it, Mom," Joan piped in, looking at our father.

"It's true," I said. "We talked about this already."

"I don't remember having that discussion! Tell me when I told you to throw our beautiful tree into the river."

She can't be serious, I thought to myself. She's being dramatic. Maybe she's upset that Joan and I left her alone with my father. No, that's what she prefers. Maybe she's upset that we came back.

"We talked about it the other day. I told you I heard that's what you're supposed to do—throw it in the river so it's not sitting out with the trash on trash day. It makes a place for the fish to live. Like a nest."

"The fish seemed happy with what we did," Joan said, sounding like a considerate six-year-old.

"It's littering, that's what it is: littering!" our mother said with finality. "And what, the fish were happy? Oh, Joan, please!"

"What?" said Joan, exasperated.

"How is it littering?" I was getting annoyed. "It's recycling!"

"What is?" said our father, groggy and blinking. "What's littering?"

"Oh, no! Did we wake you up?" my mother, Joan, and I all said, delighted, in unison.

12

Thanksgiving at Auntie E's this year was tense but short. We said we were tired and left after dinner. No one argued with us. Auntie E cried and gave us each a hug and then hugged us both at the same time. We just said, "It's OK. It's OK. We're OK. It's OK." It was like a little song we sang to her. Our cousins stayed off the topic but asked if we wanted to go to a hockey game. It was their way, I knew, of being kind. There was talk of Uncle Steve showing up.

Joan brought a pie; it was praised. It was fine, the whole day. It was their job to make us feel integrated, normal, welcome. We did. I did feel welcome. I don't know about Joan. She was polite and talkative, like a flight attendant. I thought to myself, Bring this up with her later. I took her aside and gestured to a framed picture Auntie E had of our family on the beach. I was fourteen and Joan was sixteen. We both had terrible hairstyles: I had a rattail; she had an asymmetrical bowl cut that was meant to look as if she were wearing a beret—a beret made out of her own hair. I pointed to us in the photo and lowered my head in true humiliation. I thought she would laugh.

"Warren, don't," she said sternly.

"What's wrong with you?" I asked quietly.

"Cut it out," she said. "I'm not in the mood to joke around."

"What?"

She walked away from me and into the kitchen, where Auntie E was cramming her hand down the garbage disposal because a teaspoon had fallen in.

"Let me," I heard Joan say from the kitchen. "I have thin hands."

Joan had sustained her crappy mood for the rest of the visit and insisted that we listen to the radio (with no discussion) on the way home. When we got home, Mike had left a note on the kitchen window. Joan sat down at the table to read it. Oh, Mike left a note! I thought to myself, Praise the Lord!

"What does it say?" I asked.

"He came by an hour ago. We should have left earlier."

"Are you joking?"

"What? No. Why?"

"Because Auntie E looked devastated enough when we left. If we left any earlier she would have thrown herself under our tires. You can't tell me you didn't notice."

"I didn't," Joan said, lying.

"Well, she looked wounded."

"She always looks like that. *You* could have stayed if you felt so bad."

"What?"

"You could have stayed longer. I'd been wanting to go for hours."

"But we couldn't. Besides, how was I supposed to get home if I stayed? I didn't want to stay, anyway. I wanted to come back."

"Right. So we came back."

"Right, Joan. Jesus, what is your problem? Why are you being this way?"

"You wanted to leave, and we left. Now we're here, and I'm mad that I missed Mike."

"So call him. Or he'll stop by later. Why have you been in such a crap-ass mood? You wanted to leave Auntie E's house too. Don't make it out that it was just me wanting to go. We both wanted to go."

"So we left, Warren."

It's moments like these when I want to tell Joan that she's going to be a terrible mother.

"Yes, we left, but before, for the entire time we were there, you wouldn't even talk to me." I had meant to bring this up at another time. What might have been a productive discussion was soon to be a full-force defensive blowout. Here we go, I thought.

"Jesus, Warren, give me a break!" Joan said, exasperated. "I didn't ignore you, I just thought I should talk to our relatives. We can't *both* be moping around. It's depressing."

"It *is* depressing!"

"That's what I said."

"Everything is depressing." I was spitting.

"Besides, I can talk to you whenever."

"But you don't! Not anymore. And what are you talking about that *I'm* moping around? Do you realize what a tremendous bitch you are?"

"Shut up. I'm sorry. I'm in a bad mood. I'm sorry that you feel like I ignored you. I didn't mean to make you feel that way. I'm sorry. I'm annoyed because I missed Mike and I wasted an entire day at Auntie E's house. OK?"

"*You* wasted an entire day? I was at her house too. I had to go too. You remember me, your brother, only surviving kin, next to you at dinner? We were there together, if you care to remember."

"Shut up, Warren," she moaned. "Don't make me feel bad. You know I love you, so please don't make me feel bad about this. I didn't mean that *you* were a waste of an afternoon."

"You're completely insane," I said.

We sat at the table, looking down at the mail. Joan ran the edge of the note along the inside of her fingers.

"Do you want to go to the quarries?" I asked her. "It's still light out. We can go and then walk through the woods to the beach and then back home."

"In a little while. I'm going upstairs to use the phone."

Because Mike's father is a fisherman and his mother used to be a cook at an inn in town, they have different ways of preparing a turkey. They buy a huge bird, over thirty pounds, from a local farm. They clean and scrub it and prick it all over with needles and skewers. They fill a plastic trash barrel with seawater. They throw in whole bulbs of peeled garlic, handfuls of herbs, and two large cups of black pepper. They pour in bottles of wine. They heat honey so it pours smoothly and dissolves quickly in the mix. They stir it with the handle of a shovel and lower the bird in. It marinates in the mixture for two days before it goes into the oven for six hours. When it is cut, the meat looks wet and sweats on your plate. The skin is evenly browned, and you barely need to use a knife to cut it. Even reheated, the meat is moist, with the rich flavor and scent of the ocean. They eat it with pumpkin chutney and brown-sugared beets. Joan said she'd never tasted better turkey in her life. She told me this the morning after Thanksgiving. An hour after we'd gotten back from Auntie E's, while I was in my room listening to the radio, she'd taken her bike and gone to Mike's house. It took me at least an hour to realize that she'd left.

13

During my hours alone in the house I have designed a way to fold sheets without help. I used to watch my mother fold sheets; she pinned the wide part of the fabric under her chin with her arms outstretched like someone about to perform a dramatic bow. This method of folding made her tongue stick out of her mouth. Even as she was talking to me, her tongue would poke out of her mouth. I realize now that it was a product of that particular stage in the folding process: pinning the sheet under the chin can make the tongue poke from the mouth.

"Ugh, Mom, don't do that!" I would say to her, because it was unsettling to see her pointed maroon tongue. One summer, when I was holding an ice cream cone, I asked her if she wanted some. I paid too much attention to how she took a taste—I was concerned about how much she was taking and how much would be left for me. I remember her tongue coming out and licking the scoop. It was a horrible thing to watch. Her strange slender tongue stiffened to a point, jabbing little dents into the ice cream. When I had spent the day on a boat, all day on the stern where the waves leapt up and splashed me, I came home with the taste of salt on my skin. "Taste my skin," I said to her innocently, with my arm reached out. Obligingly, her weird slender tongue carved a little moat into my arm and cleared away a gauzy strip of salt.

"Don't do what?" she'd reply, grabbing the halved sheet from under her chin, swiftly folding it again into a narrow band.

"Stick your tongue out. It's gross."

*"Please pardon me, your highness."

My mother needed me or Joan or my father there in the beginning stages of the sheet folding. She was thin, with blue eyes and a slim nose that turned up at the tip, and she wasn't tall enough to fold a queen-sized sheet in half by herself. She hated to see clean laundry hitting the floor.

I have created a new method she would be proud of—though she could not imitate it because I am at least seven inches taller than she was. With my way, no laundry touches the floor. Especially not the sheets, blankets, and pillowcases that were on their bed. I removed them yesterday while Joan was out. After they were washed and dried I took them out of the dryer and cleaned out the lint trap. I scooped up the glob of lint with my fingers; it was the size of a crab apple or a bulb. I put it in a box that used to hold recipe cards.

I thought about the white curtains I had tried to fix and how badly I had gone about it. When we put them back up in the living room, I couldn't see that they were ruined. "They aren't ruined," Joan said to me. "They look good, probably better than before. But you still didn't have to do it."

I don't know why I thought I had ruined them, or why I tried to fix them, or why I thought they needed to be fixed. The house is still falling apart, though we don't talk about it anymore; rather, we talk about it less than we used to, which was rarely. The leak in the pantry is worse. The rain soaks the backs of all the boxes of food as it trickles through the buckled wallpaper. But the outside looks good. Someone told me today that our father did a great job of painting it. Or had he touched it up recently? the person asked. I didn't know what to say, so I said yes. It was the guy from the hardware store. He knows. Everyone knows our story. So why did he ask me?

What an asshole was my father's favorite thing to say. "What an asshole," he'd say to the car passing in the wrong lane while we drove on the highway to the nursery. "What an asshole," of the man in the boat who was pouring out the contents of his cooler—halves of uneaten subs still in wax paper, dented cans of soda—into the water near the boatyard. "You little assholes," he said to us, laughing. We were children, and Joan and I had hidden his cigarettes. We were making him promise that his habit would end with that pack. *Say it out loud, and we'll give them back.* It was a child's bargain. We didn't understand that he could go buy more or he might have some stashed somewhere else, in another of his coats. We didn't understand there was no way in the world that he was going to do what we asked.

I take one single flat queen-sized sheet in my arms, making sure that no part of it touches the floor. I root around in the mass of fabric until I have found the four corners. Then, I slowly open the sheet, gathering clumps in my fists to keep it from completely unfurling. My mother was right: when laundry hits the floor it collects every single particle of dirt. If the corners I have blindly attempted to pair in my hands are mismatched, this is the time, before the sheet is expanded any further, to discover it. Once those corrections are made, I stretch the sheet out as far as my arms will go to line up the sheet's outside edges. By this point, the sheet is almost folded in half and some adjusting—a rolling motion with the fingers—is necessary. Once it is perfect, or close, by pinching small sections of the fabric I inch my hands into the center of the folded sheet to fold it again in half. Pinch and slide, pinch and slide, gathering the sheet as I go. By now it's the size of a towel or an infant's blanket, and can be folded a few more times, depending on what space is left in the linen closet, currently overstuffed with old sleeping bags, quilts, my mother's sewing projects, and my father's long underwear hanging on a hook.

All this came about during a conversation Joan and I had about cleaning. We were in the diner. It was the afternoon when we sat in the booth by the window for such a long time. I was impressed with us; we had a frank discussion about what we had to do. But then again we were avoiding talking about what a jerk Joan was on Thanksgiving. I said we should clean our parents' room together and she agreed. "I hate this," she moaned.

We agreed we would clean the upstairs on Friday, which was yesterday. But yesterday Joan didn't come back from Christmas shopping until late. She went with her friend Grace. They both walked in last night while I was in the kitchen making macaroni and cheese from a box.

"Hey, Warren," Grace said in her breathy voice, the voice of an airhead, except that she was an honors student. She took off her thin suede jacket to reveal a snug-fitting white turtleneck sweater, which I gawked at helplessly.

"Warren," Joan said, scowling, "what's going on?"

"Where did you guys go?" I watched Joan washing her hands at the sink. I was pissed that she was late and pissed that she was nonchalantly washing her hands and thinking nothing was wrong. Joan is so dim! She doesn't care about me!

"Shopping!" Grace sang cheerfully.

"Shopping," said Joan. "I was looking for something for Mike." She looked disheartened. "But I can't find anything." Grace looked at her and frowned.

"That's too bad," I said, without sympathy, "but I thought we were going to clean Mom and Dad's room today."

"Shit. That's right," she said, as if actually surprised. "I'm sorry."

Grace frowned more deeply. I wanted her to leave. She looked back and forth between us.

"Well, let's do it now," Joan said.

"We can't do it now, Joan."

"Why not?"

Joan knew why not.

"Why not?" she repeated.

"Because it's too late. It's already dark out. And"—I stammered, glancing at Grace—"it's too late to do it now, Joan."

"Oh, Warren. Let's just do it now. We'll do it together and it won't take that long. What difference does it make if it's dark out?"

I didn't know what she meant by "together." Did she mean herself, Grace, and me? Grace looked worried, taking her hair down from a high ponytail and putting it back up.

"Grace," I began.

"Why don't I go home and I'll call you later about tomorrow," Grace said quickly, pulling her coat off the back of the chair.

"No," Joan snapped, "you don't have to go. It's not going to take that long to clean a room, Grace. Just stay."

Grace looked confused. For a smart person, I thought, this is sad. Just go, Grace, I wanted to say. You don't have to do Joan's bidding; that's my job.

"I thought you were going to come home earlier so we could clean it and have it finished before we ate," I said.

"I already ate," Joan said. "We ate at the mall."

"You already ate? At the mall?"

"We ate at Wong's," Grace said, with a weak smile, patting her stomach to indicate that food was inside.

"Joan," I said, "we talked about this the other day. We made a plan for tonight."

"I know, but Grace came over so we could hang out. We'll clean tomorrow. We don't have to go up there in the dark. I don't want to either."

"Didn't we talk about cleaning up there the other day? And we agreed we would do it on Friday. Today is Friday."

"I know. We'll do it tomorrow when I get back from work. I'll be out by eleven. You'll be here, right?" I saw Joan cast a quick glance over at Grace when she said this. It was an all-knowing glance, one that said, See, like I said, he never leaves the house. I hated Joan for making me look like a housebound freak. "So, that's good. I'm sorry I forgot about tonight. We'll do it tomorrow. Together."

From the corner of my eye I could see that Grace looked relieved, sensing the end of the argument. She smiled at us with warmth and sympathy.

"Well, I did my half already."

"What?" Joan asked.

"What?" Grace piped.

"You heard me. And, Joan, why would you eat at Wong's? That place is foul."

Grace touched her stomach.

"You did your half already? What is that supposed to mean?"

"It means I already cleaned my half. All you have to do is vacuum and clean the windows."

"No, what does 'your half' mean? What constitutes 'half?'"

"I did half the work," I said definitively. "For the record, Wong's is gross, and I can't believe you ate there. I heard they keep the food out on the counters overnight."

"Warren!" Joan said shrilly. "Jesus! Grace wanted Chinese and there's nothing else at the mall but Wong's."

Grace cowered in her chair.

"It's gross. You didn't come home. You should have called. So now you can do your half whenever it's convenient for you." Grace looked harrowed, which made me feel bad.

"I forgot! I was looking for presents. *Your* present too, if you must know."

"She was," Grace said timidly, smoothing her hair. "We looked forever!"

"Your present to me would be to come back here and help me take Mom and Dad's sheets and blankets off their bed to wash and fold and put away."

"You put them away? Are you insane? Warren, I'm not going to use their sheets! You're not going to use their sheets either! Why did you put them in the closet with the other things?"

Grace got up and put on her coat. She looked rattled but determined to leave.

"Hold on, Grace!" Joan commanded.

"Joan, this is awkward, I'm sorry. I'm going to go home."

"No, wait," Joan insisted, but more calmly. "Just wait. Don't go."

I felt a swell of pride that Joan and I had forced Grace out.

"I put them in there because that's where they go," I continued. "What was I supposed to do, throw them out? Burn them in the yard?"

Joan turned back to me. "Yes, throw them out or put them away or do something that isn't putting them with the rest of our sheets and things. Warren, think about it."

"Joan, I'll call you later," Grace said softly, putting on her mittens. She looked over at me. "'Bye, Warren. Sorry."

"Wait!" Joan shouted. Grace froze at the door.

"Joan, it's OK," she said. "I'll call you later."

"No," she said.

"They're clean now, what's the difference?" I interrupted.

"No, they're not, they're not clean now!" she shrieked, whipping her face back at me.

"If you didn't want them in the linen closet, you should have been here to recommend somewhere else to put them."

"I was shopping for presents!" She looked at Grace for support. Grace was looking at the floor, leaning against the doorjamb.

"That's the stupidest excuse I've ever heard! It's obvious you just didn't want to help me."

"Warren," she said coldly, "you think everything is obvious."

"Don't start that, Joan." I seethed. "Why don't you just let her leave?" I gestured to Grace, who stood between us with her coat, hat, and mittens on.

"Warren, you are such an ass sometimes."

"I was here, like we agreed. Friday."

"And you went ahead and did it—*your half.*"

"Just go, Grace," I said to her.

She looked at Joan, who nodded and said, "Just go. It's all right."

Grace disappeared out the door and into the dark. A cold rush of air came into the kitchen. Joan and I stood looking at each other, she leaning against the sink with her arms folded defiantly, me standing by the stove stirring the bright orange powdered cheese into the macaroni.

"Now what?" Joan asked.

"Now what what?"

"Are you going to tell me exactly what you did up there?"

"I didn't do half, but at least I did something," I said.

"What was it that you did?"

"I did their laundry. I told you."

"Why did you do their laundry, Warren? Of all things to do."

"I don't know. You should have been here."

"You're right." She paused. "I know it. I should have come back."

"Thank you."

"And I should have guessed you'd go ahead and do it yourself."

"I waited, and then I had to at least start something."

"You always have to start something."

The light above the sink flickered. Joan took her scarf off the chair where it was draped over her heavy winter coat. As soon as the scarf lifted from the coat the chair tipped over. She wrapped the scarf around her neck, picked the chair up, and sat down quickly, before it could tip over again.

"What else did you do today?" she asked, in an exhausted voice.

"I figured out a way to fold a sheet without its touching the ground."

"What?"

"While I was doing their laundry, I figured out a way."

"What are you talking about?"

"I can fold a sheet by myself."

"A fitted sheet?"

"No. Well, probably. But so far my system applies only to a top sheet."

"Warren, what's wrong with you?" She grinned, perplexed.

"It's a revolutionary technique."

"Is that so?"

"It is."

"How?"

"I'll explain."

14

We had used the sheets and blankets from Joan's bed to make a place for our mother to sleep on the couch. This was when our father was on his last legs and our mother was losing her shit. We came home and found her at the kitchen table wearing our father's coat, smoking one of his cigarettes, and finishing off the last ounces of a large bottle of white wine. Joan had been at the bakery. She picked me up from the library and we went and got coffee and drove to the beach, where we sat in the car and watched the people and the water. We waited for the sun to curl around the snowy peak of Quick Island.

Joan had brought me some lemon bread she had already crumbled in the bag. We popped the ragged scraps in our mouths as we talked.

"I'm actually afraid to go back home," I said.

"No kidding. Me too."

"Was Mom at the hospital all day?" I asked. "Did you see her this morning?"

"She left before I left. Her car was gone."

"She's home now?"

"I drove by before I picked you up. Her car's there; she's home."

"Well, we should go back."

"I know."

"When this woman in the weird hat with the dogs gets to the end of the beach, we'll go home," I said.

"Or when those people in jogging outfits near the flagpole leave, we'll go," Joan proposed.

"When Quick is completely dark."

"When the tide's up over the rocks."

"When there's no one on the beach anymore."

"When there's no one left. Then we'll go back."

We walked in the kitchen door and found our mother singing. The radio was tuned to the public radio station. She was singing "My One and Only Love."

"Oh, shit," Joan said.

"We should have come back earlier," I said.

My mother sang with a weird warble to her voice. Tears had run down her face, and her eye makeup was smeared. "I'm all alone in the house," she sang, to the tune of the song. "My love's alone in the hospital ward," she sang, "and I'm alone in the house."

We tried to get her upstairs but she would not go; we got into an argument. Joan became upset and started to cry. We resolved to make a bed on the couch for her. "I'm afraid to go up there," our mother said to us drunkenly. "I'm afraid to be up there alone."

I told Joan to go upstairs and get some stuff to make a bed for our mother while I tried to get her into the living room. My mother was more mobile and less resistant than the last time I'd tried to move her. I could tell when I hoisted her up into my arms because she relaxed against me. She gave in.

"Just listen to me," she said, as I walked her the way an adult walks a child, the child's feet on the adult's feet, in a sort of dance or game. "Just listen to me; stay with me," she said.

"We're making you a place to sleep on the couch, Mom," I said to her.

"I don't need that, you don't have to," she said, in a flattered voice.

"We do, though, Mom. There's nothing else to do, because you won't go upstairs."

"That's right. I won't go upstairs."

Joan had taken sheets and tucked them tightly in and around the cushions of the couch. A white comforter lay like a meringue over the sheets. In an instant our mother vanished beneath it; she dived into the bed. I got a bottle of water and put it by the couch. "He's dying," said our mother in a small voice. "He's going to die and I'm going to be alone."

"You won't be alone, Mom, you'll have us," we said, trying to sound sincere and caring but feeling mechanical, mute, and irrelevant.

"I know, I know, I know," she said. "Alone."

Once our mother fell asleep, Joan and I went upstairs. I went into my room and she went into hers. A few minutes later she came in through the connecting door.

"I used my sheets and blankets to make Mom's bed on the couch."

"Why?"

"I don't know. I was sort of panicked, I guess."

"That was dumb." I smiled.

"Can I sleep here?" she asked.

"Why don't you get some stuff from the linen closet?"

"Because it's a pain and I'm tired and I have to get up early. Can I just sleep here? Please?"

"OK," I said, and turned off the light. "Hurry up. And no snoring."

I woke up suddenly; it was still dark. Joan was shaking my shoulder and saying something to me. I looked at the digital display of the clock radio, but the numbers were incomprehensible. Joan had pulled back the blankets on her side of the bed and was saying something I couldn't quite understand. She had turned on the small lamp beside the bed.

"Warren, wake up," she said to me. "Warren!"

"Are you going to work now?" I asked, disoriented.

"No, not now. You have to get out of the bed."

"Why? When are you going to work? Why are you up? Is it Mom?"

"Warren, get out of the bed," she said, with mild urgency. "We have to remake it."

"Why?"

"Come on, get out for a second. There's blood in your bed."

"There's what in the bed?"

"I'm sorry, Warren—I bled in your bed."

15

I saw Valerie this afternoon. She was with a young boy, her son. I thought about the night when I last saw her, almost a week ago, when the workmen were putting up the Christmas tree in the Town Square. She was with all those children as their chaperon. It made sense now; her child must have been among them.

I could not take my eyes off them. She and the child were standing together on the bus, which was crowded with people on their way back from Christmas shopping at the wharf. Everyone was hidden inside down parkas with large shopping bags at their feet. I was coming back from the library. The heater on the bus was broken, so everyone huddled together, strangers against strangers, and Valerie's son pushed himself up against her legs and tucked his head under her coat. She had one hand against the back of his head while the other steadied them against the metal pole near the back door of the bus. She smiled warmly at her son, who looked up at her. He was small, wearing a snowsuit and a fleece hat with brown pointed ears stitched to the top. He held on to her as the bus buckled and lurched, and she held on to him as his body swayed against hers. They barely spoke at all and I couldn't hear what they were saying. I was at the back of the bus, crammed in between the window and an old woman who smelled like a fireplace.

Valerie's pale skin had pink circles on her cheeks. When she took off her mitten to push some hair from her face and retrieve a tissue from her pocket, I watched the delicate white hand emerge. I decided it was the most beautiful thing I had ever seen. Why didn't anyone else on the bus notice this display of unapologetic devotion and love? Why weren't other people on the bus in awe as I was? No one seemed to notice them.

Valerie had been a year ahead of Joan in school. I barely knew her; Joan was in a few of her classes. Joan said she did not appear very smart except in things like art, but she was quiet and was probably holding out—jealousy and pettiness could have factored into Joan's low appraisal. I used to see Val walking on the sidewalk around town. I didn't know where she lived or what her family was like. I think she lived with her grandparents on Crow's Point. She was old enough for me not to know the specific details of her life.

That is, until she started to work at Marshland Nursery. She started a few years ago in the fall, after she'd graduated. I saw her in the potting shed and was reminded of the time I'd seen her at the quarries the previous summer, lying on an old beach towel in an orange two-piece bathing suit. I remember my mother's comment: A pretty redhead like her should not wear orange. She had white skin that tanned a yellow-gold in the summer. I remember watching her pick her way along the rocks of the quarry, delicately, like a deer seeking secure footing among shale. Her bathing suit was held to her lean body by strings tied in bow-tied knots. I remember watching the bows wag back and forth as she moved, wondering what would happen, *what would happen,* if they were to come undone. I pictured the suit unfurled as she swam free of it, her pale body flashing like a fish beneath the green water.

The first time I came across her in the nursery, in the potting shed, she'd caught me off guard. I was waiting for my father and wandering around aimlessly. She was sitting quietly on a stool in the back greenhouses of the nursery, surrounded by dark soil, her hair tied back with a white elastic band. Coming upon her, with her pale skin and calm expression, I thought she looked like a statue excavated from the earth.

She worked in the potting shed for a while. Joan and I were still in school, and sometimes Joan worked in the flower shop at the nursery on the weekends. I didn't work there at all because I had a job at the library, which was far more interesting, if less cool.

The summer before Joan's senior year, she gave up her catering job to work at the bakery. My father wouldn't let Joan work at the nursery more than two days a week, because he didn't think it was fair to the other employees. That was when he promoted Valerie to work in the flower shop. He said he believed she was artistic and would have a knack for arranging. No one else seemed to care, but Joan freaked out and exploded one day early that summer. "Why did you give her my job?"

"There was no job until I saw she could do it and wanted it," he replied plainly. "So I asked her."

"I could do it too!" Joan said. "I would have wanted it! I've worked there forever—ask Helen!" Helen was a tiny Asian woman with long wiry hair and doll-like features who ran the flower shop. She loved Joan, whom she called "Roan," which I thought was the best thing I'd ever heard.

"Joan, it's a waste to have Val in the back if she is better suited to work with the flowers. Don't get bent out of shape. You have a new job at the bakery, anyway."

"Only because you never asked me if I wanted to work in the flower shop! Why didn't you ask me?"

"Because we didn't need to hire anyone else, Joanie."

"What about Valerie? You took her!"

"She was already on the payroll," he said with finality, and went upstairs.

My father didn't think he was doing anything wrong. I think he thought he was doing the right thing by not giving the job to someone in the family. I couldn't tell whether or not Val did a good job. Everything looked the same as it always had: rows of flowers in paper cones in the freezer, arrangements with ivy and cranberry branches spilling out of baskets and vases in leafy explosions. Val just seemed to be doing what Joan was doing.

"Yeah," Joan sneered. "Stealing all my ideas."

The unfairness of the situation was something I only really understood through Joan's devastation. I had no professional interest in the nursery, but I liked it there, so I could empathize with her exile. The air in the greenhouses was wet and pungent from sprinklers that sprayed a fine mist over the plants, whose leaves, in their constant wetness, gave off a thick jungle scent. There were metal-winged heaters with red coils hanging by chains from the roof, and I would walk slowly beneath them and feel the intense focused heat beating down on my head. Rows and rows of tiny sprigs of green, each in its separate cup of soil, stretched out endlessly in the potting shed. There were signs naming each plant and illustrations for what they would look like in bloom, though in their cups they all looked like grass.

There were four large greenhouses, plus a dirt-packed lot where trees, house plants, and perennials were sold during the spring and summer. I remember Joan and I used to run through the rows of trees during one of the many games we'd invented for ourselves. The trees were dense; it was a maze we wound our way through, though in reality the lot was barely an acre. In the fall, ten or twenty cars could park there.

In winter they would string up lights and bring in Christmas trees from Canada and Vermont to sell. I used to go and watch my father bitch out the people who brought bare, diseased, and dying trees. I remember one time when he refused to pay a guy who had brought a whole load of trees from up north. My father said they were "crap-ass." "It's Christmas!" the guy said to my father. "Exactly," my father barked at him. "Don't take me for a fucking ride!" Our father always picked the best tree on the lot for us and kept it in a bucket of fresh water in the back before he brought it home, strapped like a deer to the top of his truck.

16

I watch the steady mist of snow pour down outside the window. This is the first snow of the winter, and it's been falling for the last few days. I am looking for my old piano music books in the recycling basket. I have been searching for them all day; it makes me insane to think they might have been thrown out.

Through the gauze of flurries outside I see a truck coming up the driveway, parting the snow and creating fluffy drifts as it moves toward the house. I can hear the gravel and seashells of the driveway getting crushed under the plow. We didn't order this. I don't remember writing a check to have the driveway plowed. It's easy enough to park the car on the street near the mailbox and walk up and down the snow path. That's what we do.

I look through the truck's windshield. Mike is behind the wheel. His hat is pulled down low over his eyes, but I can see his thin straight nose and pointed chin, white as quartz above his dark blue anorak. This must be the return favor he was referring to the other day when I bumped into him at work.

I was at the library, working with Mrs. Caldwell on the second floor, at the main desk. She is my boss. I've worked with her since middle school. She is tall, a widow, and looks the part of a librarian, with her long gray braid wound in a bun, cardigan sweaters, and an assortment of knee-length plaid skirts worn with nude-colored nylons. She's an older woman whom I've always found attractive; she makes me wonder what she looked like when she was young. Her face is long and slender, with large glass brown eyes; she looks like a friendly calf. As with any woman who winds a long braid into a cinnamon roll–sized bun, I cannot help wanting to see what she looks like with it unwound, undone and spread out across her back and shoulders. How long is it really? Since we know each other relatively well, I took the chance and asked her once if she ever took it down. "When I sleep—and of course when it needs to be brushed," she told me, in an informative way.

I was retouching some paint on the banister of the staircase in the main lobby. Mrs. Caldwell was at the main desk telling me about which of her children were not coming to visit this Christmas and how that made her reflect on the possibility that she may have been a bad mother. She was telling me and everyone else in the main lobby of the library, since there was a steady stream of people coming and going, dropping off books, asking questions, and reading the plastic-covered magazines in the informal reading area by the fireplace.

A school field trip flooded through the main doors, and twenty children wrapped in winter coats waddled in. They were shepherded by two older teachers and three young teenage girls, who looked shabby and troubling and who I knew were affiliated with some program that paired them with lower-school classes in hopes of reforming their wayward lives. One of the three girls was pregnant, and her old winter coat looked like it might bust its zipper.

I looked down at the class and watched as Mrs. Caldwell scurried out from behind her desk with her hands out in front of her, ready to pinch some cheeks. "It's cold, it's so cold, it's cold out! Ooh, you come inside and get out of the cold! Ooh!" She closed the heavy door behind them and worked her way back into the crowd. She was over all of them at once, rubbing her hands on their coats and peering down into their hoods. It was amazing—she made her way through their little mob, touching, patting, and rubbing each kid while maintaining a conversation with the two teachers in charge. "Yes, downstairs, downstairs, the reading room's just been vacuumed. If the heat's not working Warren'll be down to give the radiator a kick!" I imagined that she could perhaps be the best mother on the face of the earth. If I were her child, I would be rushing home every Christmas, every holiday, always.

From where I sat near the top steps of the curving staircase, I could survey the action. I recognized Valerie's son in the back of the group, under the arm of one of the teenage girls. Valerie's son was wearing the hat with the pointed ears, and he was talking to a boy next to him. Most of the children were holding hands, which was a strange and disarming thing to see. Disarming in its sweetness and utter lack of anything else. All the children gabbed away in the lobby of the library, their voices combined into a chirping muddle. Mitten in mitten, glove in glove, they passed by the stairway toward the back staircase and I peered down on them, like a bird perched, or a cat caught, or a plastic bag snagged and unnoticed in the branches of a tree.

Downstairs in the children's reading room the radiator is erratic, and Mrs. Caldwell told me to go down see that it was working. It was hard to get to. I had to step through the field of children, strewn around, as their boots and coats were in the hallway, on the room's worn shag carpet.

It was almost soundless among them, except for the voice of one of the teachers, who was doing her best to make herself comfortable in a miniature chair while she read to them. I was amazed at their attention, which was unwavering. I felt a prick of jealousy for their lives. Sit and listen to a story. Apple juice in a paper cup, a ginger snap. Rest on a mat.

I envied the children's calm and composure. What did they know? Nothing much yet. I stared at them and listened to the story myself, something about a girl who lost her favorite music box and a boy who got pulled by his kite all around mainland China.

Soon the kids' attention started to wander, and they began to chatter and laugh and become unruly, which was entertaining to witness. The teacher who was reading the story had given up and joined forces with the others in an attempt to restore order. I looked for Valerie's son among the melee and spotted him sitting upright against a bookshelf, with his legs folded under him Indian style. He looked spaced out. A lamp was lit on the table next to him, and the light fell over the top of his head and highlighted the waves in his dark hair. This was the first time I had noticed his hair, because it was the first time I had seen him without a hat. His hair was not deep red like Valerie's, it was dark brown with a slight curl to it. I couldn't help thinking of Joan, because her hair is like that, only long and wild. Mine is too, though a lighter brown, and short. "It's unfair," my mother would say, because her hair was fine and blond and was so often filled with static she had to smooth it down with a small squirt of moisturizer cream. "It's unfair—look at this," she'd say, picking up a thin clump of her hair from her shoulder. "You two are the lucky ducks. You've got your father's hair."

I went upstairs into Periodicals to pull out the old magazines for recycling. Mrs. Caldwell was still at the main desk, talking to some old ladies.

"Is the heat on down there, Warren?" she asked.

"Yes. I just had to play around with the knob," I said.

"Yes, that's right." She smiled at me, smiled at the old ladies, and smiled all around the room in an indiscriminate way.

Only a few people were in Periodicals when I walked in. It was not the usual assortment of elderly people in the green leather reading chairs folding and refolding the newspapers—fisherman types, baby-sitters, PTA affiliates, the women who worked at the yarn store or town hall who'd come in to read *People* magazine. The room was nearly empty except for an ancient-looking man dropping nickels in the copier and a tall dark-haired guy I quickly recognized as Mike.

"Hey, Warren," he whispered, as he strode over to where I had quickly sat down, behind the desk in the corner by the window. He was wearing a puffy down coat and work pants, smiling his crooked, harmless grin.

"Hey," I said, picking up the label gun and loading it with thin red adhesive tape.

"How's it going?" he asked. Two seconds into our conversation and I could already tell he was nervous. I wanted to say, Don't be nervous. Be an asshole or something. Have a personality.

"OK. Everything is going OK." I drew out the O sound in OK. I sounded like a jerk, I knew, as I punched the letters into the tape in an overly determined way.

"OK. Cool. I want to—I mean, can I ask you something?" he said. "I want your advice about what I should get Joan for Christmas."

"Oh." This took me by surprise. I didn't even know what *I* was going to get Joan for Christmas.

"I figure you know her best," he added.

"You are correct," I said.

"That's what I figured. That's why I came by."

"So, you'd say that you *don't* know her?" I asked.

"No, I do know her, but I just don't know what to get her for a present. Something nice, something she'll like, like a book or something."

"We don't sell books here at the library." I thought to myself, *I'm an asshole.*

"I know that." He shrugged. "It's just an idea, because I know she likes to read and knows a lot about books."

"I read way more than Joan. She hardly finishes half the books even *I* give to her."

"OK." He looked confused. Obviously, I thought, he wasn't used to having interactions like this. It shed some light on perhaps why Joan liked him so much. He sat down and pulled the chair up closer to the desk. His face re-formed into its usual expression of eager calm, like a dog that appears at your chair and just wants you to place your hand lightly on its head. "Yeah, she's always so busy, so I want to get her something that she likes—but not something that will stress her out."

"Oh, but that could be anything." I said. My mild slandering of Joan caught me by surprise.

"Jewelry?" he asked. "Does she have a lot of that? It's kind of a lame gift."

"Yes, it is. Or it can be. You wouldn't know it, but she has a lot of it she doesn't wear."

"And not a book. No books, right?"

"Well, I mean, she likes books. Yes. We both do. Like I said, I read more than she does and everything, but she likes to read, yes. You could get her a book and she'd like it, I'm sure. Depending on the book, obviously."

"Well, that's the thing. What book should I get her? You know her best. What would she like?"

"I don't know, actually. I'd have to think."

We were facing each other, me behind the desk and him in the chair across from me, leaning forward with his elbows on his knees. He was doing this as a way to keep our conversational noise down, as we had already gotten a dirty look from a hunched-over woman who had come to read her horoscope on the back page of the paper.

"Go ahead and think. I'll just sit here and wait." He leaned back and grinned at nothing in particular. His unself-conscious calm and ease inspired both annoyance and awe in me. What makes a person this way? I wondered.

"Or should I go? Do you want to talk later? I can swing by later." He was all apologies, accommodations.

In the small distance that separated us I noticed that his eyes were not at all like the elves' eyes in the book we had read when we were young. I saw that they were a striking green color, like water in a tide pool, and not small and impish, dark and simply drawn. Mike was less like a real elf— that is, like the elves in the book—than I had thought. Though his nose was upturned and he had an innocence that was completely foreign to me, I realized as I spoke directly to him, as I looked at him without malice, he became himself and less and less like an elf on the page. This was disappointing.

"No, you can stay here," I was surprised to hear myself say. "It doesn't really matter. You're not distracting me. Nothing does," I added, without knowing what exactly I meant.

I was hoping Mrs. Caldwell would come in and ask me to do something that needed to be done somewhere else in the library, somewhere nonemployees were forbidden, but I could hear her having a conversation in the lobby. She was explaining, to someone who whispered his responses, about which children of hers weren't coming home for Christmas and how that made her reconsider all sorts of things.

"What makes her happy do you think?" We were sitting in the cab of Mike's truck, waiting for the engine to warm up. It was six-thirty and already pitch dark in the parking lot behind the library. "Because she can be so tough."

"What?" I had been thinking about what sort of compromise I had succumbed to by accepting Mike's offer of a ride home. My reasons were confused, though the bitter cold, the habitually late town bus, and the long walk up the hill and across the cove were major factors in my decision.

Still, the fact that I felt a little flattered by Mike's choice to sit around the library until it closed, just so he could ask me questions about Joan and me, what we liked and didn't like, remained stubbornly in my head. I brooded over why I was sitting in the cab of the truck whereas normally I would be alone on the bus or walking up Granite Street banging on my Walkman, trying to get the last ounce of juice out of the batteries. I couldn't make sense of any of it.

It had been a strange day, and not an easy one. I was too tired to refuse Mike's offer. He had helped me stack some books on the second floor, though I had to redo them, since he didn't quite understand how the separate sets of call numbers worked. The whole day had been strange. Just thinking about Valerie's son left me puzzled and adrift, uncertain about my fixation on him and his mother. I thought about my parents. While I was punching cards earlier that morning, it occurred to me, suddenly and without reason, that they had died. They were gone, and Joan and I were alone. And just looking at Mike, just listening to him being *so nice, so considerate,* made me want to start crying. I couldn't say why I was feeling so bad. It had just turned out to be a difficult day. A long time ago I had accepted that days could be inexplicably difficult. That's the only way I found I could manage.

"What do you think would make Joan happy?" His breath shot out in a mist that clouded around the steering wheel. His teeth glowed green from the dashboard lights. I was thinking, *This is where Joan sits on all their rides together to plow snow. This is what he looks like to her as they drive around all night.* I looked at him and discovered something.

This was my revelation: Mike Mitchell was not a bad-looking guy. He was tall and thin, and though clearly not as smart as I was, he was, at that moment, completely focused on one thing: Joan's happiness. He had a simple objective, and it was Joan. I was certain he wasn't really thinking about the actual depth of his task, the actual things he might have to do to make her happy; that didn't seem to ruffle or deter him. He just wanted to get her a present that for the time being would make her happy, happy to have the gift and happy to have him.

And I realized it was she who was the reason he came up and talked to me in the first place. She was why I was invited into his truck. All of this because he wanted to be nice to me. All because he cares about Joan who cares about me—this was his reason. It was clear. It was obvious. What was I thinking? Why was I making it complex? Why was I sitting with him in the cab of the truck when this has nothing to do with me?

I wished he had never come back, but that was pointless. I wished Joan were strong enough to sustain the anger and hatred she had had for him while he was gone, but that was futile. She seemed to be fixated on him more deeply now than ever before. I wished I had had the sense to suck it up, wait out in the cold, and take the fucking bus home.

For a split second I felt like I was going to throw up. I was tired. Again, it had been a terrible day. I thought of Joan at home, sitting at the kitchen table reading the paper or watching TV. I felt ashamed, duplicitous, humiliated, a wimp.

"Soup in a bowl," I said.

"What?"

"She loves soup in a bowl. It's the little things, you know."

I didn't want him having any more information. I was sick of giving him things, and I was tired of talking about Joan.

"Wait, what?" he said, dumbfounded.

The period of silence that followed was taken up by him toying with the pull-throttle of the truck and me thinking more about the unruly class of children and my inability to be consistently helpful and kind to Mike. I thought about how stupid he was and how mean I could be. I thought how simple and free of sarcasm he seemed to remain, and how spiteful and skeptical I was of him and people like him.

I brooded on how obnoxious the soup-in-a-bowl comment was. I wondered if he was the type to remember things like that and hold a grudge. I thought about Joan at home and what she would say when I got out of Mike's truck—if she would be pleased or be pissed. I thought about Valerie's son sitting quietly on the floor, staring at the rug as if in a trance. I thought about my mother in the garden and my father's sleeping face, how he slept all the time during the last days of his sickness. I thought about how things had changed and how I would not be able to listen to Joan's complaints about Mike again. And how I would not be able to ignore them either.

17

"I have a hilarious idea," Joan says to me, coming in the door laughing.

"And what might that be?" I ask, grateful for her arrival, having been alone at home all day.

"I heard that the Polar Bear Club is swimming out near Tuck's Point this afternoon," Joan says giddily.

"That's a fucking hilarious idea," I say.

"No, we should go watch them! It'll be funny!"

"You're right. There's nothing funnier than watching old people in bathing suits splash around in arctic-temperature seawater."

"Come on, it'll be good to get out of the house. I guarantee it will be amusing."

"I'm sure it will be in some way. But I don't understand why you'd be into it. It doesn't seem like you at all to want to go and be a spectator."

"We're not going to be spectators, exactly—we'll stay in the car and watch. Or we'll hide. We're not going to be seen; we're going to spy!"

"You're the person who gave me all that shit for spying on the kids on Halloween! You said it was perverted!"

"It was vaguely perverted, but only because it was your idea and you're a pervert. I'll go by myself. I was just asking if you want to join me."

"Of course I do!"

We drive to Tuck's Point, which is a spit of sand and rock that juts out the back of the Nature Reserve. We park in the parking lot and make our way quietly to the path that leads through the woods. There are laminated plaques on posts situated at scenic parts of the trail, and on each plaque is a poem that Joan insists there is no time to read. "We'll come back another day, when we're not in a rush," she assures me. I don't mind. I've read them hundreds of times.

"I'm wondering if we should have parked the car somewhere else and walked in—you know, to keep us covered," she says.

"Joan, I don't think it's such a big deal. If we get 'caught,' we can just say we're on a walk or something. I doubt anyone will really care."

"OK, fine. We just have to be quiet."

Joan moves slowly along the packed dirt path, carefully avoiding twigs and small piles of dry leaves; I follow behind her. Our progress is slow because she is concerned that the tracks we make in the shallow drifts of snow will give us away.

"Squanto, can we pick up the pace here? It's not exactly warm out," I say.

"We have to find a good spot where we can see them but they can't see us," Joan says.

"Yes, of course we do."

We find a large boulder to hide behind about ten yards from where the path spills down the embankment onto the sand. We have an open view of the entire beach and of the group of people ("polar bears") who are standing around wearing running pants, fleece jackets, and knit hats with large yarn pom-poms. Of the fifteen people on the beach, ten of them are elderly, at least in their seventies, three are in their fifties; one is a thirtyish-looking guy; and one is a child, a girl, hopping up and down to keep warm.

"Wow, what a crew," I say.

"Shhhhh!"

We watch as they get revved up, pound and rub on one another's backs, and yell "Are you ready?" loudly in the air. They laugh and pass around a steaming thermos, and everyone takes swigs. The sun is low, and its deep golden light illuminates the group with the effect of firelight. I look closely at the people and recognize some faces but no one I exactly know.

As I watch them, I find I don't feel as skeptical about the assembly as I thought I would. These people seem tight—friends in an aggressively appreciative way. They all like to jump in freezing-cold water, and they have found each other, so how about that?

"Do you think that little girl is going to go in?" I ask Joan. "She'll wait on the beach, right? Because, won't it stunt her growth or something?"

"Hold on," she says, scrutinizing the crowd. "They're getting ready. The clothes are coming off."

"Great."

Everyone at once, as if signaled by some unheard bell, starts shedding clothes. Everyone, thankfully, is wearing some kind of bathing suit underneath their outfits, though all the men wear small Speedo-type trunks. I envy their lack of embarrassment, their nonchalance at how the temperature humiliates their privates. The women wear skirted one-piece bathing suits and one or two don swimming caps, which is entertaining to watch as they snap the caps onto their scalps. The little girl wears a regular little girl's bathing suit, though she keeps a white tank top on over it.

Once they are disrobed, they all join hands in a line and begin to walk slowly toward the water's edge. They crow and cackle and laugh in the frigid air, and their skin begins to glow, luminous white against the deep green water. When they reach the water they stop, ankle-high in the gentle waves, and howl, in unison, loudly in the call of a wolf.

"That's taking it a bit too far, don't you think?" I ask Joan.

"Yes, I do," she says, with an uneasy look.

"Is that what a polar bear sounds like?" I ask, staring.

"Maybe it is," Joan replies, rapt.

They proceed forward in their line, all at once, everyone in step except the little girl, who hops up and down moaning, making little splashes. Everyone else is still whooping and hollering and singing songs that sound religious. They continue walking until their heads, one by one, the shortest first, disappear under the dark water. And once they submerge, they explode violently out, shoot up, and shriek, shaking their heads violently and splashing around. Everyone cheers loudly and heartily for them.

Every inch of my skin is covered in bumps; my groin aches. I lean against Joan and she leans against me and we sit there in wonder.

"Oh, my God, Dad would have loved this," I say.

"I'm sure he did this at least once. I can just imagine him down here. I have to ask Mike if he knows whether Dad ever came out with these guys."

"How would Mike know?"

"Because he's the one who told me about this happening today in the first place."

"Is Mike in the Polar Bear Club? Please say no."

"God, no, he thinks it's crazy. But his dad's in it."

"What? Oh, no, Joan!"

"I know, it's crazy. You'd never guess."

"Does Mike know you came out to watch?"

"No! He'd die if he knew I came out here!"

"Then, tell me, why are we here again? For the laughs?"

"Yes. And to see Mike's dad."

"Don't you see him enough already? I mean without having to see him cavorting around in a tiny bathing suit in the middle of winter?"

"It's just not the same." Joan gets a weird coy look on her face.

"You're here to check out Mike's father? That's twisted!"

"Not check him out—I'm just here to see. You know, to look at him. Get an idea."

"What kind of idea?" I feel sick.

"You know, what Mike might look like when he's older. See what I might have to look forward to . . . or maybe not."

"This is fucked up."

"No it's not. You have to admit, it's ingenious."

"And useful, I'm sure you'd say."

"Yes, quite useful."

"I don't understand this at all." I feel the need to jump into the bracing water myself.

"Well, I don't really expect you to."

18

When my father was released from the hospital last January, he and I went driving in his truck down near the river. I drove because he was not allowed to operate a vehicle. His condition was that he was "on death's door"—those were his words. He got to come home from the hospital a week after New Year's because he had leveled out and his doctors saw this might be his last chance. Two days after Christmas he had had a seizure in bed while my mother was sleeping next to him, and it took us twenty minutes to hear her screaming. Joan and I were playing the radio in the kitchen, joking and dancing around, making the breakfast we planned to bring up to them on two blue lacquer trays.

It was January, but we were having a thaw. The weather had been eerie all winter: biting cold and wind, snow and sleet, and then a sudden warm day out of nowhere, where the sun was shining and everyone was out on the sidewalks and in town, walking their dogs, saying Can you believe this? to one another.

My father asked me to take him out in the truck; he said he needed new air. My mother was out of the house for once. As soon as she left he called me onto the sun porch where he sat, as always, looking out over the ocean.

"Let's go for a ride," he said.

"In the car?"

"In the car."

"Are you sure we should?" I asked him.

"Certain," he said.

"Aren't you supposed to stay indoors?" I asked.

"I'm supposed to be alive," he said.

There was no point in reassuring him that he *was* alive—breathing and thinking, looking at me with a terrible, inscrutable expression. But I said it anyway. "You *are* alive."

"I feel like a piece of furniture," he said, "but useless."

I knew what he meant. Every day was the same for him: Joan or me offering him the same three beverages, the same mealy, bland food substitutes, at scheduled intervals throughout the day. He wore a blue robe and brown slippers, and on colder days he donned a light-blue knit cap with a red maple-leaf design. Each day replicated itself, like the waves he'd watch out the window, dividing and merging, indistinguishable.

"It's not going to kill me to try something new," my father said to me.

"Mom will go ballistic if she comes home and you're gone."

"At some point that'll be the case," he said. "Let's go out while I'm still able to come back."

"Jesus, Dad. What a way to look at it."

He was still bandaged up. He wore a neck brace because his neck was weak from all the times they had to remove this or that, a tumor or some cells to test in a dish. I drove slowly, cautiously, trying to avoid the many potholes our town is known to ignore. My father winced each time the car bucked over the uneven road.

"I'm sorry," I said to him.

"Not a problem," he said, through gritted teeth.

We drove to Scallop Point and parked in the parking lot of the Inn, which had a view of the ocean and the many small chains of islands offshore.

"The Pilgrims named these islands after animals," he said, as if it was new information when he had been telling us for our entire lives, "and for the few things that they brought with them. And the things they wished they had brought. And the things they missed most." His throat was sore, but he labored on.

We named the islands that we could see, but he grew tired, so I filled in most of the words while he nodded and drank a weak mixture of apple juice and seltzer water I had made for him and put in a plastic bottle: Hope Chest, Buckle, Mule, Minnow, Old Dory Landing, Biscuit, and Sow.

"Where should we go?" I asked him. "I think we should go home."

"I think we should just drive around," he said.

The sun was low in the sky because it was four in the afternoon; it gleamed above the water like a coin. We drove west, inland and therefore into darkness. "Do you want anything to eat?" I asked.

"No. This is good." He tapped the plastic bottle resting on his knee.

"OK. Tell me, though, OK?"

"I'll say something."

"So, I guess I'll just drive around now."

"All around," he said.

We drove along the river, which had flooded from the rain and the warm weather onto the low fields that surround its banks and the road beside it. The tips of the tall grass peered above the water's surface and swayed as if in wind, though it was the river's hidden current that caused the ghostly movement. A white farmhouse in the middle of the field appeared to be balanced on glass; the water crept up to its walls. The yard had vanished. I remember, years ago, riding my bike past the house and taking a bunch of small green grapes from the arbor next to the garage. It was stealing, but I couldn't resist—they were perfect looking, dusty green with waxen leaves, a satisfying heft in my hand. In the end, the grapes were hard and sour and inedible and I ripped them from their stems and threw them like pellet shot (with that satisfying sound) into the river.

When we drove by I could see the grape arbor was submerged, but in the dusk I couldn't see if the vines were dried and clinging to the wood, the way our trumpet vine looks in the winter—pitiful—as if it might never come back to life.

We came to the stop sign at the four-way intersection. River Road, which goes along the river and eventually over the stone bridge—from which Joan and I had dropped the Christmas tree into the ice—was blockaded with orange and white sawhorses and three flares, hissing on wire tripods on the pavement. The truck's headlights shone on the sawhorses and showed that the water had come up just behind them. The road was completely flooded, and I could see the current working its way from the field, over the road, and into the woods, where the thinnest trees were already beginning to bow. I looked at my father, who was looking at the water.

"Go in," he said. "Let's go in."

I maneuvered the truck to the left of the sawhorses, where there was more room between the blockade and the ditch on the side of the road. I was cautious and edged the truck through in first gear. From where we were on the road, about a quarter mile from the stone bridge, the water had risen far beyond its banks. I had never seen flooding this severe before.

As the truck inched closer to where the road was no longer pavement but a swift flowing sheet of brackish water, I turned to look at my father, who had been silent since goading me beyond the blockade. He stared out through the windshield and watched the water flickering wildly in the headlights' steady beams. He rolled down his window and we both jumped as the truck filled with the deafening sound of the river—an eerie noise, the sound of an invisible stadium, packed and unruly.

"Let's go in," my father said to me. "All the way."

"Why?" I asked.

"Let's see how deep it gets," he said.

"Up to here," I said. "Obviously, up to this part of the road. It's strong. Look how it's pushing over all the trees in the woods. It's up to the trunks of those trees by the road."

"Let's go in," he repeated.

I put the truck in gear and slowly released the clutch. I was afraid he would think I was a wimp if I refused. We rolled forward, into the shallowest part of the swollen river.

After ten feet the river water already covered the bottom quarter of the tires; I opened my door and leaned out. It was up to the hubcaps; and the chrome glinted in the reflected light off the river. I put my hand in the water that rushed under the chassis of the truck; it was cold and pushed hard against my hand. I was closer to the river's noise, which at this distance was like the sound of an exhaled breath—a thousand released breaths— against my face.

I was afraid to drive too fast into the water because it was getting deep quickly. I stayed in first gear the whole time, rolling slowly into the flood. We were still on the first part of the flooded road, and I was visualizing what lay ahead: a large tree would be on the right, where Salem Road intersects with River Road.

As we drove, the water level reached the middle of the tires. I could hear the water sucking out of the treads as the tires turned. We had not yet reached the intersection at Salem Road, which I figured would be halfway to the stone bridge. My father said, "Keep it moving; don't let it idle."

"OK," I said. "Should I shift?"

"No, don't. It's getting deep fast."

Once, when Joan, my father, and I were out on the boat, we got stuck in the marsh. We'd missed the tide and had to wait until it came in again to lift us out of the muddy puddle we sat lolling in. All three of us went walking in the marsh to look for deer and cranberries. I remember that he walked between us and held our hands, lifted us both up on either side of him over the muddiest patches of ground, to protect the cuffs of our pants.

As the evening drew on, the cold wind blew in with the tide and we waded back through the rank mud to the boat. We sat up against our father as the boat gradually lifted beneath us. We sang some songs that Joan and I knew from school. Joan taught my father the words to sing along with me. Joan, like my mother, has such a pretty voice, and she sang by herself and beckoned us in when our parts came around.

We sat in the boat with a wool blanket over our laps as the twilight thickened above the trees on the western side of the marsh. Then we were off, rocking in the narrow channel, the sky replete with the wings of bats.

Finally, the large dead tree was in sight and Salem Road's green sign hovered above the water on a slanted pole. It flashed in the way road signs flash, the way an animal's eyes flash, when they're struck by headlights. "Salem Road. Should we take it and get out of here?" I asked. I didn't know what he was going to say. I thought he might be scared. He was sick and was going to die—we all knew this, he knew this; we had talked about it a few months earlier, at dinner.

I think he meant to bring it up as if it were a normal topic, like what came in the mail that morning, or what we did on that particular day. He said, "I can't imagine that I'll make it," and my mother instantly started to cry and choked on a seeded roll. Joan and I sat in silence. What was there to say? We just listened to her coughing and then pounded gently on her back.

That night had been warm, one of the many unseasonably warm nights last autumn. But this was early, just after summer's end. Before dinner, I'd been outside in the yard under the trees, which were still full of leaves and the dense rinsed smell of the ocean. The trees that flanked the garden, sprawling beyond its rugged plot, still had small pink flowers covering the limbs. The trumpet vine beside the house looked luminous in the dim light, stitched to its trellis, its orange blossoms nodding in the wind. It was almost dark. There was stillness in the yard, a feeling of supreme composition and accord among everything alive around me. I wanted to stay outside, even though my mother was calling me to come in for dinner. I could see my mother and father in the kitchen window, seated at the table, waiting.

"No," my father said with a start. He looked over at me, his eyes trying, it seemed, to appear strict, though there was remorse in them, and fear. "Keep going," he said. "Salem Road will be worse."

Normally, from the intersection, the surrounding fields and the trees that line the riverbanks can be seen, but now water was everywhere—insane, rushing water—already covering the front bumper of the truck and splashing over the grille. I was trying to picture the rest of the road in my head: a bend up ahead to the left and then a straightaway that led to the stone bridge. The current was so strong I had to hold the steering wheel tightly to keep the truck from being forced over toward the side of the road. Branches and other mysterious objects slammed into the side of the truck, collected, built up like a beaver's dam. My father opened his window and tried to pull apart the branches and throw them over the cab or across the hood, but it wore him out. He started coughing and cried out; something must have torn, sutures or stitches, because a blot of blood the size of a golf ball appeared on the bandages beneath the open buttons on his flannel shirt. "Don't do that, Dad!" I cried.

"I'm trying to help you!" he snapped.

Soon, the headlights were like the lights in a fish tank, blurry and ghostly in the brown water that washed over them. We were parallel with the river's bend, and I could hear the current pressing against the truck doors. Dull metallic thuds echoed around us. I was sweating because it took a great effort to keep the car on what I believed was still the road—it was impossible to tell; the yellow line was lost deep underwater.

"We have to get out of here, the water's too high," my father said. If it gets in the engine, it will seize up."

He used to take us all on tours of the islands. He even took our dog at the time, Peanut. We all went out in the boat.

Those trips on the boat were how we learned the islands' names, and later we learned their strange shapes, from aerial maps he'd show us of the coast. Only Rattlesnake and Quahog looked vaguely like what their names suggested, and the Seven Sisters were of various shapes but close enough so you could swim from one to another, which we did. I remember my family swimming off the beach of one of the Sisters. The ocean water was cold but clear and pure; it was like swimming through glass. My mother swam near me in a dark blue bathing suit and her hair streamed behind her, a gold fan folding and spreading as she side-stroked. My father swam nearby with Joan; he swam like a dolphin: launched himself out of the water and dove back in. His legs were thick and heavily muscled; strange bulbous veins wound their way through his calves. He stood upright in the shallow water and balanced us on his shoulders. He grabbed us and threw us miles into the air, and we would land with a slap and splash far away. He held Peanut in his arms when she got tired of swimming around in circles. And then he'd throw her into the air, too, and Peanut would land and go under, come up with this shocked expression on her face, and snort around, trying to get the water out of her snout. And my father would laugh at her, splashing, suffering, even though he loved her.

He made us all swim with him from one island to the next. He cheered us on as we paddled and stroked, as we slowly made our way

across the small channel between the islands. And as we hauled ourselves up on the shore, like a tired shipwrecked family who has lost
everything but one another, he would lie down on the wet sand in
front of us. We would stand above him shivering and blue-lipped and
he'd lie there, eyes closed, in bliss, and say, "Just lie here for a second
and feel the sun on your skin." And we'd all get down on the wet sand
and lie in the sun, our bodies strewn like ravaged shells dropped
from the beaks of gulls.

The river rushed all around us; the headlights were almost of no use
anymore. We watched in horror as the shapes of drowned rabbits
and possums floated toward us and careened off the hood. Thick
clots of river insects swarmed above the headlights' glow, and bats
dove down from the darkness above us to feed before our eyes. I
began to panic. I thought of the water seeping into the engine and
the engine seizing, the fuses blowing. I imagined sitting helpless with
my father in the dark cab of his truck as the river slowly pushed us
off the edge of road into the ravine.

I tried to figure out how I would get out of the truck without getting caught in the current, which I was certain was strong enough to
pull me down and into the dense forest beyond my window. I could
not think of how to help my father, who could barely move around
the house by himself. I didn't think I'd be able to carry him through
the swiftly moving water. I was frantic to come up with a plan of how
I would save us.

I would climb on the hood of the truck and wade in the direction
of where we came from, back to the blockade to flag down a car to go
get help. If there weren't any cars, I would run to the State Police bar-
racks, which was beyond the field, on the other side of the highway. I
pictured the scene completely: me, chest deep in the water, trudging
toward the Salem Road sign, which I would be able to hold on to
safely while plotting my course. Yes, I would climb out the truck's

window and lower myself into the river from the passenger side of the hood. I would lean into the current, swiveling my torso back and forth as I trudged diagonally back in the direction we came from, keeping the large dead tree shadowed against the evening sky in full sight as a guide. I would call to my father to make sure he knew I was going for help; help was coming.

My father said suddenly, "There's the bridge!" As we came around the bend, in the little light the headlights afforded, we could see the bridge ahead of us, not more than fifty yards away. Its slender stone railings rose above the black water like two white spines. From the way the water swarmed around the truck, I could tell we were inside the river's heart. I realized there would be no chance to get out of the truck if we needed to. The doors could not be opened because the water was almost level with the outside handles. We were sealed in. I was amazed that the engine had not seized up, though it sputtered and gave off the sour smell of hot metal.

"Keep it going—the bridge is right there," my father urged. I began to feel sick; my eyes were tearing. I could see he was scared. He was swallowing loudly and his hands were tense, gripping his knees and bunching the material of his pants in his fists. He is going to die, I thought to myself; he's terrified. How could I do this? At that moment I did not think that we were going to die in the river. All I could think about was that he was going to die, that he had been dying this entire time.

The truck edged along as invisible objects slammed against the passenger side. My panic and terror gave way to a new aspect of fear—an irrational fear like a child's imaginings. I was ashamed that I was helpless to stop them. But I could not be brave. Everything that passed by the headlights suddenly appeared to me to be a human limb, or a piece of a limb, or a body, drowned but alive, disfigured and green, its features barely intact, skin hanging flimsily from the bone. I was convinced that the sudden thuds against the truck's side were not branches and trash but someone trying to grab hold, trying to get on top of the truck or trying to pull us off the road. I drove, leaning forward, my mouth dry and foul. I pictured the poor people I had read about in the newspaper who had drowned in the river, who had drowned in the quarries, those lost at sea, surrounding the truck, begging for our hands to pull them out. *I can't help you!* I wanted to scream. *I can't do a thing!*

One time, out in the boat with our father, we had to pull him from the water. Joan and I did it together. He had jumped out of the boat to fix the motor's propeller, which had been snagged with seaweed. We were in the channel, near the sandbars that sometimes surface mysteriously during the changing tides. We were cutting through a bed of kelp to avoid running too close to the bar when the motor caught, tangled with the rubbery green ribbons, and started to smoke and smell. The boat jerked suddenly and all the shells that Joan had carefully lined up on the wooden seat flew up and then clattered against the bottom of the boat. I looked back and saw my father yelling. Once we'd slowed down and stopped, he told us to sit tight. He stood up, moved to the side of the boat, and deposited himself in the water without a splash.

Joan and I watched as he tried to crank the motor into its raised position, but the seaweed had lashed the propeller to the outboard. He struggled with it before asking for his knife, which was in the tackle box underneath where we sat on red plastic flotation pillows in the front of the boat. I held the knife carefully as I moved from the front of the boat to the rear; the waves in the channel were small but large enough to keep the boat at a steady rock. I held the knife out in front of me like a torch, and it gleamed in the sun, reflecting the bright water around us. Joan watched me cautiously.

"I need the knife, Warren, give me the knife," he said, when he came up from where he struggled under the boat.

I leaned forward to where he was treading water, holding the knife with the handle toward him as my mother had always told me to. Then he began to scream. He thrashed around in the water, turning back and forth, his teeth violently clenched. He swam away from the boat a few strokes and spiraled laterally in the water. Joan and I began to scream for him; we didn't know what was happening. He swam back to the boat in a series of rapid splashes, his face twisted in a painful grimace. He moved to the side of the boat and threw his hands up for us to grab them. Joan grabbed his left hand with both her hands and I grabbed his right hand with one. I was still holding the knife in my other hand, its point aimed at my side.

"Drop the knife, Warren—Jesus Christ, put it down!" my father cried. I let the knife go and watched it disappear in the water, glinting like a fish as it descended. We pulled at him; his hands were slippery but large, and he gripped our forearms tightly. He almost pulled us into the water with him, because we were still quite small and he was panicked, writhing in the water. The weight of us on the side of the boat tipped it closer to the water and once we got him halfway over the side, he could pull himself up the rest of the way.

I remember him lying between us, panting, facedown against the fiberglass bottom of the boat, his tanned back glittering in the sun. He squirmed around like bait. "Get them off me!" he cried. "Get them off!" And Joan and I quickly set to work, peeling off the jellyfish that had affixed themselves all over his body. With each one we'd tear off and fling into the water, a red welt the color of raw meat was left in its place. We tore them off his skin, one by one, as he lay between us stiffened and clenched, breathing heavily, biting his fists, screaming, "Jesus Christ! Jesus fucking Christ!"

"Jesus Christ, look at that!" my father said in a startled whisper. We had reached the bridge and begun gradually to climb up its arc. The headlights lifted out from under the surface of the water and revealed three shapes caught in between the stone railing of the bridge. "What are they," I asked, "people? Are they alive?"

"No. I can't tell. I don't know. I can't see."

We inched up the incline of the bridge and saw they were the drowned bodies of three deer, splayed, their limbs dragging in the current like loose grass. The headlights hit the eyes of one of the deer, and they flashed green and blue. Their coats were soaked and glittered black. One deer was turned on its side and its white belly glowed above the surface, bright as ice or a sheet of perfectly clean cloth.

"Couldn't they run away?" I asked, like a child who didn't know anything, who just asked questions. "How did they get caught?"

"I don't know," my father said, in a quiet voice. "Maybe they were sleeping."

We were on the crest of the bridge; the headlights were above the water and showed a short stretch of flooded river and then the other side of the road. We could see another blockade up ahead, the faint red lights of the flares and two shadows of sawhorses standing side by side about fifteen feet from where the river had crept up and over the road.

19

I am superstitious—and in the worst way. I believed he would be saved. I believed the night of the flood was a sign. That we had survived the river meant my father would live. But it didn't mean anything. Five days later he died in bed while my mother was downstairs finding a record to play on the stereo. She used to turn it up loud so he could hear it in their bedroom, on the third floor. There was no real reason to search for a record, because she always played the same one. It was a classical piece by a composer who had spelled out the name of his beloved in the phrases of the music. The notes rose and fell and completed the woman's name. My mother sang along with it and called out, "Isn't this beautiful? Can you imagine being that woman?"

Joan and I were not there. We were together, at the bakery; she was mopping the tiled floor and I was icing a cake for her. Patsy, the manager, was there with us; we were laughing and having a good time. While everything was happening at home, we were at the bakery, joking around like idiots.

My mother holed herself up and planned the funeral. She refused to include Joan and me in the planning. "This is mine to do—this is all I have," she told us sternly.

Then the funeral came. How do I remember that day? I remember more, I think, the stunned process of going through my mother's things, her receipts, her notes, her address book, to get the name of the priest, the number of a caterer, the times and schedules of the cemetery. I remember all this because it wasn't long after my father's funeral that we had make arrangements for my mother's.

It was clear that she couldn't handle being alive after he died. She made it clear. But we didn't know what exactly that meant, for her or for us. I tried to imagine what was in store in our future. I imagined a long recovery for Joan and me, in particular, and for our mother—a mourning period without visible end. But there would be hope. I held out some hope that she would recover, that we would recover; we would survive together, under the same roof. The fact that we would be together made our devastation bearable.

In the time after his death, Joan and I steeled ourselves, and this became our mode of dealing with our mother. It was necessary, for every day she dismissed our efforts to get close to her, showing rancor toward our solicitude. She became a changed person; grief made her our adversary, for reasons we couldn't understand or question. Our mode of grieving for our father was expressed through function and usefulness. It was a form of giving, becoming something strong our mother could lean on—or, rather, something she could throw herself against. This wasn't something we'd planned. Her grief was so potent, so wretched, so bone-marrow deep that ours in comparison, if only for its unshaped confusion, felt flimsy, unsubstantial, even though we knew we deserved to have it.

"We have lost our father!" I would say to Joan, crying on her bed.

"This was our loss too!" she would sob.

But our mother's was a sadness that projected, sprayed out, and settled, like a fine invisible dust. Invisible until you catch sight of it shifting, swirling in a shaft of light, and suddenly you become aware that it is all around, it is everywhere, and you are living inside its cloud.

Our father's funeral was short and well attended. It was on a cold day in the middle of February. Inside the church it took a while for the heat to turn on, so we wore our coats. Before the people arrived, Joan and I hurried about and did what the priest told us to do. We checked on our mother every other minute, and she'd wave us off from where she sat silently, in the second pew from the altar. I would look over and see her silver head, her eyes motionless and blank, or we would hear her crying, her sobs echoing off the high stone ceilings as we helped move a table or take the heavy nylon cover off the organ's brilliant pipes.

At eight o'clock, Richard and my father's other friend, Andy, showed up. They brought Maurice from the nursery to help. I was relieved to see Richard. He was my father's best friend. He was our family friend; thank God he's here, I found myself thinking. But of course he would be here. For some reason the fact that he had come made me feel, in some way, reinforced. Andy looked pale and nauseated, hung over, wearing an unfortunate blazer that was too small for him. Joan said to Andy, "Oh, you look really nice," because he'd made an effort to dress up. He was on the verge of tears.

At nine, people started coming in. I could hear the sound of boot soles grinding the rock salt into the granite steps of the church. The radiators were clanking as the spiraled pipes worked hard to fill the vast space with heat. Each time the doors opened, a fresh blast of freezing air would flood down the central aisle and siphon down each pew. My mother asked that Joan and I sit on either side of her; she asked that we not leave. The priest had suggested that she stand toward the back of the church and greet people as they come in, "to receive their respects." She looked at him blankly and said, "I don't think so." She told us, once we were seated, "I'm not standing back there like some ridiculous hostess."

When I was summoned to help Richard, Andy, and Maurice with the ashes, my mother grabbed my arm, panicked. "Where are you going?" she asked.

"I have to help with the ashes, Mom," I said gently.

"Oh, God!" she cried. "Joan, he has to help them," and she buried her head in Joan's shoulder.

I remember walking down the aisle, my hand gently resting on the top of the red lacquer box my mother had found for the ashes. Half of his ashes had already been placed in the sea. I looked at the faces of the other men, and their eyes were filled with tears. I looked at their various-shaped hands, their condition of wear. We all walked in time to the music, which came from the organ hidden in the apse. I looked at the windows; their stories were darkened because of the gray day roiling outside. The wings of the angels in the windows looked tarnished and grim, like the wings of swans I'd seen floating in loose formations around the saltwater pond near our house. I could not discern the stories in the windows; I was not able to consider their meanings. We were moving at a steady pace down the red carpeted aisle of the church. I looked at the people in the pews, their heads in ordered rows like the stones in the cemetery where the remaining half of him would be placed in the ground later that morning. There were more people than I'd expected would come, though the pews weren't nearly full. I was relieved by this, and dismayed.

I knew almost everyone there, but I was not in the right state of mind to tally up numbers or make associations. I felt anguish and hopelessness; I felt hollowed out. Somewhere, I knew, he was under my hand. Between my hand and my father, the brilliant lacquer box intervened, smooth and glossy as oil or a gem. Inside the box we wheeled toward the priest, the thing that was my father lay—fractured, a pile of ash, powder, and grit in no way resembling a man.

We got to the front of the church and the priest descended from the altar; he swung a smoking sphere from a chain in his hand. Somewhere, it seemed, a bell was ringing, but it was the clasp on the sphere, banging against its latch as it moved through the air. I looked back over the congregation; all the faces had tissues rising around their eyes like white blooms. I saw my mother and Joan, disconsolate, their paired form crushed together into a soft pyramid. I saw a portion of a town come out on this cold morning. It was touching. It was terrifying. I was afraid to talk to them. At the end of it, I was afraid they might ask to have a word with me.

Far in the back of the church, where the shadows of the balcony seeped down along the walls and into the side aisles, I saw a flash of copper, of red. Above the doors, above the congregation, the church's rose window pulsed as the clouds behind it fought the light back with their gradations of gray. And the glowing red light, set richly and reassuringly against the black shadows of coats and hats, shone brightly like the horns of the trumpet vine, luminous in a summer's dusk. It was not a piece of cut glass from the window, punctured by light from behind. It was not the small flames of the votive candles, packed on their risers, flickering, perishing in their own wax. I saw the red hair of Valerie in the back of the church, as she raised and lowered her head, and her pale skin, and her white hand rising to wipe her eyes with a soft yellow handkerchief.

20

December is the worst month; the house is dry, dry, dry. Every day I complain about this to Joan, and she agrees with me, but offers no solutions. The only humidifier we have broke because my mother ran it day and night and, inevitably, without water, so the motor burned out. Now that it's cold again and the radiators are pumping out their arid heat, our skin is dry and our hair feels brittle.

I went out the other day and bought five aluminum roasting pans to fill with water and put on the radiators. I'd heard this recommended on the radio. When Joan saw them, she asked in an unhelpful way, "Is it healthy for us to be breathing those particles?" referring to the bubbles that had formed at the floor and sides of the tray and the amount of water that had already evaporated.

Every day now I go around the house and refill the pans; they dry out quickly and get caked with a mysterious white film when the water is completely gone. Joan might be right about particles. But I laugh every time I refill them in the bathtub or kitchen sink. SUPPORT THE BOTTOM, it says on the base of the tin. I showed Joan and we both laughed. "Support the bottom!" we yelled, and slapped each other's butts.

The difference is that I laugh almost every time I refill the pans and she laughed only once, because she never does the refilling. She rarely notices them sitting empty and dry on the radiators, or anything else that needs to be done. I think I know how my mother felt when we neglected our rooms or left dishes in the sink. I think I know a bit more about how my mother might have felt.

When my mother asked "What's Mike been up to, Joan?" weeks after Mike had left town, it illustrated how little she knew about what was going on in our lives. This was last November or December; I don't remember when she asked this question, since it seemed like all the time. But it was at the end of November when Mike left and Joan spiraled into a deep, unreachable sadness, because he told her he didn't know where exactly he was going or when he was coming back.

"But where would you go?" she asked.

"Anywhere," he replied.

That began the months when Joan sulked around in an unprecedented way. We couldn't afford this, as my father was enduring another round of radiation, this time on his colon, and my mother, as his full-time nurse, was making more efforts to further remove herself from our general vicinity. There was enough darkness in the house, and Joan's brand, which relied on an audience to make its point, was something I could not commit my full attention to. I knew she was in pain, but who wasn't? Pain was redundant in our house.

"Please, Warren, I don't want to sleep alone," Joan would say back then, in the days of her abandonment, standing in my room in her nightgown.

"Sleep in your own bed," I'd say to her.

"Noooooooo," she'd say, in a low moan. "Come on." And she'd jump under the covers and pretend to be asleep before I could say anything else.

I didn't really mind, and that was good, because I didn't really have a choice. The problem was that she was a restless sleeper and hoarded all the blankets and left drool spots on the pillowcases and shouted mysterious phrases like "Please! I don't know how to play cribbage!" in her sleep.

Still, in truth, I enjoyed it. I liked that she would come in every night and we would lie in bed and talk. I had never heard someone's voice so close to my face. I had never slept with anyone else in my bed before. It took some getting used to, the weight of someone else on the mattress, the warmth another body emits, her hair spilling over her pillow and onto mine. More than once I woke up with her arms around my ribs, her head resting gently against my back. And this worried me. I was afraid my mother would find us and think we were doing something wrong.

But we weren't doing anything wrong. Besides, there was nothing I could do to deter her. I didn't understand completely why she came in and I was never capable of sending her back through the door that connected our rooms. It was easier just to let her have her way.

"Come on, Warren," she'd say in an irritated way, when I put up a fight. "Come on, Warren, I'm all alone. I don't want to sleep by myself." Then she'd jump in.

"No!" I'd insist. "Get out!"

Then she'd use a facial expression that was part pleading, part imperious, and part flirtatious, which was weird to me—that she'd do that, pull the flirtatious thing. Because it worked, even though I was her brother. I'd always give in and let her sleep with me, but not for any other reason than to make her stop speaking to me that way—make her quit using the tactics she probably used on Mike and other guys who had the hots for her.

But back in those days, I barely knew Mike at all. I'd decided it was because Joan kept him to herself and because of my own inability to engage with him when I saw him around town. To say we didn't get along would be wrong, because we weren't given the chance. Plus, I never gave him a chance. I hated him in the beginning of their relationship, which I felt I was entitled to do, since he took all of Joan's attention and energy and didn't even bother with the rest of us. He should have insisted on spending time with her family. He should have forced Joan to let him come over and hang out. Joan should have known that someone like me would have liked something like that. Sometimes when I thought about it, the whole thing was Joan's fault and he left her for good reason.

I remember last January when things were growing tense between them. Joan and I were sitting in the kitchen with our mother. I looked up, and Mike's head was in the window. When Joan saw him, her face flew into a panicked twist, which got me worried.

He wouldn't even come in, though I had, as a kind host should, invited him. "No, thanks, Warren, I'll wait out here," he said. He did not look well. His skin was an odd turnip color, and his green eyes had dark streaks around the lids and redness spreading toward his temples. I wondered if he had been crying, which intrigued me and for an instant made me interested in what sort of emotions he might be capable of.

Joan whipped her coat off the back of my chair. "No, Warren, no, he can't come in; we're going out."

"Joan," my mother said in a serious way, "what's going on?" She stood up and looked back and forth between Joan and Mike.

"Where are you guys going?" I asked innocently. This question was my way of making the awkward situation more awkward, for clearly they had no plan.

"Warren, please," my mother snapped. She handed Joan her scarf from where it was slung over a chair.

"I don't know. Where do you want to go, Joan?" Mike asked, with an inappropriate lilt, given the extreme sense of terror he had engendered in her.

"I don't know, Mike, where should we go?" Joan asked—as if they might *actually* be going somewhere. "Wherever you want. You decide." She looked over at my mother, who gave her a worried look.

Mike said, "We can go anywhere."

I was going to say, Well, not quite anywhere . . . but I decided to keep my mouth shut.

"Mike," my mother said suddenly, "why not come in for some food? We were just planning what to have for dinner."

This was not true. We had been listening to our mother's highly detailed account of her day at the hospital. She had just been telling us about how she bitched out one of the nurses for not attending to my father in a sufficiently compassionate way.

"Please, Mike, come inside," my mother said.

"Mom," Joan said cautiously, "I think we have to go."

"Won't you come in?" my mother said again, smiling weakly at Mike. "Warren, take his coat."

"He's wearing his coat," I said.

"Warren," my mother said to me sternly, "please try and help the situation."

"What's the situation?" I asked her. The sudden atmosphere of panic in the kitchen was not clear to me. Joan never acted normally around Mike anyway; her behavior now was just a new version of how weird she already was. Though she did look stricken, and Mike looked stunned, standing across the kitchen from each other, with my mother and me in between.

"Warren," my mother said, looking at me as if I held the key to all resolution.

"Mike," I said, "are you hungry?"

"I think we're going to go," Joan said quickly.

"Yeah," said Mike. "Thanks, though."

My mother raced up to Joan as she made her way toward the door. "Joan!" she said in a stern whisper. "Joan. Don't let him leave. Make him stay."

21

Joan, my mother, and I were crying in the kitchen when the paramedics rushed out of the house, rushed as if there were still a life to save. I had seen him already. I saw it was not my father; it was a replica lying in his bed. A version of someone I vaguely recognized, like a poorly sculpted celebrity in a wax museum, one that takes some time to recognize, one you laugh at because it's barely done right.

When Joan and I got home from the bakery, where we had been joking around and acting like idiots with Patsy, my mother was crying in the kitchen. "What is it?" we asked her. "What's happened, Mom?" She was putting on water for tea. She had a tray laid out with two cups and a stack of plain-tasting crackers.

The music was playing on the stereo—the same record we all knew by heart at this point. My mother brought us into her arms, and Joan and I started to cry. Part of my crying was out of fear, because Joan and I had just been talking about this—that our mother was not well, that she was losing her mind. We could only wonder what she might be like when our father was gone. This was the day we would begin to know.

We stood there fused, our arms around one another, my jaw against Joan's head and her cheek pressed against our mother's forehead, who shuddered between us. We supported her, enveloped her; she was caught securely between us like a pearl.

I went upstairs and Joan stayed with my mother and called the ambulance. I wanted to leave the house altogether, but where would be a safe place to go? I passed the stereo in the living room in time to see the record player's arm eerily swing back to the start of the record. As I walked up the stairs, the scratching and crackling of the needle finding the record's groove echoed against the narrow plaster stairwell. But as I climbed the stairs the music began to recede, as if the notes couldn't bear to follow me beyond the second floor.

When I reached the third floor I saw their door was open and a shaft of sunlight glared against it, the bleak harsh light of winter against the white door. I moved along the hall, trailing my hands along the bamboo-ridged wallpaper, which produced a tingling feeling in my fingertips, and a clicking sound, as I went. I was not afraid.

The air on the third floor was not congested but it was not fresh. It was a new atmosphere to come upon. There was no longer a sense that sickness and sorrow clogged the upper rooms of the house; something seemed rinsed about the place. But I remember being reluctant to breathe the air, take it in deeply. I was afraid of its taste.

It was terrible to find him, as if it were really he, lying in bed with the breathing tube up his nostrils and the newspaper in his hands. He was something completely different but disguised as someone I knew. He was a body, emptied. This seems obvious now. What did I expect to find? He was gone by the time I discovered him. I thought of how they say; I found the body. Because that is what it is. It is like saying, I found the rind. I found the husk.

I knelt beside him and cried. I took hold of his hands, and the newspaper fell into its separate leaves. The flutterings of their fall and the distinct sound of paper sliding against the wood floor were all there was to hear in the room. There was a smell he gave off, of talc and soot and soap. His skin had changed, was changing before me, pale white into gray into beige into yellow, the way a teabag changes color as it dries on the edge of a saucer.

The paramedics came and got him. Joan kept my mother downstairs. I watched the way they went at him, like a pit crew on a car. I watched them maneuver his limbs onto the gurney, tucking them around his body. I wanted to say, Keep the sheet over his face, because they had taken off the one I had drawn over him. I wanted to say, Don't take out the body bag, because I was afraid they would. I was terrified of the black rubber bag, even though I had only seen it on TV. But suddenly it appeared, and in moments it was put under and around him, and then the sound came, the deep groan of the metal zipper clenching its teeth together as it was sealed shut.

When they took him downstairs I followed behind the red EMT jumpsuits, cramming down the stairwell, angling the gurney that slammed the wooden banister as they went. I thought about Joan and my mother in the kitchen, how they would see this violent little parade move past them in the kitchen, all the men in red and my father in his black sheath. I wanted to run down and prepare them, but I was speechless, immobile, trapped at the back of the procession.

In the kitchen Joan and my mother were embracing in a way that looked painful, grabbing on to each other with hands in the shape of claws. By the time I got to them and joined their desperate clutch, all of us heaving the desperate breath of the helpless, the paramedics were in the yard heading for the ambulance. They were racing and racing. I heard the siren blow as the lights turned on, flashing all over the walls of the kitchen.

We sat with my mother in the waiting room of the emergency unit. After a while it was impossible to produce any more tears. It was more painful to cry than to just sit there with the dull weight, like the cotton that blocks the mouth of the aspirin bottle, behind our eyes. Joan and I sat on either side of her, and she cooed and rocked between us, gently bumping up against our shoulders like a boat tethered to two posts.

22

Oh, dear the eye that softly looks,
Oh, dear the heart that fondly loves;
Though but a tender babe thou art,
The graces all grow up with thee.

Joan and I are singing. She is standing at the piano and I am at the keyboard playing. Outside, the water is black and the running lights from the passing boats are reflected clearly; the ocean is calm, the waves are small. It's like the old days, we say to each other. This is what we used to do, together and with our parents. When they weren't up for it, Joan and I would sing alone, sometimes to entertain them but mostly to entertain ourselves; all the nice carols reduced to jokes and screaming fits of laughter. It is this reason—that we used to do this on our own, for our own pleasure—that makes it possible to do now. But still, it's not easy. We turn the pages delicately; we sing with reserve, as if we're afraid we'll be caught, as if we might wake someone up. But we're enjoying this. Joan and I are singing.

It is Christmas Eve day, and Joan came home this afternoon in a pensive mood because Mike is working all night. She informed me that this went against her plans of their spending the evening together. He's working on the fishing boat that is charged with bringing in the catch for family feasts tomorrow afternoon. It is a tradition in our town. People line up at the docks in the morning, waiting in cars in their bathrobes.

So the Christmas miracle in our house is that Joan isn't a ball of misery, given Mike's choice to go out on the freezing ocean with a couple of ragged, surly fishermen rather than spend the day with her. I'm not sure what she had planned. She hadn't mentioned anything to me. I assumed we were going to be together, which we are, but the fact that she had plans that didn't include me makes me less appreciative of her rallying, agreeing to stand at the piano to sing our favorite carols.

Since the episode at the library, whenever I see Mike around town I have avoided talking to him. I don't want to risk another chat about Joan or another confusing ride in the truck. The other day I was in the bookstore, poking around the new books and harassing Mrs. Kestrel, the owner, to see if I could inspect the book catalogs of what's coming out when.

"Can I choose some books for the next order?" I asked her.

She shook her fluffy brown head at me. "No. With your taste, Warren," she said coldly, "you'd be the only one buying them. And I have to order at least fifty. And you'd only buy one and then I'd go broke. That's bad business."

"But superb customer service," I said.

Mrs. Kestrel writes a column in the local paper and manages to mention her business aplomb in some form or another every week. Part of my asking to order a book is to annoy her, since she already has a number of issues with me, which I don't respect. Professionally, she resents me because I work at the library, an institution that she believes takes potential customers away from her store. She resents me on a personal level because my mother gave her the heave-ho as a friend a few years ago. My mother accused her of being too high maintenance, too clingy, too close—and she was, calling our house all the time, always stopping by, bringing gifts for no particular occasion. She became a joke to us; we joked about how desperate she was for our mother's attentions, which, we all knew, was futile. She also resents Joan, and therefore me by association, because once Joan botched a cake order for her daughter's birthday party.

"I guess I might find what I need in the library," I say, putting the catalog down on the counter and climbing the spiral staircase to the loft.

"Not when you want it, Warren," she calls after me, "and I can guarantee it won't be new!"

I saw Mike from the second-story window of the bookshop. I was sitting in an overstuffed chair looking at a photography book of Civil War battleground sites that have been covered over by malls and movie theaters. His head was down as he loped across the street, his breath steaming, puffing steadily out of his mouth. And yet he seemed directed—something about his gait suggested he had a specific destination—so I pondered the limited amount of information I had about him in order to come up with some logical trajectory. There was nothing I could imagine; nothing about him suggested anything interesting, bad or good. And yet I watched him trudge along until he was just a vague blue smear in the tangle of branches of the bare fruit trees lined up along the park's perimeter.

This past fall I saw Mrs. Kestrel at the beach. I was alone, coming up the wooden walkway that arches over the dunes where tiny endangered birds make their nests and where the Conservation Society has put up fences so people don't tromp all over their eggs. Mrs. Kestrel was standing in the parking lot making a racket, slapping the soles of her shoes together before getting in her car.

"I didn't see you out there on the beach," she said to me brightly.

"I know," I said in a factual way, which made it sound like I had successfully hidden from her. "I didn't see you out there either."

"How are you doing, Warren? How's Joan?" she asked. In truth, she was always nice to us; she even tried to be nice after our mother dumped her. She had the sincere face and mannerisms of an old woman, though I don't think she was all that old or all that sincere. She was wearing a white floppy-brimmed hat and an irrational amount of jewelry for walking on the beach. The pendant on her coat was large and brass-colored, and it glinted in the sun. I thought about how a bird might see it from the air and swoop down and try to grab it from her chest. I had an image of the bird carrying her up in its beak, screaming, high into the sky.

"We're doing all right. Just plugging along." I didn't want to talk. Only moments before, I was alone on the beach, walking backward against the wind, out to the sandbar and back. I sat at the end of the bar for as long as I could stand the cold and watched the seals rise out of the water, their eyes watching me—or probably just surveying the shoreline.

"Oh, Warren, you are both so brave. But I can't believe it's easy for either of you." She started taking a few steps toward me. She had a meaningful expression on her face, which annoyed me. I knew my feelings toward her were tainted by my mother's opinions; I didn't even really know Mrs. Kestrel. But it was easier to be irritated by her than to be empathic. Besides, she openly criticized Mrs. Caldwell and the library in her newspaper column and had once told my mother that she didn't approve of the crass language bandied about in our household.

"Do you know how to ask for help or where to go to for help?" she asked, in what I feared would become a lecture on spiritualism. She was emotional; my mother once complained that she was a raw nerve and too new-age.

I felt conflicted, probably because I was caught off guard, having been alone on the beach that morning. Mrs. Kestrel genuinely appeared enveloped in sadness, standing beside her sporty red hatchback. She had that frown some women have because they feel things very deeply and have never been told they sometimes take them too far. She held her hat on her head with her left hand and hooked her white sneakers with the fingers in her right hand. She moved toward me, along the gravel, slowly and painfully because she was in her sock feet. I wanted to go because she was making me feel sorry for her—sorry that she was affected so profoundly by the sadness of our situation.

"Are you and Joan OK?" she began again. "You know there are a lot of people in town you could talk to. A lot of people wonder how you both are; we worry about you."

For some reason it had not occurred to me that other people would be worried about us. It was enough to endure the sympathetic stares in the grocery store and the library. It had not occurred to me that other people would actually be concerned and that their concern might be long-term. I don't know why I hadn't thought about that.

"I think we'll be fine," I said.

"How do you survive? What do you do?" She took her hand off the top of her hat and covered her mouth. She began to cry, and in the strong wind her hat flew off. She put her head down, dropped her shoes on the sandy dirt, and sobbed. Her hat rolled along, pushed by the wind, flipping along the cold parking lot. I ran after it. I retrieved it from where it had gotten trapped in the slats of a snow fence. I walked over and gave it back to her, where she stood still crying.

"I'm sorry," I said. "I'm sorry about all of this."

After singing all our favorite carols at the piano, Joan and I go into the kitchen, where food has been cooking all morning.

"We should call Auntie E," Joan says with trepidation.

"I know. I have a feeling she's just going to show up tomorrow morning."

"She left all those messages, and if we call her and deal with her now, maybe we can head her off at the pass." Joan sounds a little too serious.

"Wait—how many messages did she leave?" I ask. "I heard only one."

"No, she left—probably—ten over the last week. I just erased them all."

"I never heard any of them," I say.

"Warren, it doesn't matter. You've heard one, you've heard them all."

"I was afraid you'd say that," I said.

I don't see why having Auntie E over would be that bad. She can be pretty funny. And she loves us. It *is* the holidays, after all.

"She can't be deterred, Joan," I say. "Remember the time when we were little and she came over early Easter morning to make up an egg hunt for us?"

"Yes, and all the eggs were old and she forgot where she hid them and the whole house ended up smelling rotten."

"The house smells as it is," I say.

"Shut up, it smells good!" Joan lashes out. "You don't have to have any food if you're going to complain about the way it smells!"

"Whoa! I meant that the house smells *in general*—not that it smells because of your cooking," I say, backing away.

"Oh, sorry." Joan resumes stirring something in a saucepan, showing remorse by giving me a taste from the wooden spoon.

I find Auntie E's number in the address book and call her up. It rings and rings and finally I get her answering machine, "We cahn't come to the phone right now," her gravelly voice says.

"Hi, Auntie E, it's Warren and Joan. We're at home, and we're returning your call. It's almost Christmas, the day before. Hope you're well. Talk to you soon. Merry Christmas." I hang up the phone, feeling awkward, as if I had just prank-called someone.

"That was elegant," Joan says.

"What was I supposed to say?"

"How about, *Leave us alone*?"

"Yeah, OK, why don't you call back and say that, Joan?"

"I will, Warren. Really. *Merry Christmas, Auntie E. Please leave us alone.*"

23

I'm in the living room and Joan's still in the kitchen. She's relegated me to other parts of the house while she prepares our meal. She told me I was in her way.

The phone rings. Joan bounds into the living room from the kitchen, her hair flying up behind her. "It's Mike, it's Mike, it's Mike," she chirps. I feel the evening begin to evaporate around me.

I snatch the cordless phone up triumphantly. Joan stands over me looking irked, her hand stretched out.

"Hello," I say, waiting to hear the three-second pause before Mike's voice sputters into life on the other end.

"Brother Warren! It's your Uncle Steve." The line is crackling and it's hard to hear. Joan shakes her hand around as if to say *Give me the phone, give me the phone!*

I look at her and hand her the phone.

"Honey?" she coos into the receiver.

Her coy little smile dissolves. I stare at her smugly from the couch.

"It's Joan, yes. Sorry, Uncle Steve. How are you?" She looks at me with hatred. I am filled with glee, squirming around the couch like, as my father used to say, a pig in shit.

"He wants to come and visit," she says in a grave voice, after she hangs up. "His plan is to come and stay, get a visa, and try to get a job."

"He's a Canadian citizen? When did that happen?"

"I don't know, but he has to get a visa to live here longer than six months."

"That's what he's planning—to live in the States for more than six months?" The idea of Uncle Steve living with us makes me terribly nervous. Ominous images of him wearing a red bikini bathing suit around the house, cooking at the stove, getting the mail, reading the paper—they all make me want to throw up. "Did he say he wants to live with us?"

"Sort of. He didn't mention anyone else."

"What about Auntie E?"

"He just said he wanted to be close to his family."

"Exactly. Auntie E. He can live with her."

"Whatever, Warren, but I think he wants to live here," Joan says.

"Why now?"

"Because, Warren, what he told me was, when Mom died, he lost a sister. He said it again and again: 'I lost a sister.' And he feels bad that he wasn't there for her or for us." Joan sounds sympathetic but exhausted—and hopeless.

I turn the phrase over and over in my head: I lost a sister. It takes me a few seconds to apply it to myself, and when it sets in, I pause and make myself feel its meaning. I lost a sister. I look up at Joan, who is looking straight at me. I lost a sister. This is my sister. I lost her. I stop myself from thinking about it any further.

"Do you believe him?"

"I don't know. I don't even know him well enough to know if he's being sincere. As far as I knew he was living in Canada because he was considered a criminal here. That's what Dad always told us. But now he wants to come back."

"God."

"I know."

"Did he say anything about money? About what Mom and Dad left us?"

"I don't know. Why?" Joan's eyes roll around in their sockets, going back over the conversation in her head.

"Because that's what he was asking me that time I talked to him. He tried to be cagey about it, but he couldn't manage. He just blurted it out."

"What did you tell him?"

"I hung up. No. I told him we were fine, and *then* I hung up. I told him I was late to meet you at the diner."

"Which you were, terribly late," Joan says, with a slight smile. "But no, he didn't ask me about the money, he just asked me, about a million times, how we were. I told him we were doing OK. He seems to think we're losing our minds. He has this impression that we're closing ourselves in the house and not coming out. I told him we both have jobs."

"I heard you say that, but I didn't know what it meant." I had been listening intently, but I could not discern anything from the conversation, because Uncle Steve was doing most of the talking. Joan was barely able to get a word in.

"I'm afraid he's been talking to Auntie E and they've been coming up with weird ideas," Joan concluded.

"Always a possibility. I guess we should call her and see what she says."

"You call her," Joan says frankly. "I've done my time."

"Fine."

This time when I call Auntie E something weird happens after I finish dialing: I hear a series of clicks and beeps and then a message alerting me that my call is being forwarded to a cellular number.

What's wrong? Joan mouths.

"Hold on," I say, listening to the robotic click and whir over the connection. "Here we go."

"Yvonne Howard—hello?" a smoky voice garbles on the other end. The sound of a static-filled radio fills the background.

"Auntie E?"

"Warren?" The voice lilts roughly.

"It's Warren. Where are you? Why is the connection so bad?"

"I had my home and work phone bounced to my cell. I'm actually almost at your exit. I'll be there in a jiff, babe."

"What?" I look up at Joan.

What? she mouths again.

"You're coming over?" I blurt.

"Almost there—is Joan with you?"

"She's right here," I say. Joan winces.

"Good! See ya in a few!"

She hangs up. I look at Joan and she looks back at me. My immediate reaction is to jump up and run around the house, draw the curtains closed, lock the doors, turn off the lights, and hurry upstairs. We have devised a system of what to do with people we don't want to deal with. But this time it is too late. By the time I explain to Joan that Auntie E is on her way over, literally minutes away, there is no time to do all we have to do to create the appearance that no one is at home. And she knows we're here. We can't hide from her.

Once, Auntie E came and stayed with us when our parents went out for the evening. They were going to Richard and Mona's house. Usually they stayed out late. Sometimes they stayed out all night and returned in the morning, pretending that they got up early when we came down into the kitchen. But I could always tell when they hadn't come home. I would stay up and wait for their car in the driveway. I would be up worrying all night, afraid that something had happened to them. I never really knew what took place on those nights out with their friends. Only, on one occasion I did see what went on—it was once when they had friends over and woke me up. I saw what they were doing.

We were young and happy about the fact that Auntie E was coming to stay with us for the night. She assured my parents that everything would be fine and stood on the porch with us, waving as their car pulled out of the driveway. Once they were out of sight, she hurried to her car and produced three huge white bags from behind the front seat. Fast food. It was illegal in our house—fast food and unhealthy food of all varieties.

Auntie E insisted that our mother wouldn't find out and set to work unpacking the bags in the kitchen. Immediately the heavy scent of oil, salt, and multilevel hamburgers filled the room. Joan and I were excited as we grabbed long limp french fries from the bottom of the bag, wolfed them by the cluster, and wiped our shining greasy fingers on our jeans. Auntie E removed some dense-looking shakes from a brown cardboard tray and put them in the refrigerator. Joan and I danced around her, ketchup packets between our fingers, feeling the contents squish around in their narrow plastic sleeves. The entire experience was too much, the excitement and lawlessness, and periodically I would take a quick look out the window in case our parents' car was crawling back up toward the house.

"These are cold." Auntie E frowned as she opened the Styrofoam shell the hamburgers came in and probed her long red fingernail in between the buns. "Let's warm them up, shall we?" Joan gave her a cookie sheet and we put them in the oven to heat. "Do you want your shakes now while we wait for the burgers?" Auntie E asked, her eyes wide with excitement.

Just the idea of shakes, fundamentally a dessert-type food, *before* the actual meal sent us over the edge. I looked out the window. No car. Joan and I looked at each other; we shared a crazed excitement. We nodded furiously and took the cold cups in our hands, punctured the slits in the plastic lid with the thick striped straws, and plunged them in. The first taste was icy—the ice crystals were large and clicked minutely against my teeth; I crunched them with vigor. Then the sugary chemical surge of the shake hit my tongue, not so much a flavor as a sensation, cold and sweet, all thick slush. Joan and I braced ourselves against the refrigerator, in shock, in awe, our mouths in a fish's puckered suck.

"Bring them in the living room. Let's see what's on TV tonight."

Again we looked at each other, eyes popping, mouth working at the straws. *Bring the shakes in the living room. What's on TV tonight.* Auntie E had been at the house for a total of twenty minutes, and already the strictest rules were flying out the window. We loved her. We wanted her to stay.

As we sat on the couch, drinking our shakes and checking the newspaper, we noticed a suspicious smell in the air: food mixed with gas mixed with plastic. We ran into the kitchen and saw wispy strands of smoke spilling out of the cracks of the oven door. Joan and I opened the windows and Auntie E opened the oven. She took out the tray with an oven mitt and put it on the counter next to the sink. Once the smoke was cleared and the smell had died down, we gathered around the tray.

Everything looked normal at first. The Styrofoam shells appeared untouched and unmarred. Nothing was burned. But when Auntie E attempted to open them up, undo the little clasp at the front of each one, it wouldn't give. She tried to pry it open with her clawlike nails, but it would not split. On closer inspection we saw that the shells had shrunk, had perfectly reduced in shape and size to form-fit the burgers inside. We were astounded. The burgers were hermetically sealed in the plastic shells, coated over and completely trapped. Their lingering smell devastated us; it was the most unfair moment of our lives. We stood over the three useless objects, picked them up, and attempted to peel the Styrofoam off, but it was no use. There was nothing we could do. They were ruined.

Joan and I exchanged a look of utter despair; we knew the shape of each other's faces when subjected to such extremes. Auntie E peered down at us with a regretful expression, one that showed worry that we might slip into hysteria. But it didn't happen. Joan and I had our moment and quickly dismissed our disappointment; there was no need to get upset—or, rather, there was no point. Perhaps because the eating of fast food was so forbidden, the ruining of it was somewhat of a relief—this made our resolve more intense, since we'd not given in completely.

Moments after the plastic-shelled burgers were put back in their large white bag to be thrown out at some discreet location by Auntie E, Joan and I set to work. We cleaned the cookie sheet and scrubbed down the countertops. We searched for and swept up the drinking straws' white paper wrappings that we'd flung to the floor with crazed anticipation. Auntie E stood back and watched us. We told her to put on her coat if she thought she'd get cold; we opened all the windows.

"What are you kids doing?" she asked in shock, putting on her coat.

"She'll know," I told her.

"They'll immediately notice the smell," Joan said.

"But who knows when they're going to be back? They said late!" Auntie E pleaded. "Come on, it'll be fine!" We handed her the white bag filled with refuse, still stinking heavily of gas and plastic, the faint tinge of meat.

"You can never be too sure," I told her. "This is about rules."

"In a way," Joan said, looking at me, "it's best that this is how it turned out."

"I thought it would be nice," Auntie E said, to no one in particular. "I thought it would be a treat for you two."

24

My parents rarely entertained at our house. But it was not completely unusual to come home and find them out on the sun porch with Richard and his girlfriend Mona, Mrs. Kestrel (before she was cast out), and Andy, or other people of greater or lesser significance in their lives. If they did entertain, it was the same small group of people. I recognized their cars. I knew whose voices were whose when I walked into the kitchen. This small group would gather at our house or someone else's, or go out on a boat, or have a picnic on Quahog Island, or go to The Mill for dinner and stay until it closed. My parents would come home late and knock all the things off the kitchen table: mail, car keys.

When our parents' friends came over to our house, they all were welcoming and wanted Joan and me to join them. But it was best to stay out of it. When they presided over the sun porch, it was an uncomfortable place to be because by the time we sat down in whatever free seat or spot was left among them, the wine had been poured and poured and poured.

I remember once I came downstairs because they'd woken me up. They were being loud and I was drawn to them. Something smelled strange. I worried that something had caught on fire; I'd pictured a candle knocked over and the couch in flames.

They were all out on the sun porch when I came down. The candles were dim, spitting in the pools of wax that had collected in the wide cups of the brass candlesticks. Everyone lounged about, flung over their chairs like coats, their limbs obscured in the dim light. My mother was asleep on the wicker couch. My father, Richard, and Andy were bleary-eyed, struggling toward one another as they passed a small metal pipe among them. Mona, Richard's girlfriend, sat curled up next to Richard on the orange velvet couch, with her head tilted back. When the pipe got to her, she shook her head slowly back and forth, and a few wiry clumps of her hair sprayed out from their clip. I watched the scene from behind the windowed wall that separates the living room from the sun porch.

Joan had gone to sleep hours before. I realized how long ago that had been when the clock next to me chimed three loud notes. We had been talking about how depressing the scene downstairs was—the levels of humiliation we had to endure every time they entertained, Mom being a drunk and Dad saying gross things.

Richard opened his mouth loosely, like a blowfish, and the smoke came out in an impressive column, aimed directly at my father. A dense cloud gathered above the group when all the mouths had emptied. Mona moved and came to life; she asked Richard something that made him smile and pat her shoulder. I think she wanted to go home. She fell back against the side of the couch.

My father and Andy were in two different chairs, one wicker and one wingback, facing Richard and Mona on the couch. The table between them was congested with dessert plates, coffee cups, and the requisite nine hundred empty wine bottles. Richard motioned to Andy to give him the pipe, and Andy took another hit and handed it over, coughed a bit, and then laughed at nothing, alone. We always used to see Andy around town with small scraps of blood-dotted toilet paper stuck to his face. He would forget about them, I think, and go about his day with these little bloody scraps all around his lips and above the collar of his uniform, which was a blue one-piece delivery suit. He delivered dry cleaning.

Richard took the pipe and drew a long hit. He looked at my father and grinned with his mouth tightly closed. He turned to the side and put Mona in a gentle headlock. He took her face in his hands and put his mouth over hers. I saw the smoke spill out of the spaces between their joined mouths. Mona woke up and began to cough slightly, but then a weak smile came over her face and she began to kiss Richard. They kissed for a few minutes, openmouthed, their tongues wet and shiny, their wetness silvery in the light of the candles. My father and Andy sat in their chairs and watched. I could see my father from where I stood behind the leaded glass window; he leaned back slightly and focused on them as if he were watching television. He glanced over at my mother, who was still asleep on the small couch, a wool army blanket covering most of her body. My father leaned to the side and said something to Andy, who smiled and said something back. Then Andy said something to Richard, who stopped kissing Mona for a minute and looked at them.

Mona was limp like a doll, supported by Richard on the couch. Her head was loose and heavy and her hair was wild, fully sprung from its clasp. She had a tough-looking but pretty face, creased from spending so much time out in people's gardens, landscaping the nicer properties around town. Her hair was thick but coarse, like the tail of a horse or a brush used to polish shoes. Mona had muscular arms and legs, both visible through her red tank top and beige canvas shorts. I looked at her face as Richard held it up with one hand. She looked at peace. Richard was talking to my father; his eyes were swollen and his neat bank of white teeth glowed inside his tanned face, flashing as he spoke. There was something perverse about his expression, there was exhaustion, too—and an eagerness to please, as well.

Richard was always kind to us. He worked with my father at the nursery and would always give us tours of the greenhouses when we were young. His face was gentle, with high cheekbones and widely spaced eyes. His voice was deep, yet his laugh was high-pitched—it trilled like a whistle or a bird. It cracked us up. When we were children, he liked to try and make us laugh.

Richard turned away from my father and began kissing Mona again. She groggily came back to life and started to kiss him back. Richard sat up straight and turned his shoulders toward Mona, took her hand, and placed it on his leg, right above the knee, below the hem of his shorts. Her hand grabbed the place it had been set and squeezed. My father and Andy leaned farther back in their chairs. Richard started kissing Mona's neck, pushing her hair away from her shoulders, and kissed her tanned clavicle. She seemed oblivious to everything except Richard's head, which was eagerly pecking a line across her chest. She leaned forward and repositioned herself so that she was sidesaddle on the couch. Her hand was gently rubbing Richard's leg and he opened his legs up wide so that his shorts gaped. Her hand remained where it was, at the edge of the shorts' material, tracing her fingernails back and forth along the hem.

I thought they were going to stop. But they progressed. Suddenly Richard had his hands on her breasts and was squeezing them over her tank top. He massaged them in a circular motion while he kissed her mouth. I could see her white bra flash through the tank top's armholes as he moved her shirt around. Andy was shifting around in his chair. My father kept looking over at my mother, who hadn't moved since I had arrived at my place behind the windowed wall in the living room.

I had only fooled around with a girl once—it was John's sister, Cindy. I was over at their house one afternoon in tenth grade, and it was just me and John and Cindy sitting around, keeping an eye on their two younger sisters while their mother was at aerobics, which was held at a roller rink in the town next to ours. We had been watching movies they'd taped off cable, late-night movies that John kept hidden between the mattress and box spring of his bed. His little sisters were in the basement, playing with dolls whose brightly colored hair emitted different fruity aromas.

John had to go on his paper route. I told him I'd go with him but he said he went on his bike and they had only girls' bikes, which I would break if I were to ride one. I was going to call home to get picked up but Cindy said she'd drive me. She only had her permit, but their parents let her drive anyway, because the younger sisters needed to be shuttled back and forth to their ballet, tap, and jazz dance classes.

John left. Cindy told me that she had to get her car keys in her room and I should come with her. We went into her parents' room, which was an extra room built onto the back of the house. It was long and narrow, with high windows along the upper part of the walls, like in a basement or a bunker. At one end of the room was a sliding glass door that went out into the backyard and had a view of the aboveground pool and its various inflatable animals and rafts floating around in random formations. Every now and then what looked like a head would appear at the edge of the pool. I thought it was someone swimming, someone spying on us in the house. But it was a basketball, half bleached from the sun and chlorine.

Misty, their dog, was panting on the other side of the door. She had drooled pasty white goo all over the glass. Cindy walked over and let her in and said, "No barking, Misty! No barking!" The room was cool because the air conditioner was on. I didn't know what we were doing in her parents' room—I figured we were looking for the car keys. Cindy didn't say anything to me as she began to strip the blankets and sheets off her parents' bed. "Help me," she said finally, pulling at the bottom sheet, whose corner was caught between the mattress and the wall. I picked up the corner of the mattress and the sheet flew free; it snapped and fluttered in the air between us. Soon there was nothing on the bed but the satiny quilted mattress cover, glossy in the dense shafts of summer light that came in through the high windows. Cindy slid across the mattress on her stomach. "We used to slide around on mattresses when we were little," she said. I stood patting Misty, who had to be held down or she would start jumping.

"Yeah," I said.

"Warren?" Cindy asked.

"Uh-huh?" I replied. I figured she was doing chores, starting the laundry before she took me home.

"Take off your shirt and come over here," she said, in a voice one would use to give clear, helpful directions to a stranger.

Richard reached down, took Mona's hand, and put it firmly against the fly of his shorts. He stopped kissing her for a moment while he held it there. He attempted to guide it into the opened leg of his shorts; he pulled her over toward him so that the hand could maneuver inside. His other hand reached around her waist and made its way to her lower back. I could see the top of her underwear, pink with a thin white waistband.

I kept my shirt on and sat down on the corner of the bed. Misty started to thump her tail against the rug, ready to jump around in her hyper way. "Misty, no! Misty, stay!" Cindy commanded.

"Come on, Warren," she said to me quietly. She slid over behind me and put her chin on my shoulder. Jesus, I thought to myself. What do I do?

Cindy put her hands on my shoulders and pulled me down onto my back. She flipped around me and straddled my chest, sitting with all her weight on my stomach. This could just be a game, I thought to myself: the strong, the weak. She was a bully; I knew that for a fact—I'd seen her slap John around a lot.

I put my hands on her hips, which she liked. She gave me a smile of appreciation and said "Ha!" Misty was making noise, and I looked over to see her little shaggy head at the edge of the bed.

"Go lie down, Misty," Cindy said sternly.

I could hear a record player playing downstairs. I imagined Cindy's sisters down there with their dolls and doll clothes and miniature cars and plastic furniture. I was afraid they would come upstairs, we wouldn't hear them, and they would throw open the bedroom door.

Cindy took off her T-shirt and put my hands on her breasts, which were pressed up against her thin chest by her bra. "Take it off me," she said to me as we kissed, her tongue whirling in quick circles around in my mouth.

"I don't know how it works," I said pathetically.

She laughed, a light fluttering laugh, which made me feel stupid. She showed me how the clasp, hidden in the front, unhooked, released. Her breasts fell forward and filled my hands.

I remember thinking at that moment, *This is interesting.* Even though I was confused, trying to get a handle on what was going on, I thought for a moment, *This is odd. This is good.* Cindy leaned forward so that her chest was pressing against my forehead; I felt her hardened nipples brush across the bridge of my nose.

And then I had my mouth on them, and I was licking them, aware of my awkward lips and tongue and hoping I was not being too doglike, reckless, or inattentive. She made a whistling sound between her teeth and dug her nails into my hair, and I felt the tiny silver charms of her bracelet tapping softly against my temples.

Misty was running around the bed, jumping up, standing on her hind legs with her paws on the mattress. She started barking and whining, her nails scraping the linoleum floor as she hopped about in a nervous way. "Misty! No!" Cindy hissed; she snapped her fingers at the dog. She rolled off me, still holding the back of my head with one hand as she undid her shorts with the other. "Hold on," she said, and pushed me gently to the side; in one second she had slipped off her shorts and underwear and threw them onto the floor. Then she smiled, lying naked against the shiny copper-colored mattress cover. I looked at her body; her skin was bright white where her bathing suit bottoms had been. I stared. She had a fine layer of sweat on her forehead and lower back; she smelled like lotion and salt and grape chewing gum.

"I want to see you," she said, and turned over, showing every white inch of her body. I was afraid to take off my clothes in front of her. I still had all my clothes on—I had never been naked in front of anyone. She had already grabbed at my jeans before and slid her hand into the front pocket. That was something. I stopped what I was doing—I was touching her breasts with the tips of my fingers—I had to stop because her hand had gotten ahold of me. I had gotten hold of myself so many times, and this time the difference was astounding.

Misty was running around the bed, barking loudly. The music had stopped downstairs and I was going to get up and say no, we should stop. But I didn't. I couldn't say a thing. The dog jumped all the way up on the bed and then jumped down to the floor the way show dogs in the circus do. The music started up again downstairs. Cindy was kneeling on the mattress; we were kissing and she was touching my face.

"You're pretty, Warren," she said, looking me square in the eyes. "You are," she whispered.

I thought I might cry. I put my arms around her and felt her smooth soft skin with my hands. I reached down and traced the small indent of her back, around to her hipbones. Her hands unbuttoned my jeans and I lifted myself up so she could pull them down past my thighs. She put her hands between my legs and held them still against the skin. She began lightly brushing her fingers against me, delicately, and then up inside my underwear, a series of movements and gestures. I felt the mattress's surface, oily and yet dry, against the backs of my legs, against my back as she pushed up my shirt, slid my underwear down around my knees. I thought of the deaf people I would see signing to each other, how they move their hands with precision and speed, how what they do with their hands is a language that has meaning.

Misty was nosing around our clothes, which sat in small piles on the bedroom floor. I could hear the little girls in the basement, screaming, fighting over their dolls. I thought about John and where he might be in town, how many houses he had left to go. I started to get uneasy, upset, and Cindy could tell I was getting distracted. I was convinced we would be caught. I thought about how I would leave, what I would say, how I would get home. Then I felt Cindy's hair fall against my stomach. I felt the dampness of her tongue on my hip. I looked up and saw the top of her head move in a purposeful way across my stomach. I had nothing on. "Don't worry, Warren," she said.

I couldn't watch the rest. I was afraid someone would see me, find me standing there in the dark living room watching with a hard-on pressing out against the thin material of the hospital pants I wore as pajamas. I wanted to watch more but I was sickened by it. My heart was going to burst inside my chest. My father shifted and twitched in his seat, my mother was a sleeping heap, a pile of limbs and silver hair spilling from underneath the heavy wool blanket. I looked over at Richard and Mona. Things had progressed, as I'd feared, as I'd hoped. He had pushed up her tank top to just below her chin. He pushed her breasts upward so that they swelled above the bra's white cups. He pulled the bra down and the breasts came out, large dark nipples, which Richard immediately set his mouth to. A thin layer of spit covered them and they gave off a wet shimmer.

I looked at Mona and saw she was asleep; her hand was unmoving, lost in the dark shadow beneath Richard's untucked flannel shirt. Richard was losing his focus, dropping his head, jerking it back up, and clumsily putting it against Mona's chest, his tongue hanging out like a dog's. I looked at my father, who had passed out. Andy was gone too, his hand clutching his jeans in an obvious way. The candles were almost out. I waited until they were completely extinguished, so I would not have to worry once I'd gone upstairs to bed.

25

Today is Christmas, and Joan and I have decided to go to Singing Beach. It's freezing, and once we're out of the car we wonder why we've come, whose bright idea this was. The beach is empty and I am relieved. There are a few seagulls standing around on the rocks and four or five loons floating in the water offshore.

"They look huge out there—I thought they were dogs," I say.

"What?" Joan screams into the wind. "They're loons. The white on their heads is their winter plumage."

"I was just saying," I begin.

"No," she says, staring out over the water at the black shapes disappearing under the water. "I see what you're saying."

"OK," I say, "that's good. I'm glad."

We walk along the beach near where the water laps up against the rocks, where the gulls have congregated in a loud clump of white and dirty gray. They have scattered shells all around, and the broken purple pieces look like bright petals against the smooth gray sand.

The tide is low and the beach is at its best for singing. It is something about the air and the water and the size of the sand's grain. Something about the movement, the twist of the foot against the sand, incising the sand's irregular surface. These things, plus others, I'm sure, combine to make the beach sing. Though it barely sounds like a song at all. It's more like a squeak or a wheeze.

Joan and I twist around and do a ridiculous dance to make the sand sing, and from beneath our soles it delivers its sad noises. It is a whimper beneath us. We walk on. "Walk on," we say to each other, because at one point we'd seen a movie where some people are on horseback and say to their horses, "Walk on," to get them moving again.

For Christmas, I'd gotten Joan two books and a hand-dyed scarf made by a girl I knew from the library. One of the books I got Joan was a collection of short stories written by literally unknown writers, anonymous writers. The other was a cookbook of breads and desserts with interesting calligraphic titles on each of the pages and collage-type illustrations featuring canceled stamps indicating where the recipes originated. I hoped she would like the gifts. I was incapable of not seeking her approval; in the end I wanted to please her alone. When she opened the gifts she threw the scarf around her neck and hugged me in her tight clenched embrace. Together we pored through the cookbook, and I showed her the particular things that reminded me of her, drawings of braided and creatively shaped breads, the things that convinced me that this book would be perfect for her. And she agreed it was perfect. We were in agreement, and it was Christmas.

We sat in the living room all morning, the gray sky on the other side of the windows assembling and reassembling its various fabrics above the water. Our faces were taxed from sleep, since we'd rolled out of bed and come directly downstairs. We sat in silence, in that just-awakened state that discourages movement or conversation. Neither of us had the sense to get up and turn on the stereo—Joan had only put on the kettle. We looked around the room or closed our eyes and lay back against the pillows on the couch. There was no need to wait for anyone to come down the stairs; there was no waiting anymore. We had in the room all that comprised the holiday: the ficus tree decorated with white lights and a few ornaments, our gifts, wrapped and arranged beneath it, Joan and me, and the strange task ahead of us of inventing the day.

Joan gave me a set of watercolor pencils. She went all out and bought me the 72-pencil set. She also got me a book on how a cathedral is built. The book is filled with minuscule illustrations and scientific diagrams, intensely detailed plans, and tiny people drawn to scale. I remember looking at the book in the bookstore and having Mrs. Kestrel take it and put it behind the counter when I put it down. It was up front near the register; she had told me someone asked her to set it aside.

In the most elaborately decorated package was a new set of sheets for my bed. They were pale blue, the color of snow at night. I looked up at Joan because I didn't know what to say; it was a bizarre gift. She looked at me eagerly.

"Do you like the color?" she asked.

"Yes, I do like it," I said.

"I knew it," she said. There was no reason to disagree with the gift, because it was perfectly nice. But I was taken aback. Why new sheets? I asked myself. What kind of present is this? Joan read my reaction. "You need new sheets," she said.

We reach the end of the beach, where The Chimneys, an imposing and beautiful mansion, sits up on the cliff. A few years ago I had a summer job up there, mowing the lawn and helping the gardener trim the topiary in the formal garden. The brown-shingled house looms on an overhanging granite cliff, behind a row of different types of trees, whose many kinds of leaves I would endlessly rake into piles around the lawn. My father knew the gardener, Milo, and that's how I got the job. I remember my father was happy to hear that I wanted the job and happier when it turned out that I enjoyed it.

From where Joan and I stand on the sand, the house looks phony, like a set on a stage stabilized by plywood buttresses and sandbags from behind. I had been inside a few times—once to return a TV remote control that I found out on the lawn. It must have fallen out the window, I told Mr. Loring, the ninety-two-year-old man who lived there alone—alone since his mother had passed away years ago. Sometimes I'd be on the tractor, cutting the rough grass down by the edge of the yard, and I'd see him out on the beach, raking the seaweed into large piles, which he'd pick up by hand, little by little, and put into a wheelbarrow to dump behind the boathouse. I would watch him at his task, with his frail arms, his face shaded beneath a broad straw hat, in dark blue pants and flat white sneakers; he pushed the wheelbarrow over the sand's ridges and gaps, straining, backing it up, pushing it through the soft sand. I thought, What if he dies while I'm watching him? He's an old man—he could die right now. But he never did. He's still alive.

As Joan and I look at the massive house, I imagine him inside, swishing around wearing his slippers and silk robe, half tied around his normal outfit of pressed gray pants and a clean white pinstriped shirt. I had seen him watching me from the windows as I traced and cut the complicated pattern on the lawn that was necessary to achieve the perfect diagonal stripes that radiate from the garden's perimeter of hedges.

"It's your art," he had said to me once, taking me by surprise as I was dumping the grass clippings into the compost bin behind the tractor shed.

"What?" I was staggered. "I mean, excuse me?"

"You do it perfectly every time. It's your art," he said, looking pleased.

"No, it's not. It's just cutting the lawn. Turning the wheel at the right times." I tried to sound polite, but he was making me uneasy.

He was standing beneath a low branch of the large tree that shaded us. Up close I saw that one of his eyes was completely yellow; a gauzy film covered the white part and the iris. It looked submerged, like something suspended and blurry beneath ice. Although I imagined that his teeth were false, they were straight and white and reassuring—perhaps it was his smile that was reassuring, though it was strange, too, because it seemed fixed.

He stood waiflike and frail in the dappled shadows, wearing his neat outfit with red socks and indoor shoes. His hair was gray and thin but perfectly combed into a small wave above his forehead. From a few yards away he might have been mistaken for a young boy, still slight and on the cusp of growth, dressed up to go to church. But I was close up and saw that every inch of his skin was lined and folded, loosely attached. I thought, How did he get out here without me noticing? How does he rake the beach all day without keeling over or snapping in half? He moved closer to me.

"No, it's not that, no," he said smiling. "It's not just cutting the lawn and turning the wheel and, indeed, not just dumping the grass back here."

I was trying to figure out, given the situation, the most polite way to act. I resolved to shut up and nod my head periodically. But this was not easy because I was a bit freaked; his fogged eye was eerie, his grin ambiguous. I kept wishing Milo would show up and yell at me for slacking off. But I could hear him far off by the pond weed-whacking the reeds. Every now and then a flotilla of ducks would rise noisily into the air, which meant he was harassing them.

"Well, I don't know, but thank you," I stammered.

"Do you know what I mean when I say it's your art?" he asked, with an air of intrigue and drama, punctuated by raising his hand up toward me in an odd gesture, as if he were cautiously throwing something delicate for me to catch.

"No," I said frankly. "I don't know what you mean." Now leave me alone to cut your lawn, I thought.

I didn't like that he was talking about me. I didn't like that he had formulated some ideas about me while he watched me drive around on the tractor from his high windows. I was suddenly uncomfortable about the entire encounter and wished we were not standing awkwardly in the otherwise shaded and peaceful copse between the yard and the sea.

"I just cut the lawn," I said, hoping he'd think I was dim and a waste of his time and energy—considering what a commodity both must be in his case.

"You don't just cut the lawn, boy," he pressed. The term *boy* hit me like a dart. "But clearly you don't want to endeavor into conversation with me." He made a face like he had smelled something unpleasant and turned away, looking up toward the house looming over the cliff.

Then, of course, I felt bad. What was the harm in endeavoring into conversation? What was he going to do? The last thing I wanted was for him to tell Milo that he didn't want some obnoxious brat on his property, and for Milo to tell my father.

"No, it's OK. I mean, it's fine. I don't really know what you mean, but it's fine." Even though I said this, and sounded apologetic while saying it, I was becoming aware, in the back of my mind, that there was something more going on here, a little drama playing out between us.

His face was lighted by a look of satisfaction. "Well, then. Yes. That's right." He glowed and continued. "What I mean, dear, is that I see you on the tractor going around and around, and you have this look on your face. So serious." I noticed that he was wearing slippers: satiny scarlet-colored mules. He paused for a moment. "So intense," he rasped, sounding fascinated.

I raked the grass, tamped the pile down. "Oh."

"All morning," he began again, "that face, so focused, driving around in the hot sun."

I visualized a gigantic face driving a tractor in the hot sun.

"And the lawn, in the end," he continued, sweeping his arm in a hula-like gesture, "is always perfection."

"Well, that's good," I said, in a robotic way. "I'm glad." Even if he did think I was obnoxious and maybe disrespectful, in the end he was aware of my doing a quality job, and my father couldn't really get angry with me for that.

"Yes, dear, it is good; be glad." He smiled.

I worked with Milo for a few summers and this had been the first real encounter I'd had with Mr. Loring. It was when my father first fell ill. It was around the time when we first started to become officially worried about him. My mother was in the design stages of what would become a seamless skin of stress and worry. Joan and I were feeling the pressure of their illnesses and were quickly learning what little power we had in the situation. It was when we were in the beginning phase of helplessness.

Mr. Loring had his eyes fixed on me; he was talking on and on, but I wasn't listening. I looked up at his house and imagined all the rooms. I pictured clocks, desks, and framed oil portraits bearing austere expressions; beds with curtains and posts; striped, patterned, flowered wallpaper; plants in the sunroom whose vines and leaves and blossoms I could see from the front lawn at the base of the cliff. I pictured living in the house—not with Mr. Loring, because he would be dead; I would not have to worry about that. I would live in this amazing house by myself or with my family—they would get better in this house; their health would improve with these views, these grounds. Or maybe I would live with Joan. Joan would come and live with me, and every day we would go and visit our parents, or we would invite them over. Or we could walk on the beach or swim; we could do what we wanted.

"Do you think it's an art? Are you serious?" I asked Mr. Loring, in a voice Joan would use to manipulate Mike.

Joan runs down to the water. The tide is low but it is coming in rapidly. My hair feels stiff and clumpy in the cold salt air—I left my hat in the car and my ears are numb. I watch Joan standing at the edge of the water, looking down at the minuscule waves that have begun to push the tide forward up the beach.

I run after her. My boots are heavy and make deep ruts in the sand. When I reach her she says, "You're insane," because she's watched me tromp clumsily toward her. I just look at her and shrug, breathing heavily. From this we invent a game. We go about measuring my stride by using our boot lengths as means of calculation. My stride is five of my boots long, seven and a bit more of Joan's. We play around for the next half hour, running at full speed and measuring the strides. We do this until we are sweating inside our coats and the cold air around us is irrelevant.

A square-headed dog arrives, panting, on a leash with someone we know on the other end. "Merry Christmas!" the person's voice says warmly.

"Merry Christmas," we say in unison, automatically, like children.

I look up from the sand and see Valerie standing in a long quilted down coat with plastic clips cinching it closed. She has a thick rough-looking scarf wrapped around her neck that trails down her back; it flaps in the wind like a waving arm. She is wearing the snug knit cap I'd seen her wearing on the bus; the yarn of her mittens matches the hat. It is the first time in a long while that I've had a chance to look her in the face, which I blatantly do, staring at her gray eyes and pale skin. She smiles at me and looks over at Joan and smiles. There is a moment of silence between us as the dog finds a shell and starts to crunch it loudly.

"No, Tess, no, drop it, drop!" Valerie cries to the dog. She bends down and attempts to dig out the broken shell from between the dog's teeth. I look down and see blood dripping out of the dog's mouth; Valerie's fingers are covered and she's moaning, "Oh no. Oh no—you're bleeding!" She looks up at us with a painful and worried expression. "She's cut her mouth on the shell!"

I think, Where is her son? Who's taking care of him?

Joan leads Valerie and the dog down to the edge of the water. Joan and Valerie cup their hands and wash out the dog's mouth, using their fingers to rout out the shell's tiny shards. I always thought

Joan hated Valerie for taking her job at the nursery. Even though it was our father's doing and Valerie had no choice either way, I was under the impression that Joan maintained the grudge. Why wouldn't she? She seemed to hold it against my father forever.

"What are you guys doing out here?" Valerie asks, her face bright with a genuine curiosity—and relief, because the dog seems to be OK, sniffing around the sand and seaweed.

"You know, just walking the beach," Joan explains. "It's nice, because no one is here. Or, it's just not crowded."

"I know. It *is* nice."

"What are you doing today?" I ask Valerie, trying to get over my shock at what a civil and boring exchange has just taken place between the two of them.

"I guess the same thing. I left Jake with my grandmother because I start work in an hour. I had some extra time and figured I'd give Tess a run."

"I thought the nursery was usually closed today and tomorrow," I say.

"Warren!" Joan looks at me sharply.

"What?" I look at Joan, who is embarrassed for me for some reason; she looks at Valerie with apology.

"I'm sorry," I blurt.

"It is, I guess," began Valerie. "It's all right, Joan." She smiles at me weakly. "Don't worry about it, Warren."

"Val doesn't work at the nursery anymore, Warren."

"I waitress at The Surf," she says, and she picks up her foot to show her black high-top sneakers with Velcro ankle support.

"Oh. OK. I didn't know you'd left the nursery." How was I supposed to know where she worked now? Joan is always trying to make me look stupid in front of people. I have to remember to bring this up with her later.

"Do you want to walk with us to the end of the beach?" Joan asks

Valerie. She lets the dog go free and we take turns throwing driftwood for it into the water. At first Valerie doesn't want the dog to get wet because it will smell up the car and the seats will get damp, but then she smiles and in her kind way says, "Whatever—it's Christmas."

We walk to the end of the beach and back up the dunes to the parking lot. Joan and Valerie talk mostly about Helen at the nursery, Jake, and Joan's job at the bakery. Again, Joan astounds me by extending a job offer for Valerie to come and work at the bakery if she wants. Every now and then I chime in and add something, but it's clear, ever since I made the mistake of thinking Valerie worked at the nursery, that I am to keep my trap shut.

We wave to Valerie as she drives away. Joan and I sit down on a bench and look at the ocean, as we've done a million times before, all our lives. The tide has risen and covers over where we played our clumsy and pointless game of measuring our strides. It is only three in the afternoon and already the light is dissolving, as if sopped up by the rising water. No lights can be seen through the trees near The Chimneys; no one is home at the mansion.

"Should we go home?" I say. "It just gets colder as it gets darker."

"I know, but not yet," Joan says, as if deep in thought.

"Hold on—why did you yell at me in front of Valerie? What was so bad about me not knowing she doesn't work at the nursery any-more?"

"Because, Warren, she got fired, you ass," Joan says.

"What? When?"

"Don't even say 'why?' Warren."

"Why?" I whisper intensely. "No, really, when did she get the ax?"

"Right before she had her kid. Right before Jake."

"Richard fired her? That's insane."

"Not Richard," Joan said.

"Helen?"

"No, Warren. Pay attention."

"I am! Who fired her?"

"Dad fired her."

"Why?"

"Because he was a fucking selfish, irresponsible bastard, that's why."

"Well, OK then."

When I thought about Valerie, a little slide show played in my head of all the images I had collected of her. There was Valerie walking on the sidewalk with our neighbors' children for whom she used to baby-sit. Valerie wearing an orange string bikini laid out on a pink towel at the quarries. Valerie at the nursery surrounded by flowers, her hair tied back, her long fingers working away. Valerie in the church and then outside, among the stone markers in the cemetery.

In the cemetery, Joan and I had knelt at the perfectly cut hole in the earth. The ground was frozen and I marveled at how it had been done; the sides were smooth and the angles were square. We knelt at the hole with roses in our hands. We pulled off the blooms—they were huge, from the hothouse—the heavy petals came loose in our palms and those that did not fall off we tore from the roseheads. There was barely any resistance as the petals pulled free. I remember the waxy feeling in my hands as I spread my fingers over the grave and watched the petals fall into the chamber of soil, listened to them sigh against the glossy lids of the casket, the lacquer box.

We went through the same ritual with both of our parents. The casket was our mother's; it was the second one, the second ceremony. The first was for our father in the lacquer box. We didn't know about this custom of crumbling the roses until our mother had led us to the edge of our father's grave. She motioned to us and showed us, emphatically, almost angrily, as if to say, Tear these flowers to pieces, rip them apart, throw them into the hole—disassemble them—and we will bury them with him.

When we finished, I peered down into the hole and saw the pile of rose blossoms and petals. I saw the red box glowing beneath them. I saw the black soil, dusted with snow and ice from the morning's frost. The box gleamed like a jewel in a shadowed alcove. I peered down at it; the day was getting darker because the clouds were dense, threatening to snow. It was freezing. My mother huddled against Joan, crying, her large tears falling from her face and landing on the dark lapels of her coat, where they remained, fixed. I looked at them, the tears intact, round like pearls but transparent and glassy on her coat, as if frozen in place.

The day was gray, sewn into place at every edge, but with color occurring at odd intervals around us: Joan's blue stone earrings, the tiny red flecks of cranberries in the arrangement by the gravestone, the opal in my mother's ring pulsating as it emerged from her narrow leather glove. Inside the stand of birch trees, the white paper fluttering from the trunks, I saw the same flash of red—Valerie leaned against a tree. Against the static of black and white trunks, I saw her red hair, her slender white hand glowing like an ivory clasp against her coat.

"I thought you hated Valerie," I tell Joan.

"Because why?"

"Because she took your job."

"Dad gave her my job. For a while I felt petty hatred—because she had what I wanted. I didn't hate *her*; I hated Dad for giving it to her."

"That was obvious."

"I suppose."

We are in the beach parking lot; the car won't start. It's four in the afternoon, and the dusk is at that point of deception—I thought I saw a child in the brush near the dunes, but it was a trash barrel lying on its side. Joan and I stare out through the windshield and over the water; slowly the lights on the harbor spindles become visible, blinking vaguely against the competing blackness of sky and water.

"Try it again," I tell Joan, and she turns the key. An ominous clicking noise comes from under the hood.

"Fuck!" she says, and she aggressively turns the key on and off, on and off.

"If you snap the key off in the ignition, we're screwed," I tell her.

"Shut up," she says.

"We could walk back into town."

"And leave the car?"

"I doubt someone's going to take it. They can't get it to go anywhere."

"Someone might trash it."

Maybe. Our mother's car once got trashed when she left it overnight at the train station. Some kids smashed two windows, ripped apart the seats and glove compartment, and shoved broken glass into the ignition.

"No one's going to trash it on Christmas," I reassure her.

"Since when do you have faith in people?" Joan sneers, zipping up her coat and getting out of the car.

"Since never," I tell her.

We go to the diner, which is open and depressingly full, given that it's Christmas. Most people are at the counter on stools. None of the waitresses we know are on duty this evening. This is heartening; maybe they have families and lives beyond working here. Why wouldn't they?

Joan and I sit down at the booth near the window. No sooner are we served our coffee than the outrageously large blue eyes of Auntie E appear suddenly at the window beside us. We both jump at the sight of her. She has removed a glove and is tapping the large diamond in her pinkie ring against the glass to get our attention. Thankfully, the music in the diner, a selection of instrumental Christmas carols, is played at a volume loud enough to keep the other patrons' attention away from the flurry-covered figure grinning at us through the window.

For some reason Auntie E remains outside well after we've noticed her, well after we've waved. It's an eerie moment, because she just stands there like a robot, or like one of those motorized figurines set up in holiday dioramas at the mall. It makes me think for a split second that it's not really her but maybe her ghost—maybe she has died and this is her visitation. But then her ungloved hand holds up one finger as if to say, Hold on, and I notice a cigarette between the fingers of her other hand. She turns away from us slightly, takes a last drag, drops the butt on the ground, and grinds it into the snowy cement. She looks up to see if we're watching. Joan is taking our coats and putting them next to her, filling the empty space next to her in the booth. Today Auntie E's hair looks brittle, yellow, like the synthetic hair of the angel on top of the Christmas tree the diner has set up beside the pastry cooler.

She bustles in, scraping her boots along the tile floor, scuffing off the mat. "It's colder up here than at home. Why is that?" Auntie E asks in a loud voice, apparently soliciting the answer from anyone in the diner.

"Hi, Auntie E, merry Christmas," says Joan brightly, safely padded into inaccessibility by our coats. "We just saw you yesterday. Why are you back? It's nice to see you again." Joan manages to make it sound like this is a very pleasant surprise.

It's true. We did see her yesterday. An instant after I'd hung up with her on her cell phone, she appeared at our door. But it turned out she hadn't planned to stay—she just wanted to drop off our gifts on the porch. "I didn't think you'd be home, so I made some arrangements in the area," she'd said, when we opened the door. I didn't know exactly what this meant, but it clearly was a tactic not to come inside and have the tea Joan offered her. "If I knew you were home, I'd not have made my plans. But I have a few more stops tonight. Call me Auntie Santa! All through the night!" She clucked, sounding upbeat but tired, not wholly convinced of her own cheerfulness.

Joan and I had no idea what she was talking about or whom she knew in the area that she would be visiting on Christmas Eve. But it didn't matter; it was a relief. We took the plastic bag from her hand and said thank you so much, merry Christmas, here's our present for you (fruit breads), take care, drive carefully, OK, goodbye. She was off the porch and in her car before we could close the door.

"Yes, I know. I know. We did see each other yesterday, but I felt so awful just stopping by. I really didn't think you'd be home, so I'd made plans. You never seem to be home when I call up."

We never pick up the phone, I almost say.

We sit in silence. Auntie E begins to say something but then stops, clears her throat, and looks around. "I'm sorry I ran away from you last night." She looks back and forth between us, her huge eyes quivering. "I'm so sorry. But—this is very hard."

Yikes, I think, she might start crying right now. She had looked so happy outside the window, dusted with snow, smiling away, mashing out her butt.

"No, Auntie E, I mean, yes, of course, it's OK," I stammer. "At least we got to see you for a little bit. You had friends to visit, we understand." Somehow this comes out wrong. I try to make it sound reassuring, but it doesn't; it sounds like I'm the worst actor in a middle-school play.

Joan is quiet on the other side of the table. I wonder if, in fact, she is upset with Auntie E. I am counting on Joan to restore comfort to the conversation, since she knows how to talk to Auntie E.

"Yeah. No, Warren's right, it *is* OK—totally," she says, with a level of tenderness that sounds slightly more authentic than mine did. "Please don't worry."

Auntie E orders a Diet Coke and a cup of hot water with lemon and fiddles with the gold pin that holds her scarf to her emerald-green blazer. She is sniffing and wiping her nose with a napkin from the metal dispenser on the table.

"It's colder here because we're near the water. The wind is colder off the sea," I say, as if I'm explaining it to both of them.

"Oh, well, that makes sense," says Auntie E, regaining her composure by the change of topic. She wraps her long fingers around the mug of hot water, brings the mug to her forehead, and rests it there. "It still *feels* so much colder here. How do you stay warm?" She drifts off, quietly, closing her eyes. "How do you manage?" She puts the mug on the table and covers her face with her hands. She is crying for real now. Joan and I look at each other in shock.

"Oh, Auntie E, what's wrong?" Joan says, leaning forward to grab her hand. "It's all right."

Then I say the most ridiculous thing, something a child would say but nothing I would have said when I was a child. "Yeah, Auntie E, don't cry. It's Christmas."

Joan grimaces.

I think, Auntie E is crying because she pities us. It's because we're all alone on Christmas, orphans without anyone at home. OK, I understand. I get it. And I feel confident that Joan and I know what steps to take to comfort her, to reassure her that we are OK, or that we will be. Especially with family like her so close by, we would emphasize; it makes it easier; we don't feel so alone. I look at Joan and silently strategize what we're going to say, who'll start, who'll follow up.

I begin. "Auntie E, we're OK. It's hard, yes, because it's the first Christmas—" and then it strikes me what I've said. And I think about it and feel suddenly punctured, slightly nauseated, but I continue, looking at Joan, "We're learning how to live each day."

"It's not easy," Joan picks up softly, "but every day it gets just a little bit more manageable."

"And with loving family like you, so close by—" I begin again, after Joan.

"It makes it easier, even in small ways," Joan concludes.

I'm about to start in on how it feels like such a long time ago since they died and how time has never felt so palpable to me, ever, not in my whole life. And Joan will then bring up the funerals, mention how helpful it was that Auntie E was there. How having the love of our relatives gives us strength. I find I can only start to talk about them now, Joan will say.

"No," says Auntie E. We stop talking. She unwraps her fingers from the mug of hot water, the lemon, browned and disintegrating, floating rind up on the surface.

"What?" Joan asks quietly, like a nurse.

"You don't mean that at all." Auntie E sniffs. Tears begin to fall out of her eyes again. I look around but no one seems to notice us.

"We don't mean what?" I ask, putting my hand on her forearm.

She looks over at me, her blue eyes bluer because now they are ringed with a web of bloodshot red.

"You don't mean it. It doesn't mean a thing to you that I'm close by. You don't care. You don't care at all." She sounds like an angry child scolding us through her sorrow. She puts her face in her hands.

"Auntie E, it does mean something." I try to sound sincere, and, I think, I manage to. "When we go out to lunch or—" It occurs to me that we don't do anything other than go out to lunch with her.

Joan pipes up. "And we took you to the nursery."

This is all wrong, I think—we're trying to make it sound like we don't ignore her, which we clearly do. We're taking the wrong tack. She wants us to say that we care about her and it's meaningful that she's here if we need her. That's all she wants to hear from us. I think of all the messages of hers we've deleted. I look at Joan, who looks at me with desperation.

"It may not seem like it, I guess, but it's nice to know you're just a short car ride away," I try.

She shakes her head, blowing her nose into a napkin.

"Oh, Auntie E," says Joan, "don't cry. Please."

Auntie E sits wiping her nose and the edges of her eyes, looking away from us. We sit in silence, listening to the carols play over the speakers and the general din of the diner.

"You don't want me in your lives," Auntie E says. "That's obvious to me."

"No, Auntie E. No, don't say that," I plead. I feel awful; she's miserable beside me in the booth. "We do, we do," I say with feeling. "We do, please!"

No word comes from Joan's side of the table.

"Auntie E, please, it's true—we love you!" I say.

"No, no"—she waves her hand and frowns—"there's no point. I'm sorry to bother you two like this. I suppose I should have called before I came." She slides out of the booth and takes her coat from the pile beside Joan. "I've said what I've come here to say, that's all." A mini-eruption of tears—a heave—overtakes her. We look up at her in shock. "Goodbye, dears. I think that—I don't know. This is awful." She leaves, tears streaming down her face, napkins clutched in her hand.

"Jesus Christ, Joan," I mutter, baffled and guilt-ridden. "Should we go after her? Or should we call her later? What should we do?"

Joan doesn't say a word.

26

Patsy is laughing her head off when I walk down the three steps into the bakery; I can hear her even before I open the door. It is smaller than an average-sized door because the bakery is located in the basement of one of the old mill buildings in town, and the mills were built to accommodate the average employees at the time—children.

Though obvious leadership seems nonexistent at the bakery, everyone who works there shares a love for the place. A sense of solemn vigilance and focused production falls over it in the early morning hours, when the baking is done. The women of the bakery—it's mostly women who work there—go about their work with the ardor of the pious and the efficiency of clocks.

When the river flooded last year, water filled the bakery, rose above the counters, and ruined the stores of flour, wheat, cornmeal, and sugar. The cooler's motor exploded, and all the display cases became temporary homes to fish, frogs, and the braver river otters, who'd been seen swimming back toward the current towing bags of mini muffins and scones. Snapshots of Joan, Patsy, and the other baker, Laura, adorn the brick wall above the coffee urn—photos of them thigh-high in murky water, hauling out bread tins and mixing bowls, flecks of sticks and mud and weeds on their faces, flabbergasted but smiling, salvaging the instruments of their craft.

When I walk into the bakery, Patsy is laughing her vocally impossible laugh—half crow, half kazoo. The floor's terra cotta tiles are gleaming and wet, and Patsy leans against her mop, which is submerged in a pail of dirty suds. The display cases look empty except for the fragments of muffins littering the wire shelves and a few fruit breads wrapped in plastic. It's two in the afternoon, a few days after Christmas, and Joan is in the back sweeping the floor. I've come to pick her up. Laura is sitting up on the counter, evidently so Patsy can mop under her, and wears a gratified smile that suggests she's the reason for Patsy's hysterics.

"Hey, baby boy!" Laura yells in her southern drawl. "I don't know if you want to come in here." She glances over at Patsy, whose face is red.

"No, Warren, run away while you can!" Patsy warns. "It's not safe!"

"Warren, you can come in—we're just having some sexy talk!" Laura smiles broadly.

"Get out while you can, Warren," Joan says dryly, from between the bread racks. I can tell she's serious even though she's smiling. This is her way of protecting me, I think.

Patsy's still not able to speak. She goes from shaking her head side to side, grinning, to a full-fledged raspy guffaw. Laura jumps off the counter and takes off her apron.

"Let's ask the opinion of a *man*." She smiles at me.

I want to leave, but it's too late—I've crossed the threshold, I'm down the steps. I like you, Laura. Please don't be mean to me.

"Oh, come on, Laura, as if he'll know," Joan says, coming out from the back with her bag and coat.

"He's an innocent, you tramp!" Patsy manages to cry out. "Leave him out of your wicked filthy mind!" She wipes her eyes with her shirt cuff and looks at me with a helpless smile. "Hi, Warren, how's it going?"

"Hi. Fine. I'm well," I answer her nervously.

"Now, Warren, being a male person as you are, tell me this," Laura begins. "When first out with a girl, or lady, or member of the fairer sex—what do you prefer to call her?"

"A member of the fairer sex," I say with a smile.

"Yes, right. How, then, do things proceed *beyond* the particulars?" She gives me an indulgent smile. Joan rolls her eyes and gestures to me that we should go. Patsy is shaking her head.

"I might be clearer here, I suppose, Mr. Warren, Mr. Male person. What I mean to ask is, when you take a member of the *fairer sex* out with you on a date, what is your tactical reasoning, once the date, in terms of its significant social aspects, has come to a close?"

This was a terrible idea, to come into the bakery. Why didn't I just wait in the car for Joan to come out?

"We've got to go," Joan says with a smile, looking at Laura intently in hopes that she'll stop.

Laura prances over to me and takes my hand in hers. "Now, wait just a second there, big sister." She links her arm in mine and tightens against me, I can feel the side of her breast against my elbow. "Let me ask the man of the house what, in his opinion, he thinks the ladies like."

"As if he knows, Laura!" Joan barks, exasperated. I can see Joan is taking this seriously and no one else is; this is typical of Joan, so I don't wriggle out of Laura's lock. I am prepared, if I need to, to see what I can come up with, based on the surreal experience I had with Cindy and what I've culled from the movies. Laura and I have mixed it up before, gotten into arguments or laughing fits, thoroughly annoying Joan for the basic reason of excluding her—though we never meant to, obviously. The thing is, Joan tends to get serious when other people are having fun. Joan would get annoyed even if we did include her, because in the end she always thinks our games, as with most games, are dumb.

"OK, enough—let's go, Warren." Joan tiptoes toward me over the drying tiles.

I am still wondering what exactly they were talking about when I walked in, what was making Patsy laugh so hard and Laura smile with such unfettered glee.

"These are sick girls," Joan says to me, and she pulls me away from Laura.

As we start up the stairs, Laura calls out, "Oh, Warren, we'll finish this up another time. You just keep in mind, though, what you think little girls want from a little boy in times of need. 'Bye now!"

"'Bye, you two," Patsy calls, and says something admonishing to Laura that I can't hear.

Joan and I walk up the alley to where I've parked the car near the bank.

"Sorry about that, Warren. We were giddy all morning and Laura was being particularly crude; she had a date last night, and it didn't go well."

"It's OK. I like Laura—she's insane, but she's cool. I like them both."

"I know. I do too, but they should know better."

"Than what?"

"Than to wrangle you into their gross little games." She pauses as we get into the car, she in the driver's seat. "They think it's funny, but it's mean."

"I didn't think it was mean. We were just having fun. It was funny."

"Warren, it was funny until you came in. Then it was just going to get embarrassing."

"How? They're my friends; they're not out to wreck me." I have never thought about saying this out loud, but it seems true enough.

"I'm not saying they don't like you—they do, a lot. I'm just saying that if the conversation were to continue the way it was going, it would have gotten ugly."

"How do you know?"

"Come on, Warren. Beyond what I know about you, Laura is sick and likes to take things as far as she can. It wouldn't have been fun for you. She's had quite a life, and she'll tell you all about her checkered past any time you want. I'd just recommend you not try and compare notes."

"Who says I don't have a checkered past?"

"Warren, yes, you definitely have checkers in your past. And solitaire and chess. That's not what I mean."

I almost comment on Joan's terrible attempt at a joke with the checkers-and-chess comment, but she manages to hurt my feelings slightly with the pitiful appropriateness of the word *solitaire*.

"Joan, it's not like you know everything that's happened to me in my life."

"Well, I pretty much do, Warren; you tell me everything."

"Not really. Not anymore."

"Fine—most everything. Warren, trust me; I did you a favor in there."

"Fine, whatever. Where are we going?"

"The mall."

"No! Joan, why?"

"Because that's where I want to go. I'll drop you off at home if you like, but that's where I'm going. Do you want to go home?"

At the mall, Joan and I walk around as she looks for some boots she's seen in a magazine. I'm convinced she'll have to drive into the city to find them, because they're way too cool to be at the mall. While Joan browses, I lecture her on how it's not natural to expose yourself to the mall's fluorescent lighting and ubiquitous jazzy music. It's unhealthy and can have long-term effects, I tell her. Suddenly, I realize I've been led into the men's section and she's looking for clothes for Mike. I threaten to knock over all the racks of casual slacks, and eventually Joan says we can go. It is, as every trip to the mall turns out to be, a needless waste of time.

"Do you drag Mike to the mall with you?" I ask her as we survey the tundra-like parking lot for the car.

"No way—are you joking? He would never come here with me. Grace. I go with Grace."

I laugh, and she looks at me. "Hardly," I say.

"Ha-ha—original," she says.

"Do you want to go to the movies?" I ask. At a distant point near the tire store, with its many bays for transmission and muffler services, the mall parking lot merges with the movie theater's parking lot, making the entire expanse of snow-covered pavement seem simultaneously vast and conveniently accessible.

"I don't know," Joan says.

"What else is there to do?" I ask, immediately regretting it, because for me the question has some relevance, but I'm sure Joan can come up with a million other things she would rather do.

"We could rent a movie and bring it home," Joan says. This means she wants to go home, which is fine by me, but she probably won't join me in watching the movie. She'll make plans to go out with Mike or Grace or stay up in her room primping and dancing around to stupid songs on the radio.

"Let's just go home, then," I say flatly, making it obvious that I'm not that happy with anything that's going on.

"Why don't you call John? Is he still around for Christmas break?"

If Joan had an ounce of attention not directed at herself or Mike, she'd know never to bring this up with me—or at least to do so only with delicacy. She reminds me of my mother, who at a certain point didn't even look up to see whom she was addressing. She would hear someone come in the room and just say *Joan* and start talking. It was forgivable most of the time, because she was so preoccupied with my father. But there is no excuse for Joan. She knows John and I are not friends anymore. I'd told her what had happened. One day I'd gone to her in tears, after I'd seen John in town, on the wharf.

"Let's just go home. It's fine." I feel myself migrating into a serious sulk. There is nothing worse than finding out that someone in whom you confided something very painful wasn't paying attention.

"If you want to go to the movies, let's go. There's just nothing I want to see and you'll have to pay because I didn't go to the bank machine inside. But we can go if you want to—it's fine."

* * *

John found out about what had happened between Cindy and me. How? I asked him in desperation. She told me! he screamed. We were standing on the boardwalk of the wharf, where I had run into him. This was last December. I had gone down to the wharf to get my mother some groceries from the overpriced gourmet deli near the launch. She wanted the round English butter biscuits to take to the hospital so she could have them with tea while my father had Cream of Wheat and apple juice.

I was coming out of the store and there was John, walking Misty on a leash. But when he saw me, he pretended not to notice me, steering Misty roughly in the opposite direction from where I stood.

"Hey!" I called out. Immediately my mind raced with all the reasons why he might hate me. I could only think of the standard reasons but nothing that directly related to him. He moved quickly through the cobblestone street. I ran toward him, the plastic bag of biscuits and other assorted requests banging against my leg. "Hey, wait up!" I called, when I'd almost reached him.

I was breathing hard because I'd had to run almost the entire length of the street to catch up with him. My mouth emitted dense blasts of steam, which clouded around John's face. He swatted at the air as if they were a swarm of gnats, and he looked disgusted. I stood watching him, trying to exhale calmly, moving away so as to not breathe on him. "What's going on?" I asked, trying not to sound suspicious. His face lost its look of repulsion, but not fully; he barely looked me in the eyes.

"I really don't want to talk to you, Warren," he said flatly.

"Why not? What's going on? What did I do?" I was used to this—to asking, *What did I do?* Especially to myself. It was worse having to ask someone else, someone who wasn't part of my family.

"I really don't want to see you right now. I don't want to see you or talk to you, Warren," John said, not looking at me, yanking Misty's leash because she looked like she was going to start jumping. He began to walk away.

"Hold on," I insisted, jogging alongside him, careful to turn my head when I needed to breathe.

"No, Warren, fuck you. Really, fuck off." He didn't raise his voice; he was still speaking normally, but he sounded as if he was going to cry.

It then occurred to me: What if this is about Cindy? But I could not believe she would say anything. I didn't think it mattered to her. I assured myself it had nothing to do with her. What else? What else could I have done to him?

My mind was off and running crazily. I should have told him about her. I should have told him immediately after it had happened. But what would I have said? That his sister seduced me? That I stripped naked on his parents' bed with her while he was off on his paper route and his little sisters were playing downstairs? I didn't even tell Joan. I had kept it a secret from her. I should have told her; she could have helped me figure out what to do.

I had just gotten off the bed, that day, and gone home. Cindy didn't even drive me; I just got up and left her parents' room, with her lying naked on the shiny satin-covered mattress. She was saying, Come on, Warren, I'll drive you home in a couple minutes. Come back. Please. But I just went out their front door and didn't say a word. I started walking home along the narrow shoulder of Route 1 all the way to the fairgrounds and along the river, over the bridge, back through the park woods and Big Quarry, down over the train tracks, and over to Pigeon Cove. And we never talked about it afterward, though Cindy would tease me in harsh little ways when I saw her. Which was mainly when she drove John and me to and from the beach. I never saw her otherwise, because she didn't go to the library or the bakery, and because I avoided anywhere she might be.

John started walking away and I started after him.

"I'm serious, Warren, get the fuck away from me," he said, in the voice of a pissed-off twelve-year-old. He was starting to raise his voice. We were the same age, just about seventeen.

John's family had moved to town when I was in seventh grade; he joined our class mid-year. We'd met at a classmate's birthday party on Misery Island. The party was ruined because, when we got to the island, some teenagers were already there being violent and destructive. John and I had stood next to each other that afternoon and watched as a group of long-haired boys piled trash on a fire they had built in the sand, their belt buckles flashing in the firelight. A girl and a guy were fooling around on a blanket while others stood around and watched them. We watched them too.

"That's my sister," John had said to me suddenly.

"Who?" I asked.

"The one on the blanket with the guy."

"Are you serious?"

"She's disgusting," he said, on the verge of tears.

"Why are you so mad at me? What's wrong?" I pleaded.

"You fucking well know what's wrong!" he shrieked. "Now get away from me! Jesus Christ, Warren!"

"What's wrong? Is it about Cindy?" I couldn't believe I'd said that.

"I don't want to *fucking* talk to you, Warren! So stop fucking following me!" He had a vicious expression on his face; he spat when he yelled at me.

I didn't know what to say. I never thought I'd have to talk to him about this. I'd done my best to not think about it. It began; it ended; it was over. He didn't have to know. It didn't have anything to do with him. I didn't know what to say. I said the worst thing I could have said. "It wasn't my fault."

He winced. "What?"

I was silent. He stopped where he was and looked at me with disbelief.

I wanted to say, I didn't have a choice! I wanted to say, I didn't think I'd have another chance! I wanted to say, I didn't know what I was doing and I was frightened. I was afraid to take my clothes off in front of her. I was ashamed. Does it help that I was afraid and ashamed the entire time?

Not the entire time—because I wanted to stay. I was afraid you were coming back from your paper route, I was going to say. I thought your sisters would come up from the basement and want Popsicles. They would have found us.

"I'm sorry," I stammered.

"Fuck you, Warren. You're fucking disgusting. You fucked my sister!"

"No!" I yelled. "No! It wasn't that, I didn't do that! We didn't go all the way!" I was clinging onto the misinformation with everything I had. But it didn't matter.

"Whatever, Warren. She's my fucking sister!" He looked like he was going to cry. I felt like I was going to fall apart.

"I'm sorry," I said again. "I'm sorry. I didn't know. I didn't think about it." Even though I wanted to say it was Cindy's idea, I couldn't.

"Jesus Christ! What would you do if I fucked your sister?!" John screamed. I stood silent and horrified, looking into his twisted expression. "Yeah," he said again. "What would you do if you found out that I was so fucking thoughtless I'd fucked Joan?" He looked satisfied for a moment, and then his face went slack. He moaned as if he was in pain and raked his hand through his short brown hair. He looked me in the eye and started to walk again.

I tried to catch up with him. "Don't follow me, you fucking stupid fuck!" he screamed, tears clogging his voice, buckling his stride; he pulled Misty alongside him. I watched them until they got to the end of the wharf and turned left toward the town parking lot behind the bank.

I went home. It took all my control to keep from bawling on the walk back; the plastic bag of cookies and tea, ridiculous, crinkling as it swung limply in my hand. When I walked into the kitchen I could see my mother had just gotten home from the hospital. She looked up at me from behind the refrigerator door; she looked happy to see me, almost relieved. My eyes exploded; my face was wet with tears before I could sink into a kitchen chair. I slumped over and my mother came and put her arms around me. I saw her from the corner of my eye; she rushed over to me.

I could not stop. I just pictured John's face, full of hatred and disgust and his sneering, desperate shriek: *you fucking stupid fuck!*

"I know, I know, I know, it's terrible. It's the worst thing that could happen."

What she was saying was the truth and I felt it palpably around me like smoke and cold. I began again, the crying spasms splitting through me, shaking the chair I'd slumped down in. The only sounds I could make were low sounds like a calf's plaintive bleat.

"Mom," I said. "I don't understand. Why it even happened."

"I know, I know," she repeated, in a fatigued, doleful voice. "Today is the first day when I felt my hope slipping away. Today was that day," she whispered, and she began to cry into my shoulder.

I felt her weight press deeper into me, her minute shivers across my neck. For a moment I felt a sobered clarity, long enough to understand what she had said, what she was talking about.

"Mom?"

"Oh, Warren," she moaned, and cried harder, tightening herself around me.

I couldn't say a word. She was crying for my father, and I was crying for myself. It was a terrible revelation. I am too selfish to live in this house, I decided—I shouldn't even be here, in this house, in this town. I took hold of her arms, wrapped tightly around my neck, and held my mother against me.

"I'm sorry," I said to her. "I'm sorry for everything."

"Oh, Warren," she moaned, "we all are."

27

After Christmas I called Mr. Trego. I left a message on his machine. I'd told Joan, "I'm starting my piano lessons again."

We were standing on kitchen chairs in the living room, taping up the ceiling with clear masking tape. The paint on the ceiling has begun to buckle and crack, and every now and then a weird-shaped fragment of paint falls to the floor and shatters into shards and dust. In its place is the absent shape on the ceiling, a dark yellow patch peering down on us from the expanse of fractured white. Taping was our solution since scraping and repainting the ceiling felt impossible.

"Really? Why?" she asked.

"I don't know. I don't know why I stopped in the first place."

"Well, that's a good reason."

A few days later he called back and left a message, which was unprecedented, because he loathed technology. I immediately called him back.

"Yes?" he said, when he answered the phone.

"This is Warren," I stammered.

"Warren who?" his nasally voice asked.

"Um, Warren. You left me a message a few hours ago." I was surprised that he might know another person named Warren.

"I know who you are, Warren," he said, joking or not, I couldn't tell. "You've been missing, though," he said frankly, "and you've been missed."

I didn't quite understand what he meant; it was cryptic, though he spoke in a plain way. I was not sure if he had missed me at my lessons, or if he was mad that I had stopped them. "I know. I took a break. I needed some time off."

"Time with your parents, I imagine, who have died recently. I know this. I'm very sorry, Warren."

"Yes. Thank you."

"Well, of course."

"I want to begin my lessons again," I said. I was surprised by how formal I sounded.

"That might be right."

"Yes. But wait, what do you mean?" This was something I was constantly thinking about, the meaning of what people said and how I was prone to interpret them incorrectly. Joan had taken me to task on this issue many times in the past month or so. So I was working on it at every opportunity.

"Only that it might help," he said.

"OK," I said. "When do you think you might have time? Or do you?"

"Do you know that I no longer teach at the community college?" he asked, inscrutably.

My heart sank. I thought of what it might take to find another teacher, how I would go about learning from another person. I sat down on the floor.

"I didn't know that. When did you stop teaching there?" My new objective was to hang up as soon as possible.

"I stopped when they refused me the right to audition my own students. They just sent me anyone who signed up. And some were just awful. So I left. And now all I have is my garden and my own music to look after."

"Well, that's good for you." I tried not to sound upset. "Do you know anyone who might be a good teacher for me? I'd like to start playing again."

"Warren, I said I don't teach at C.C. anymore."

"I know. Is there anyone who took your place? Or anyone you might recommend?"

"But, Warren, I still teach."

"You do? Where?"

"Out of my home."

"Where is your home?"

"Up Squam Road, behind Blunt Quarry."

"That's close by me!"

"Well, that's good news."

"When can I come?" I felt a strange excitement, as if something was finally going right, and participating in it wasn't going to ruin it. "Can it be Wednesday, at five in the afternoon?"

"It can. That sounds fine. Come on Wednesday, at five in the afternoon. Have you written it down?"

"I'm writing it down now."

"So am I."

I ride my bike up toward Blunt Quarry. It is freezing out; it feels like it's going to snow again. Joan has taken the car into the city with Mike to see an exhibit on whaling ships at the museum. They actually asked me if I wanted to go, but I was happy to say that I couldn't, I had a piano lesson.

"I'm starting my lessons again," I told them. And they both looked agreeable and asked no questions.

I had been to Blunt Quarry when I was younger, in the summer when the woods were lush and green, when the thick brush and trees conspired to make a kind of jungle. The quarry itself was small but startling to come upon because of its black granite walls and still, transparent water. Flowers grew abundantly around the quarry's ridge, because, as my father informed me, the minerals in the soil were perfect for certain flowering plants. Vines spilled down the quarry walls; yellow blooms studded the hanging tendrils like clothespins left on a line. In the water lay a thousand lily pads, thick as waffles and curled at the edges, as if they had been singed. White flowers floated among the tangle of pads or sat poised upon them, teacups on oversized saucers. When I was young, I hadn't gone to Blunt Quarry for a piano lesson; I don't remember seeing a house up there at all. I had gone with my father, who was going to gather clippings of plants to harvest them in our kitchen in small clay pots. Later he planted them in the yard, where they generally did not cooperate; they hardly ever grew. He blamed this on how close we were to the sea.

"I've been looking forward to seeing you again, Warren. You can leave your bike by the woodpile and come inside." Mr. Trego looks exactly the same as I remember. Perhaps he's gotten fatter; I scrutinize the paunch inside his cardigan.

I walk through a small mudroom, where a painted chest and a red bench are set up like a museum display against the wall. The floor is immaculate and almost glossy, so I wipe my boots aggressively on the mat by the door.

In the front room, a fire glows in the fireplace and a woman's voice seems to come directly from a bookcase. "Is this Warren; is he here?"

"Yes, Warren's just arrived," says Mr. Trego, in a ceremonious way. An older woman comes in wearing a fleece vest, light denim pants, a heavy dark red sweater, and round-lens glasses. She has short pixie-cut hair that is so uniformly white and layered it looks like a neat cap of feathers. She is smiling, as if something delightful is about to take place at any moment.

"Warren, this is my wife, Mrs. Trego."

"Please call me Meg, because I'm not your teacher. We're going to be pals." She shakes my hand. "I, unlike him, insist on informality in the house." She looks at me with kindness. "It's nice to finally meet you, Warren."

"Thank you—you too," I say, disarmed.

"This is where we will play," says Mr. Trego, and he opens the door to a music room that has a high ceiling and built in bookcases filled—overfilled—with books and boxes, records, CDs, and various objects that seem to have no consistent collectible theme. Along the wall is an old television, an empty but ornate birdcage, and a cabinet with glass doors, inside of which sit a few wooden-headed dolls leaning against one anther—an eerie slouch of silk and polished heads—each bearing a little grin. The walls of the room are painted deep brick-red, and gold-framed photographs hang from long thin wires attached with clips to the high moldings. There is an oil portrait above the fireplace of a woman in a black dress holding a leashed greyhound, whose legs are thin and chopstick-like, like the woman's fingers, which hold the dog's leash in a loose grip. The painting is dark and moody, as if done in shellac; the woman's white face gradually emerges from the gloom. It is not a beautiful face, but I am drawn to it because she looks upset.

"Who's she?" I ask.

"That was my father's sister," Mr. Trego says.

"Oh." The information means nothing to me. I notice a pendant in the shape of a spade hanging from the dog's collar.

The room is disheveled but inviting. The longer I stay in it, adjusting to the light, the more I realize how dusty everything is, how tattered the cushions and couch are, how the gray ashes from the fireplace have been tracked around the Oriental rug. For some reason—and this comes as a surprise—it's reassuring that Mr. Trego's music room seems to be in quiet, comfortable disrepair. I like it. But I can't help feeling disappointed for my own house, far down the hill, falling apart day by day, without any charm at all.

As he shows me the view of the yard, where I envision the garden sprawling in the summer months, I think to myself, *I wish I were a better player.* He mentions how in the spring the morning lilies grow through the window's sash because he always forgets to close the screens. Does he remember me as a better player? I hope he has not mistaken me for a prodigy he might have worked with in the past. I'm suddenly seized with the thought that he has mistaken me for someone with incredible talent; it's the only sensible reason for this kind hospitality. Before we go any further, are you sure you know who I am? I want to ask him.

"Our garden is quite a sight when it is in full force. When I play, I open all the windows and the garden is my audience. I lose myself to it all, Warren." He looks at me with the glittering reverie only an elderly teacher can get away with. "It is a lush place to be possessed." He gleams.

"It sounds amazing," I say, aware that I have probably used the word *amazing* at least ten times since stepping into the house. Still, I can't find much else to contribute. And Mr. Trego doesn't seem to need much from me in order to keep up his steady stream of whimsy. "Don't you like the autumn, or the winter?" I ask.

He looks troubled for a minute, pensive, and for a second I'm sure he's offended.

"I mean, do you miss the summer during the winter—since, I mean, you seem to appreciate it so much?"

"Interesting. I suppose it's all I've talked about—the summer and the garden. It's the cold I get tired of, though it's not as cold up here in the woods as where you are on the ocean."

For a moment, his consideration of me, of my being colder by the ocean, strikes me as the most thoughtful thing anyone has ever said. I look at him looking at me with the same genuine goodness that his wife radiated and suddenly feel uncomfortable, an alien in this house.

"But to answer your question, no, I love autumn and winter just as much. I guess I get nostalgic about them when it's summertime. Ask Meg—I'm sure I do. I miss them like I miss the garden and the flowers now." He looks at me and then casts a wistful look around the room. "No, I love this time of year, but it can be bleak. Because it's all about loss. You have to constantly remind yourself of that, going in. The world around you dies and freezes and the snow comes down and it gets so impossibly cold"—he pauses—"and it's not for a while that things come back to life again. And some days it's easy to lose hope that they ever will."

As I stand and listen to him, a familiar sensation arises in me—a numbness in the walls of my mouth, the distinct feeling that I'm going to vomit on the carpet. All this time I was trying to be polite, but I feel a sudden rush of contempt and anger at him and his stupid, florid artistic musings, his decorated expressive reflections on the seasons. Just think of what you're saying—who you're saying it to!

More than anger, I feel unprepared, almost suckered, completely without means to make conversation or pull myself together. I feel my eyes fill with tears and I turn away from him and look at the painting. I notice a thin silver chain around the woman's neck. This is his sister, I think—no, he said this is his father's sister. This is his aunt. I try and think of Auntie E as a distraction, and I picture her crying inconsolably in the diner as Joan and I looked on, speechless.

"Warren, I'm sorry," I hear his voice say quietly behind me. "That was an insensitive thing to say."

"No! Please, it's fine. Don't be sorry," I blurt. "I agree! That's how I feel about it too. They're my favorite months, my favorite times!" I can feel wetness on my face and frantically try to wipe it away with the cuff of my sweater. Why haven't we started the fucking lesson? I think to myself. Why do we have to get into this?

"Still, I wasn't thinking. It was thoughtless of me."

"No, please, don't be sorry." I muster up a smile and turn to look at him. "I'm OK, really."

He looks serious but gentle, showing the face of a man whose demeanor perfectly conforms to sympathy.

I should go home, I think to myself. Mr. Trego stares out the window.

"I don't hear any wonderful music!" Mrs. Trego's voice trills from the passageway. "Do you want something hot to drink before you begin?"

"That might be a good idea, yes?" he says, shrugging. "What will you have, Warren?"

"Whatever is fine," I say, trying, and failing, to sound stabilized.

"Well, Meg literally has one hundred and fifty thousand kinds of tea. She's very proud of her collection, so I suggest you come up with something specific before she asks what you'd like. Otherwise we'll be sorting through bags and leaves all afternoon and we won't get to play."

Mrs. Trego appears at the doorway and stands for a moment. "Warren, would you like something to drink before you begin?"

"Water would be fine, thank you."

She looks at me and frowns. "Water? Warren, we have more than that. You're welcome to anything we have; I have all kinds of tea."

"How about cocoa?" Mr. Trego interjects.

"We can make cocoa," she asserts, saying "co-co" in a precise way.

"That's fine," I reply, thinking the last time I had cocoa was when I was seven.

"I'll bring it in when it's made," she says, and she pulls the door closed without closing it completely.

Mr. Trego sighs and grins weakly. We move over toward the piano, and he settles himself in a comfortable-looking dining room chair.

"Sit down at the bench, Warren," he says to me, still looking apologetic. "Let's see what you remember."

28

A few days after my father's funeral, Joan and I decided that we would find professional help for my mother. Maybe we weren't giving her a fair shot—we weren't waiting to see how she would do, what form her mourning would take as time went on, how severe it would be. But we had seen what the time leading up to his death had done to her; we had seen her change, and it was worrisome. She wouldn't leave the house and she wouldn't eat the food we made for her. She wouldn't include us in her grief.

After the funeral, we couldn't reason with her because she'd convinced us that we had no claim. It wasn't outright rejection—she asked us to accept the way things were. "We're still a family," we said to her. "We're still your children; you're still our mother. Nothing has changed in those ways." She said, "I'm not saying we're not a family. I'm saying we're no longer whole."

Joan and I decided to ask around to see if anyone knew someone who could help. She would ask Patsy, who'd seen at least five therapists in the last few years, and I'd ask Mrs. Caldwell at the library, because she said she'd been known to go a little nuts at times. She told me in an austere way, "I believe in the science of the mind, and of emotion."

As my mother proved no longer able to care or to cope with the details of life, Joan and I sprang into action. We were a team, efficient and thorough, with serious facial expressions and no mincing of words.

We were impressive. The maintenance of our mother, the house, the bills, the selling of my father's truck, and the issues surrounding the nursery's changing hands were left up to us. And we dealt with them handily—the more focused we were and the more occupied we remained, the more vague and remote our own grief became.

The worst was this: When we did collapse into the awful rift of bleak, inexplicable sorrow our father left us with, we felt self-indulgent, unhelpful, unproductive. It took us away from what needed to get done. I worried that it made us appear incompetent and weak to our mother, who seemed to be growing more suspicious of us every day. She had always striven to outdo her siblings and friends at every opportunity, so that even the matter of grief seemed steeped in rivalry. She made it clear to us that she suffered the loss most acutely and out of axiomatic respect we should not contend with her; we should not challenge her devastation with our own. This left us orphaned—or, rather, I realize, this prepared us for our orphanage.

The day Patsy gave Joan the name of a woman psychiatrist who apparently specialized in grief, mourning, and loss, our mother disappeared. We had grown familiar with her immobility, her silent housebound ways, even to the point where, when she'd come down to the kitchen from her room, we knew not to speak to her. She had said, a few days after the funeral, "Please, kids, I don't want to talk; please don't look up and examine me. I'm just down here to get some crackers and cheese."

"*Examine*, Mom?" Joan asked incredulously.

"Please, Joan, don't."

We hoped that after a while our mother would get up the courage to reclaim her life and take us back in a violent, apologetic repossession. It was a matter of time, we believed. And this was what we were told by the psychiatrist. That she never left the house was just an aspect of a larger grieving process; we had to wait it out—this is also what the psychiatrist told us.

"You're saying this will get better, right? She'll be able to function on her own again, right?" asked Joan. Joan and I would talk to the psychiatrist at the same time, sitting next to each other on the couch, me on the cordless phone, she on the regular living room phone. "She'll leave the house and be normal again?" Joan asked in a desperate way. We looked at each other with halfhearted smiles, since there was no way our mother could have ever been considered normal in the first place.

"She'll find her way back, but it's not easy to lose someone very close to you," the psychiatrist urged in a tempered voice. Upon hearing this I thought, Oh, no, Mom's not going to go and see this woman. She's going to say the psychiatrist we found is too new-age.

That led immediately into my wondering about the psychiatrist's awareness and capabilities in general: The entire time she had not offered *us* sufficient consoling for *our* loss. *We* had lost someone very close to us too. *What about us?* I wanted to yell. But this was not about us; I had to remember that.

When I told Joan my doubts about the psychiatrist, she said, "You're being too hard on her. Hopefully she'll be of some help. Just because you're suspicious doesn't mean Mom will be."

"Mom's going to think she's full of shit," I said. "She's going to laugh in her face."

"Well, it might do her some good to laugh at something," Joan replied, on the verge of tears. "What else are we going to do, Warren?"

"I don't know. I have no idea."

She disappeared. We came home and the back door was open. The house was freezing, and all the curtains were blowing around the living room in a frenzy of lace. The cold air had filled the house, and as we searched for her the radiators clanked and banged around us, struggling to fight off the chill with their rations of steam. We called out for her—even after we'd searched the whole house, we called out for her. I ran into the yard and looked in the hedges, behind the shed. I looked under the porch, where the raccoons stash the garbage they steal and where we have lost a thousand croquet balls. I checked the car Joan and I had been driving around in; to see if she had stashed herself in the trunk. I could hear Joan on the phone, calling the police, calling the hospital. She ran out on the porch with the cordless phone still in her hand, her face scribed in panic. "Did you find her?"

"No!"

"No one's seen her!"

We stood in the yard. The police said they'd notify whoever was patrolling our area. The hospital said they'd not admitted anyone who fit our mother's description. "Fuck!" Joan said.

"We can't blame ourselves," I told her.

"I know, I know," she cried. "But where did she go?"

We ran to our neighbors across the street, an older married couple. They said they saw her wearing a robe in the front yard. She caught their eye because the robe was bright pink. "Is she OK?" they asked with concern.

"Where did she go—did you see where she went?" we asked.

She walked out of the yard toward the church, toward the post office, they told us. "I was going to invite her in because it was so cold out and she was just wearing a robe," said the woman.

"I didn't really watch her," said the man.

"OK," we said. "OK. Thank you." We rushed down the street toward the stone church. This made sense, we told each other; she would often go to the church to pray. She did this before. This made sense.

But the church was locked. The dark red-painted doors were fastened from within, so they didn't even budge when we pulled on the latch. We ran around to the rectory but no one was there. That didn't stop us from banging the knocker loudly, again and again against the metal plate, yelling, *Hello? Hello?* We looked at each other: What do we do? What the fuck do we do? We went out through the barren lilac bushes onto the sidewalk. We moved at a constant trot, a kind of jog and lurch, a skip quickened by fear. "Joan!" I would cry out from moment to moment. "Warren!" She would cry, grabbing my arm, her eyes round and terrified.

We covered the entire area around our house, the perimeter of where she might have gone in the brief time we had been out. We had no way of knowing when she left and how fast she was on her feet. She moved slowly, lethargically around the house, but we couldn't assume she'd be that way outdoors in the cold.

Joan suggested we go to Little Quarry, because it was the only place close by that we hadn't checked. I agreed, but I was afraid. We ran up the road and cut through the lawns of the houses that bordered the woods where the granite had been quarried. The sky above us was beginning to dim in the afternoon hours; we ran under a scrawled cloud of bare branches. The light was silvery and opaque; the trees were sturdy, as if made of stone, all around us like columns.

"What do we do when we find her?" I asked Joan.

"We bring her home," she said.

What I meant was something different, which I knew Joan understood, but she wouldn't encourage me. We just ran through the woods.

We got to the quarry. I scanned the water for the pink robe. I looked everywhere for it and imagined what hue it would assume underwater, submerged or half submerged or floating among the shapes of ice. There were patches of ice along the edge, against the granite walls, like shards left from a broken pane; it looked as if the quarry's center had been shattered. Some kids must have thrown large rocks in to break the ice.

I didn't see the pink robe. We ran down to where there was an entry point—where bathers can enter the water on a series of descending stones. It was growing darker; the woods around us seemed to hold the evening and dispel it gradually, like smoke, into the air.

On a flat rock surrounded by thin glassy ice, twenty feet from the bank where we stood, we saw the bright pink robe slumped over, leaning on its side. The robe had always been very pink, but outside in the open air, in the faint twilight, it was luminous and kinetic, quavering against the deep slate color of the water and the granite walls that surrounded it. My mother's pale hair shone silver above it. She didn't move. We were still as well. We didn't know what to say. We were relieved and afraid. We made our way out to her, stepping carefully on the rocks that led in a neat path to where she sat, shivering and blue on a rock in the middle of the water.

"Mom?" Joan said softly.

The robe didn't stir. We stood over her, crowded on the flat rock as if under an umbrella. The wind whipped inside the quarry's walls. We stayed close to the rock's center; ice radiated around the rock's edge in a frilled cuff.

"Mom?" Joan said again. Joan looked at me with vacant eyes, her mouth slightly opened. The task of getting our mother safely off the rock to the embankment, through the woods, and home was impossible to imagine. I suspected that she was drunk and we would have to fight her to get her back.

She wasn't drunk, she was impaired by medication. We tried to pull her up but it was like pulling on a doll.

"We're going to take you home now, Mom," I said, in the voice I had created for instances like this: determined and in control. "Otherwise you're going to freeze out here. Let's go, Mom."

"I know. I'm freezing. I'm only wearing my robe." She looked up at us with a bewildered expression.

"Come on, Mom," Joan pleaded. "Stand up and we'll take you home."

"I'll help you, Mom." I tried bending down and putting my arms under her armpits.

"Kids, this is so embarrassing: I'm out of the house with my robe on," she said. "Give me something to wear!" She sounded like a child. She seemed to have no vision, no ability to gauge where we were. She looked at us as if we were strangers, or through us as if we were ghosts.

Joan had no discernible expression on her face. She was looking down at my mother, who was shivering and blue-lipped. Joan removed her scarf and tied it securely around my mother's neck. "Here, wear this," she said quietly.

"Thank you, Joan," she said tamping it down against her chest and straightening the knot. "That's better. That's better."

29

In the car back from the mall I ask Joan about Christmas Day.

"I don't remember. What happened?"

An obvious lie. "What do you mean you don't remember? It wasn't that long ago. We went to the diner from the beach after the car wouldn't start, and Auntie E showed up out of nowhere."

"Oh, yeah," she says.

"Well, we haven't heard from her since then. It's been two weeks—almost."

"It has?"

"Doesn't that bother you? Don't you feel bad about it?"

"Do you feel bad about it?"

"Yes, I feel bad. She basically came all the way out to ask us to accept her as family and we basically told her no. That's terrible, and I do feel bad about it."

"Really?" she says thoughtfully. "I don't know. I don't know if it really is that terrible."

"Of course it is! She was wrecked! When she left she was sobbing into a napkin!"

"I know. I'm not saying I'm glad she was upset, because it's painful to see her like that. I do feel terrible about that part of it."

She slows the car down, turns off the highway at Grapevine Road, and continues.

"I'm just saying, even though it was hard to have that conversation,

I think it's good that it happened. I think it's good that we had it."

"In what way is it good? What good comes out of Auntie E feeling like we don't want her in our family anymore?"

"Here we go," Joan says, rolling her eyes.

"Seriously."

"OK, seriously. I don't know if any real good can come out of it, because she's going to be hurt," Joan began, "but what I take as the value of that conversation is that now she knows the story. Now she knows what she came to find out. She must at least be relieved that she knows, even though it hurts." Joan pauses.

I'm confused.

"For me," she continues, "it was like with Mike, when he left me and left town and didn't tell me anything; I was tortured. Every day I would torture myself wondering what I had done, what was going on, if he was coming back or if I was supposed to go and find him or what. I had no idea what the story was. And it ruined me. You remember. I was destroyed, I hated life."

"And you were a total pain in the ass to live with," I add.

"Whatever. The point is, at least with Auntie E, she knows. She doesn't have to go through all the shit that I did."

I look at Joan. She has been speaking with such authority, with surprisingly little verbal clutter, and yet making no sense. I want very badly to understand what she is saying but I have a hard time following the parallels she is offering: herself and Auntie E, her getting mysteriously dumped by Mike and Auntie E getting dumped by us.

"It's better for everyone that Auntie E not be a part of our lives— it will be easier in the long run," she says decisively.

"Joan, do you really believe that? Is that why you didn't say anything when she was crying at the diner, because you agreed with her?"

"I didn't say anything because I didn't know what to say. I felt awful that she was so upset, but I didn't feel like I could comfort her in the way she wanted. I would have been lying to her."

"Maybe that's true, but sometimes maybe you just have to comfort someone when they need to be comforted."

"Not if it's going to mislead them."

"How would saying that we still wanted Auntie E to be our aunt be misleading?"

"Because we don't want her to be."

"Yes, we do! That's crazy! What are you talking about? Of course we do. I know she's annoying and embarrassing, but, shit, she's our aunt and our relative, and we don't have many of them left. Why not try and keep the family we do have?"

"Because they're insane and we don't need them."

"What?"

"We have to start over now. You and I are the only family we've ever really had, and you know it. We never felt close to anyone else." Joan's tone of voice is forceful, eerily professional. I think back to how she acted, in this exact same way, last Thanksgiving at Auntie E's house. This plan of hers may have been set in action a long time ago. "We can choose the people we want in our lives, Warren. It's one of the only things we have now—the only thing Mom and Dad left us. We can choose what we want."

"You're completely insane!" I say. "You mean *you* can choose."

"I don't recall an outpouring of emotion toward Auntie E on your part either. You weren't exactly taking her into your arms like family."

"But at least I tried! Besides, I was in shock. I kept on thinking about our conversation about Uncle Steve and all the crazy shit he pulls and how he and Auntie E are probably in cahoots and are probably planning something. And then she started crying and I was totally caught off guard. And I felt bad for her!"

"See, that's just it: Uncle Steve—we can't have that. We can't keep worrying about whether he'll show up at some point. We have to make the break now."

"It's just so harsh."

"I know it is, but it's what we have to do. We have to take what we have, take what is ours, and move on."

"Joan, it doesn't have to be so extreme. We don't have to do anything, really, if we don't want. We can just patch things up with Auntie E and let things go on normally. But you sound like we have to take some action, like we have to follow some plan."

"There is no plan. There are only things we have to do to keep us sane, for the future especially."

"The future! What does the future hold for us, Miss Mystic? What's our fate? A life of complete isolation, locked all alone in our house?" Frankly the idea doesn't seem like a bad one, but I'm surprised to find that Joan might be adopting a bit of my hermitlike impulses she's found so annoying all our lives.

"Warren"—she narrows her gaze at me—"we're not going to be alone. I have Mike and you. And you have me. We can start there."

"I just think this is kind of fucked up."

"I knew you would."

"I don't get it, Joan."

"Oh, I know, but you will. You have to trust me that it's for the best."

"Wow."

"What, wow?"

"You've never said that to me before."

"Said what?"

"Trust me." I look at her.

"Why?"

"Because," I say, "I've always trusted you."

The roads are clear and salted, so that the pavement looks filmy, as if covered in chalk dust or flour. We take Grapevine Road to Haskell, up toward Route 1A. The thick clouds begin to break apart over the water, near the Sanctuary's peninsula and Tuck's Point, where we had spied on Mike's father and the rest of the polar bears. Now and then it snows a bit, and we watch as the snowflakes swirl around and accumulate along the edges of the windshield wipers. When Joan turns the wipers on, we watch as they smear the flakes into two filmy arcs.

"Let's go and see them," I say.

"Who?"

"Mom and Dad," I say.

"OK," Joan replies.

"When's the last time you went to see them?"

"I don't remember. When have you?"

"Probably about a week ago."

"Oh."

Joan takes the turn toward the hill where Mr. Trego lives and stops at the stop sign. "Let's get them some flowers," she says.

"They'll die right away in the cold."

"It doesn't matter. Let's get them some."

"OK," I say. "Let's go see Richard and get some flowers."

"We'll tell him, 'We need some flowers to put at the graves of our parents. Do you remember them? Our dad, who gave you this place?'" Joan says with a bitter smile.

"Maybe he'll charge us for them."

"That fucker probably will."

30

A week or so after my father's funeral we went to the nursery. Richard had asked us to come. This was where we had been when our mother went missing.

Joan and I drove to the nursery without knowing exactly why Richard wanted to meet with us. Although we weren't present, my father had officially signed the place over to Richard before he died and had explained the deal to us, but only in the simplest terms. We were all in his hospital room at the time, and my mother sat at his side and insisted that he limit his explanation to a few short phrases, in order to preserve his strength. But we had faith in the fact that the deal was transacted honestly. Why wouldn't it be? Richard, in my eyes, was the picture of honesty—if not honesty, then the picture of warmth and authenticity, and therefore the least likely person to try and hurt us.

At my father's funeral, Richard had protected us. I'd told him my mother didn't want to speak to anyone—none of us wanted to—and he kept everyone away. Joan and I stayed close by him and kept our mother safely between us. Like a guardian he accompanied us through every stage of the occasion, splitting apart the crowd like a ship through rough waves.

We figured Richard was going to explain to us the terms of the agreement and perhaps our part in it, if we had one. I was looking forward to seeing him because he was like family, a comfort, and had said on the phone that he looked forward to seeing us too.

We felt relieved, driving down the driveway, out into the world. Even though it was winter we rolled down the windows, as if to be closer to the lives that went on around us. We had agreed not to worry about our mother; she'd been in her room all day. It felt good to be out of the house.

The nursery looked disheveled because some of the last vestiges of the Christmas decorations were still up. The yard where Christmas trees were sold had an emptied look to it; bags of peat were stacked in their taut plastic blocks, frozen beneath a flimsy swag of pine boughs. Strings of fat bulb lights hung around the perimeter of the barren area, swinging in the cold wind that blew from the marsh. As we walked to the door Joan stopped at the holly plants, lined up along the walkway, and took a sprig of holly between her gloved fingers. "Should we get one of these for the house?" she said. "Mom might like it."

"Maybe," I said.

Inside, the place was almost completely empty; it was just about closing time. Helen, the diminutive Asian woman who runs the flower shop, jumped up and clapped her hands when she saw Joan. "Roan!" she cried. She was sweeping the floor, and she came over to give Joan and me each a hug.

"Thank you for the beautiful arrangement you made for our father," I said to her.

"Aw, no." She frowned and looked up at us with her old eyes, glassy and black like beads beneath her lids. She hugged us again and shook her head. She walked over to the table and took two small orchids from a plastic bucket and handed them to us.

"Thank you, Helen," Joan said.

"Thank you," I said.

Richard popped his head out from the back and asked us into the office that used to be our father's. Nothing much had been changed, which was reassuring. I believed it was out of respect. Richard sat behind the desk, which was covered with catalogs, invoices, seed packets, and scraps of green ribbon.

"I know this isn't easy for you, and I know your mom's having a tough time with it all, too," Richard began. "You guys are such great kids, I'm sure you're taking good care of her." He looked back and forth from Joan to me with a serious but gentle expression. "But I wanted you to come over today so I could explain some details. I don't think it's wise for your mom to come just yet—I think it would be too hard." He shifted in his chair uncomfortably. "You guys should know how your dad came to give me this place, and how it affects you, or will affect you, in the long term or short, or maybe never, directly—I don't know; in many ways it's up to you. In any case, I think he'd want you to know what went on, since it was his, and you guys basically grew up here."

Joan and I sat quietly in our chairs facing him, feeling no need to contribute anything beyond a nod or smile. It was nice to have someone talk to us without fear and without anxiety—someone who could actually look us in the eye.

"Before your father passed away, he offered to sell me the nursery in exchange for a sum that would directly go to both of you and your mother. I agreed to those terms along with a few minor caveats. He asked, in exchange for a slight modification in selling price, that I keep the name, Marshland Nursery, and most of the advertising and marketing, as it was mostly his idea and he wanted to leave something behind."

That my father's idea of leaving something behind was the nursery's name and some of its advertising concepts made me feel suddenly wounded. I looked over at Joan to see if see looked offended, but she seemed unaffected, listening attentively to Richard.

"He asked me that should I want to build on to the existing building, that I do so within set parameters and use the architects he'd hired two years ago to build the back greenhouses and potting sheds, because we've developed a relationship with them." Richard leafed through some pages of a long document that, every now and then, he held up for us to see, showing us particular clauses and paragraphs.

"Finally—and he emphasized this point—if I was going to sell the nursery for any reason whatsoever, that I was to inform you about my decision first and offer you, one or both of you along with your mother, first refusal rights. He wanted you to have this place if you wanted it. If you didn't and I was to sell it, an amount of roughly seventy-five percent would go to your mother and then to you as the original owners." Richard sat back in his chair and looked at us. "There's more to this, but I figured I'd give you the highlights. Did I make any sense at all?"

"Are you thinking about selling?" I asked. Joan looked scandalized.

"Not a bit, Warren. I love this place, and I'm flattered and touched that your dad trusted me with it. I'm not about to give it up. Why would I?"

"No kidding," Joan agreed heartily.

"I was just wondering, since you mentioned it," I said. "Maybe Joan can have her job back now," I added.

Joan flinched.

"Do you need a job, Joan?" Richard said, in a voice like Santa Claus.

"No. Warren's just being obnoxious. I'm still at the bakery, and I love it there. I don't need a job." She gave me a mean look. "I couldn't be happier."

"I appreciate your telling us this, Richard," I said. He smiled and nodded and started to say something. "But why are you, exactly?" I tried not to sound rude, but I'm certain I sounded suspicious.

"I just figured you should know. I figured your mother hadn't told you—she doesn't seem too interested in the business—and I thought maybe one of you would be—you know, in the future."

"Oh. OK," I said. "Well, Joan might be."

"Warren, shut up!" Joan snapped.

"What?"

We were like children. The nursery was our nursery.

"Yes, well, Joan, what do you think?" Richard asked, helpless in our world of private jokes and allusions. "Are you interested?"

"Not at the moment, Richard, thank you. I like the bakery. Maybe in a year or whatever, I don't know. Warren's just being obnoxious—don't listen to him."

"Well, thanks for coming in. If you want a copy of this I can run one off right now. Your mom has one at home, too, I'm sure."

"Thanks, I'm sure it's fine," I said, as we got up to leave.

"I'll let you know if there are any changes, but I don't expect any," he added cheerfully. "Take some flowers for your mother—she'd like them."

"Thanks," we said again.

He came around his desk and gave each of us an awkward hug.

"How's your mom doing, by the way?"

"She's at home," I said.

"Yeah, we'll get her some roses if that's not too much," Joan said.

"Oh, no, that's fine. Take the roses—they're in the green pails toward the back of the cooler."

"I know where they are," Joan said.

31

I am behind the front desk at the library, filling in while Mrs. Caldwell is upstairs in the office on an urgent call. It's ten in the morning, and already the reading room has filled and emptied and filled again.

Mrs. Kestrel from the bookstore comes in with her daughter, a tall, slightly chubby girl with wire-rimmed glasses and straight black hair; her face has a mashed-in look and her cheeks are flushed, as if freshly slapped. They are looking for books on standardized testing because the girl is trying to get into boarding school for next fall.

"Did you ever think about that, Warren—going away to school?" Mrs. Kestrel asks in a prying way, when she comes up to the front desk.

The question strikes me as stupid, but I manage to say, "Well, not for high school, obviously. I think about going to college sometimes, but who knows?"

"Well, Fiona's only in the sixth grade now, but if she wants an Ivy in her future she's got to start doing the work now." Fiona shrinks into her coat. "You're planning ahead, aren't you, sweetie?" She peers down at her daughter.

"I'm surprised you don't have these books in your store," I say, scanning them with the infrared barcode-reading gun. There is no point to this comment other than to shift the focus from the girl, who looks harrowed.

"No, I would never order them! They wouldn't sell at all; not in this town. Between you and me, Warren, there are few among us who want more out of life than fishing or working in a bakery."

"Excuse me?"

"Anyway, I was all ready to go to the mall when I thought, Of course! The library will have them! So I said, Forget spending money at the mall—I'll go to the library and get them for free! And look! We found the books and we found you, Warren!" She prods the child. "It's Warren. You remember his mommy, right, honey?"

Fiona stares at the floor.

"Ah, yes," I say vaguely. "The mall."

Mrs. Caldwell comes hurriedly down the main staircase, her rubber-soled clogs slapping against the carpeted runner. She is wearing her coat indoors and is rubbing her hands together furiously. Her regal bun is fastened securely to her head, dense and roped like a skein. "I'm sorry for taking so long on the phone, Warren, the oil company kept me on hold forever! They play that horrible music. I thought I was going to slip into a coma."

"Hello, Dottie, trouble heating the library?" Mrs. Kestrel asks snidely.

"Oh, hello, Susan. No—well, yes, upstairs, the radiators won't fill. Down here it's fine and downstairs and in the basement it's like a sauna, but the heat won't climb past the second floor." Mrs. Caldwell won't honor Mrs. Kestrel's tone with a retaliating bite—she's way too classy for that. She remains informative.

"Are you all set, then? Because I'm going to finish with the microfiche downstairs," I say to Mrs. Caldwell.

"Oh, yes, Warren, thank you for looking out." She smiles and waves me on toward the stairwell.

"Dottie, Warren tells me he's thinking about going off to college."

"No!" I blurt.

Mrs. Caldwell looks at me with surprise. "What? Warren, is that true? Are you applying?"

"Warren, where did you say you were applying? West Coast? Somewhere abroad?" Mrs. Kestrel asks.

"I didn't say. I don't know, actually, if I will at all."

"Wherever it is, I'm sure you can get an ambitious job in the library there, too," she assures me. "I'm sure Dottie will write you a stellar letter of recommendation."

Mrs. Caldwell looks at Mrs. Kestrel blankly and turns back to me. "Oh, Warren, it's such a relief to hear you say it." She grabs my arm. "Where are you thinking about going? Why didn't you tell me? Have you been looking at the catalogs? I suppose we should put them out, but there's never any interest. Anyway, where, Warren—where?"

"I don't know. I really haven't thought about it much. Seriously."

Mrs. Kestrel looks pleased that she's managed to create an awkward moment, if not for Mrs. Caldwell, then at least for me. She smiles and picks up her books. "Good luck, Warren. Hope that heat climbs up for you, Dottie." She hauls her daughter out the door.

"She's insane," I say.

"She's hateful," says Mrs. Caldwell. "Now, Warren—where?"

Downstairs in the archive room, the day passes quietly. Before I know it, I look out the windows and it's already dark. The library's garden covered in snow looks like pastries coated in royal icing—a confectionery term I recently learned from Patsy, who was working on an elaborate cake for a New Year's party to be thrown at The Chimneys. I stand at the window and scrutinize the darkness, trying to figure out if it's snowing, but there is nothing, no subtle shift of crystals inside the deepening evening, which is somehow disheartening. Lights turn on and off in the various windows around the library's courtyard, and I watch as the ambiguous shapes of people pass through each aperture.

I used to look up at the windows of our house when I returned from town or piano lessons or work. I liked to stand in the yard and stare up at each window, waiting for movement, a hint of who was home, whom I would find when I went through the door. Often there was no one— the windows reflected the sky back at me or revealed the curtains hanging bored and still. Sometimes I would see my mother scurry from one window to the next with the watering can, or Joan would dance by, talking on the phone with her hair put back in a brightly colored elastic. Sometimes my father would be by himself at a window, looking out at the yard, and we would see each other, on either side of the windowpane, and he would wave to me. *Come out here,* I'd wave to him. *Come inside,* he'd wave back at me. *Hold on. Wait. I'm coming.*

Every shadow passing by the library windows is a stranger. Joan is right. There is no use in doing all the same things we did when we were young. These things don't mean anything anymore; they are of no help to us. We have to start over.

I go up the back stairs to punch out in the office. Mrs. Caldwell is there with her parka's hood over her head, tapping away at lightning speed on the computer.

"I finished with most of the microfiche," I say. "There's some that doesn't seem to go into any category because the date's worn off or was snipped off by the trimmer. I'll look at them tomorrow on-screen and find out where they go."

"That would be fine. There's no need to rush, of course."

"I know. I'd just as soon get it done."

Mrs. Caldwell stops typing and turns to look at me. "Are you really thinking about going to college?" The elation in her voice is gone now; she looks at me seriously.

"I don't know. The idea just came up because Mrs. Kestrel was taking out study books for her daughter. She asked me if I ever wanted to go away to school. She was just making stupid conversation, and so was I." I feel badly that Mrs. Caldwell looks upset. Maybe she's hurt that I didn't tell her about applying to schools. But that's stupid, because I'm not; I haven't.

"I would hate to see you go, and I think I speak for everyone here," she begins, taking down her hood, "but I think it would be wonderful for you." She smiles. "I've never really talked to you about your parents—I've always tried to respect your privacy." She stops and looks down at her hands as she pulls on her gloves with a few short tugs. "Because I care for you so much. And I've always worried about you. I have." She looks at me squarely, "But I think you going to college would be wonderful. You are a hard worker and you're so bright. You should go. It would be so good for you. And you deserve it. I don't know how you feel about it—whether or not you feel you deserve it. I don't know what sense of yourself you have in that way, but I feel you deserve the kind of experience that college could offer. Really."

"To be honest, I haven't thought that hard about it—I've been thinking about other things so much these days," I say. Must we talk about this? I think about the windows and the unfamiliar shapes that passed before them. I think of how it's not snowing, how I will not walk home amid the new-falling snow. I feel suddenly bereft, unmoored.

"OK," she says quietly. "Well, I think now's a good time to think more about it. You still have time, I'm sure, to apply for fall or even next winter. There are a lot of options. I'm sure you could go wherever you wanted."

"It doesn't matter," I say.

"Don't say that." She rolls her chair over to me. "You are entitled to a life of your own." Her face looks so concerned, so empathic, it's almost too much to look at. "And you could find a place close by, so you won't have to be far from Joan."

In all the years I have worked here, throughout everything, I have not broken down in front of Mrs. Caldwell. I am proud of this. But just as she's in mid-sentence about how board scores are good for five years, I crumple against the desk. She immediately stops talking and draws me against her. I sit with my head against her narrow shoulder, dissolving.

There is no structure to this outburst, no exact trigger. I think of Joan. I cry heavily and without control. I cry for the fact that I have been given a choice, a choice I have to make for myself, a choice that will affect the people I love the most. I cry at the idea of leaving the library, leaving Joan and the house we live in. I think of how much I hate Mrs. Kestrel and how she's responsible for this breakdown. She is to blame. I cry because I'm desperately looking for someone to blame.

I bury my head in my arms and cry hard into the sleeves of my sweatshirt, heaving as Mrs. Caldwell rubs my back, and says, "Oh, Warren." I slump against her coat and listen to the clock tick its loud circular course, counting off the hours, and the radiators bang and hiss, trying to summon the steam from the basement.

"I can only imagine what goes on in your head—you're so quiet and intense," Mrs. Caldwell says softly. "What are you thinking now? What's going on?"

"I don't even know if I can go," I begin, the words muffling in my sweatshirt.

"Oh, no, I've seen your reports from school—you're a star. Joan told me, too, that you won a national award at graduation. There should be no problem in finding a good school, a top school, that will take you."

"That's not what I mean."

"Do you mean financially? There are loans and work grants and fellowships for that. Don't worry about that; you should not let that stand in your way." She rolls her chair back to where she had been at the computer. This gives me a chance to right myself fully in my chair and mop up my face. She opens the drawer and takes out a small leather book.

"I think I may have an idea."

"No, Mrs. Caldwell, you don't have to. I can figure this out on my own. It's OK." I do my best to sound capable and strong, though we both know there is no point.

"Hold on for one second. Let me at least tell you what my idea is—or, rather, who my friend is who may be of help."

"All right."

"The reason I think of him is that he recently contacted me about sponsoring a chair for the library—you know, in his name, with the money going toward helping with preservation and the special collections. I'd like to ask him if his philanthropy might extend to sponsoring one of the library's valuable employees toward getting a college education." She was getting a little worked up, which is typical of her.

I look at her blankly.

"Meaning you, Warren."

"Oh."

"Would you object if I asked him about it—you know, after we deal with the business he first called me about?"

"I don't know. I don't know if it's the right thing to do." I am hesitant because the idea of getting money from someone makes me uncomfortable. It reminds me of Uncle Steve.

"Let me just ask him. Give me your permission to act on your behalf, and we'll see what he can do for us. OK?"

"I don't know."

"Just allow me to try."

"All right."

"Good. Actually, you might know him, from the nursery and your father and all."

My heart sinks. Please, not Richard. I'm about to interject when she adds, "Phillip Loring—do you know him? He lives at The Chimneys above Singing Beach? He's an amazing man with an incredible story. He has a long history of gift giving and supporting us in the past. Do you know him, Warren?"

"I used to cut his lawn," I say sheepishly.

"Really? That's perfect! Then he already knows who you are!"

32

Joan came home and slammed the newspaper down on the kitchen table.

"Look at this fucker!" she screamed.

There was a picture of Richard in my father's old office. Next to the photo was an architectural drawing of the building that will replace the nursery. Although it's still going to be a greenhouse/nursery and some of the buildings will remain the same, it's to be expanded and become part of a chain whose headquarters are in New Jersey. The Marshland Nursery sign will be replaced with a large green sign like those gigantic illuminated ones all along Route 1. The mascot of the new chain is perhaps the worst part of all: Della Russo's Greenhouse is represented by a cartoonish, pudgy green groundhog named Della, frolicking with daisies clutched in her paw, across the words DELLA RUSSO'S GREENHOUSE & FLOWER SHOPPE.

"I knew it! I knew he was planning something! Fucker!" Joan screamed. "He never called us about this—he never asked if we wanted to buy it! And where the fuck is our seventy-five percent of the sale?" Joan shrieked as she stomped around the room.

"And why this little creature?" I had skimmed the article and was pointing in horror at Della, rotund and merry in mid-skip. In all the panic and anger I had not noticed that Mike was standing in the kitchen behind Joan. I looked at him and he shook his head, to communicate his bewilderment.

"We have to go there now! This is insane!" Joan yelled. "Get your coat, we're leaving." She turned to Mike and said quickly, "We'll drop you off at the wharf."

He nodded.

When we got to the nursery, Richard looked calm. He closed the door to his office, which had been emptied out over the past months. There was a sharp smell of disinfectants in the air, which clashed unpleasantly with the natural odors of the plants, now clustered in pockets around the store, apparently for transportation or storage.

"What's up, you guys?" Richard said, in an upbeat way.

Joan launched into action like a crazy person. "Why didn't you tell us you were selling the nursery?"

"I did. Or at least I tried; I called you to tell you in November, but no one was ever home. I had to rush with the proceedings before the holidays, so I didn't have time to wait. I figure I'd see you in town and I could tell you then."

"Did it occur to you to come over and find us? It's not like you don't know where the house is!" Joan shouted. I was impressed and proud of her.

"I did stop by, Joan," he said smoothly, "but, again, it appeared as if no one was home. I figured you might have taken a vacation."

"Oh, now, that's crap!" I said. "Come on, Richard—you know what's been going on; you know we've been home. You know we didn't go on vacation. Please, where would we go?"

Joan looked over at me, glad to see we were united, aligned.

"And today we read the paper and it turns out you sold Marshland to some stupid chain with a fucking chipmunk on the sign!" I almost laughed out loud, but I managed to maintain composure for the sake of Joan's searing invective. "You were supposed to contact us and tell us that you were selling it! We were supposed to have the option of buying it if you didn't want it!"

"You're right. You two, along with your mother, were given the option of buying it if it was going to be sold," Richard said deliberately.

"Exactly!" Joan seethed. "But as far as I could tell, we weren't given anything, either options or information or the seventy-five percent we are entitled to as original owners—unless, of course, you plan to hand over a check right now."

"I don't," Richard said quickly.

"We met right in this room and you told us all of these things—I'm just repeating what you said to us!" Joan said.

"You two and your mother are—or were—technically, the original owners. But actually, to be completely technical, your mother was the only original owner with your father because she provided half the money to start the nursery."

"So, we are entitled to that money that our mother would have otherwise received," I said, knowing now that Richard has probably done something to prevent just that.

"Not necessarily." He tried not to grin. "You see, in the contract I so thoughtfully offered to copy for you last February, it stipulates that upon death or agreed transfer of holdings and properties, the original owner forfeits all rights and claims to the property."

"Excuse me?" I asked.

"Oh, my God, this is disgusting," Joan moaned.

"I'm sorry it comes down to this, but when your mother passed away, her claim on Marshland was released. It's in this contract; it's how I was able to go through the purchase agreement without your written consent—without either of you involved at all." Richard sat back in his chair. "Kids, I'm legal in all of this."

"What the hell is wrong with you?" I yelled, standing up from my chair. "No, seriously, Richard, what the fuck is wrong with you?"

"We would have let you make the choice on your own anyway—it's not like we'd try and stop you!" Joan hissed. "But you use some fucking loophole to try to swindle us out of some money? Seriously, who are you?"

"You knew we didn't want the nursery—we only wanted to be fucking asked, fucking considered! You fucked us over as if you thought we were going to do it first!" I screamed. I caught a glimpse of Della shimmying across the letterhead of a document on the desk. "Our father gave you the nursery because he considered you to be part of our family!"

Joan and I were both on our feet, practically lurching across the desk at him.

"Your father sold me the nursery because he trusted my business savvy. What I don't think you two realize is that this is a business. It's not about family or friendships. This is about making sound business decisions."

"You probably had this planned from the start, calling my father your brother! You probably were going to do this all along. You must have been so pleased when our mother died. It must have been the happiest day in your whole miserable life!" I thought Joan was going to throttle him.

"Richard, you owe us the money that is rightfully our mother's. You know you do." I tried to introduce an aspect of reason to the conversation. He tensed up.

"Warren, there's no way I'm handing that money over to you. It's mine because I sold a property that legally belonged to me. You have no legal claim."

"This is disgusting!" Joan screamed and slammed her hand on the desk, which produced an impressively thunderous sound. She sounded exactly like our mother, shockingly like her, actually, and I had to take a moment to collect myself. "What is wrong with you, Richard?"

"Richard, you know we're not in prime shape financially." I was trying again to reason with him. "This money would help us out a lot." It was taking all my energy to keep from diving over the desk and crushing his face. In truth, our parents had left us enough money to live well and had assigned us a lawyer, with whom we communicated, to help us balance our expenses. I suppose I was offering him a final chance to redeem himself.

Joan was silent, waiting to see how Richard would respond. I sat back down on the edge of the chair.

"I see what you're saying," he started, "but I have my troubles too. I have ends to meet and bills to pay." He gave us a sorry theatrical look. I felt Joan coil up, like a cat about to go after something in the yard. "Maybe we could figure out a loan of some sort, low-interest— or no, no interest at all. Yes? I would still like to help you both. I really would like to help." His face became pathetic and imploring for a moment, which was outrageous.

Joan got up, grabbed my hand, and pulled me toward her. She turned toward Richard and screamed, "Fuck you, Richard! You should be ashamed of yourself! My father and mother would weep if they saw you right now!"

He heaved his burly frame up from his chair and started to yell back. "That's it! That is all I'm going to take from you, Joan! This world will prove to be an ugly place for you if you think you can talk to people this way! You dig yourself a hole and you climb right in!"

"I shudder to think of what you'll be like when you have kids of your own, Richard," I said.

"You have nothing! Nothing in your fucking pathetic life and nothing where your fucking heart should be! You're a fucking liar!" Joan screamed.

We walked out of his office. He kept yelling at us. We didn't slow to listen to what he said. We walked quickly together, like soldiers in perfect stride, toward the car. We passed Helen in the flower shop; she was wearing gigantic headphones and listening to her Walkman while working on a large arrangement with lilies and sticks. She looked up as we passed and waved at us in a cheerful way.

33

I found my mother. I came home and the house was quiet. I thought Joan was going to be home, but the car was gone. It turned out she was with Laura and Patsy, having drinks at the River Pub and no doubt laughing once again at the inadequacies of people in general and men in particular. She would come home soon, though.

I had been at the library. I waited for the bus for twenty-five minutes and it never came, so I walked home in the cold. When I got home I was so thankful to be there, all I could think about was lying on the heater in the window seat. I was too distracted by my own cold to notice that no lights were on in the upstairs part of the house. My mother's window was black—a rectangle punctured out of the house.

In the kitchen, one candle was sputtering, and in its dim glow I saw the top of my mother's head, her neat white part and the hair that spilled out from it onto the table. I could see the candle's flame reflected in the large green wine bottle beside her head. I moved toward her and lost my footing—something had gotten caught under my boot: marbles, I thought. I flailed around and caught myself on a chair. I reached for the light switch, and when the room was illuminated I saw her completely, sprawled out across the table, a pool of saliva and foam around her face. On the floor were ten or twenty tiny white pills and many capsules with two-colored tips, red and white.

I tried to pick her up off the table. She felt different. I had known her weight; I knew the way she felt in my arms, how her limbs gave and swung, how, when I pressed myself to her, to steady her so she could rise, there was a force pushing back. In all the times I'd had to carry her, care for her, walk her from room to room or up the stairs, I had felt something living inside her, a pulse somewhere inside her body. Now there was nothing.

I set her back down in her chair, where she slumped like a grocery bag. I thought I might vomit. I began to sweat. I called 911 and they told me to do CPR—they asked me if I knew CPR, and I said, Sort of, I think I know it; I will try but please come, please come now.

I pulled her down to the floor. I tried my best to keep her from hitting the tiles too hard; I cradled her head. I laid her on her back and opened her robe. A rank smell came out as the robe opened; her gray T-shirt smelled like trash and soil and grapes. I tried to remember what to do, how to hold my hands, flattening the palms on top of each other, and how many times to press on her ribs, above her heart. I had heard stories of people who had been saved by CPR; they lived, but their ribs had been broken while being revived. I prepared myself for that, for the sound and feeling of my mother's ribs breaking beneath my palms.

I was not able to count correctly. I kept on losing my count; I was crying. I moved up to her face and opened her mouth. I put mine on hers and blew. I could see her cheeks balloon. I could feel her teeth click against mine. I didn't know if I was doing it right, but her chest inflated slightly as I blew. Please, I thought, please. I took my mouth away from hers, and in the parting there was a tart smack. I tried to keep my tongue still in my mouth; I tried not to taste the flavor of her mouth in mine. I began the regime I had learned: I pushed against her chest and blew into her opened mouth. I blocked her nose because I could feel the air escape. Her skin was wet from my tears and from my spit, the spot I was pressing over her heart was wrinkled and sweat-stained. I worked—and she did not move.

Headlights appeared on the kitchen ceiling. I leapt up. I didn't want Joan to see this. I lunged toward the door. Outside I could hear a car door closing and then the quick blurts of a siren. I heard Joan's voice, panicked, in the driveway. *What's going on?*

"We're answering an emergency call," said a man's voice. I rushed to the door and flung myself out onto the porch. Joan was standing in the driveway looking frantic as four paramedics swarmed around and past her toward the house with a stretcher. The lights were bright, glaring up toward me; the siren had been shut off but I could hear it ringing in my head. From where I stood on the porch, the scene in the driveway was shrouded in smoke, in steam, in the exhaled breath of everyone gathered in the ambulance's headlights. Joan began to run up the hill toward me.

I met her halfway up the driveway. I couldn't speak; I was crying; my face was wet and covered in spit. Joan was screaming hysterically at me: *What? What's happening, Warren? Tell me!* The paramedics rushed into the house, their boots loud on the porch boards; I could hear the voices on their walkie-talkies reporting the scene inside. Although I could not speak clearly to Joan, I was intent on keeping her out of the kitchen. I was pushing her downhill toward the cars. And then away from the cars and into the yard, because I didn't want her to see the stretcher with our mother laid upon it when they brought her to the ambulance.

"No," I said to her again and again. "No, you can't go in!"

"Why? What is it, Warren? Warren, tell me!"

But she did not fight me; she opened up her coat and held me and we stood there wailing in the snowy yard.

She screamed, "Oh, Warren! I'm sorry! I'm so sorry!"

I screamed, "I'm sorry! I tried to save her! But I couldn't do it right!"

34

I am trying to read the music Mr. Trego has put in front of me. He seems frustrated that I can't quite get it right; it's taking more time than it used to. For some reason, I can't get my hands to sync up, play the piece through, play it well. His restlessness is obvious, but unlike before, I don't care. I am impatient with his impatience with me.

"Hold on," I say to him irritably, because I have to stop and start over every time I make a mistake. I don't accept the fact that I have to get back into playing the piano slowly; I want immediate perfection; more than ever I want evidence that I am a latent prodigy. It feels desperate and stupid. I have completely lost perspective on how I played before I stopped my lessons. Right now, as I fumble and fuck up, I think I was probably excellent.

"Just try and get through it. Don't worry if you make a mistake; you need to get through it for the sake of understanding the tempo," he says insistently.

I start over and he leans back in his chair and sighs in a dramatic way, but there is understanding in it, and pity.

"Warren." He starts up again, his voice this time steady and encouraging. "This should not be that hard for you; this is stuff you were doing years ago. After a couple of lessons you should be fine with this, and this is our third, so now just concentrate and play. You can do it, it's what you do well. Come on now."

"I *am* concentrating," I say stubbornly, staring at the music, which is a jumble of notes connected by lines and arcs and dots.

I look around the room as Mr. Trego explains some theory about "cookie cutter" chords. I look at the woman in the portrait above the fireplace. Today her dark hair and pale face look softer and more pensive than her normal austere gaze usually does. I attribute this to the light and the weather, which is overcast and freezing. The greyhound whose leash the woman holds always has the same expression of calm, its ears small as petals and its eyes narrowed, trained on something beyond the frame. Today, the darkness that surrounds them reveals more of the chair on which the woman sits, and I notice her slipper, pearl-colored beneath the hem of her dress. I look at the woman and think, She might be just a girl. She might be married; this might have been a gift to her new husband, a portrait of his young bride with his favorite dog. Or it might be her dog that she was allowed to bring with her from her parents' home when she was transported into married life.

I think of Joan, who was lying on the couch at home when I left for my lesson this morning. I had to take the car because it was too cold to ride my bike. She had just gotten up, so she was not prepared to argue; she scraped around the kitchen in her slippers and pajamas, filling the kettle and looking like crap. She went out with Mike last night and they got hammered.

"When are you coming back?" she asked, in a groggy voice.

"I'm going to the library after my lesson, to talk to Mrs. Caldwell, so probably in a few hours."

"Are you working today?"

"No, but I have to talk to her about some stuff."

"Why do you go in if you don't have to work? That's stupid," Joan said, annoyed for absolutely no reason.

"Why do you care?"

She rubbed her eyes and leaned against the counter. She looked exhausted and upset. She was just hung over. "I don't care. I mean, I do. I'm sorry. I don't know why I said that. I feel like crap."

"What did you guys do last night?"

"Nothing. We basically went to the River Pub and drank our faces off. Actually, it was just me, really—I drank my face off. Mike didn't drink that much. He saw his friends from the boat and didn't want to leave, so I just kept on drinking to pass the time." She put a hand to her stomach and tilted her head backward. "What is wrong with me?" she moaned.

I pictured Joan among the group of guys, everyone laughing and saying stupid things. She was probably laughing along with them, even though what they were saying was probably offensive to her. "I don't know what's wrong with you," I said.

She looked at me with a sour expression. "Whatever," she said.

"That's nice," I said.

Joan prepared her tea and took it into the living room. I could hear the TV turn on and her flipping the channels around in her annoying way. I don't know how Mike puts up with her.

"Do you need the car today? Because I could come back with it and you could drop me off at the library later on," I said.

She was lying on the couch with her hand over her eyes. The mug of tea sat steaming on the coffee table in front of her.

"What?" she asked wearily.

I repeated what I'd said.

"No. Do what you want. I don't care."

"Fine." I wanted to yell, I hate you! Why are you like this? I went into the kitchen and put on my coat.

"Warren?" I heard her call from the other room. The TV shut off.

"What?"

"Just come back after your lesson. OK? Don't go to the library. Just come back here afterward, OK?"

"Why? You said you don't need the car."

"Because I don't want to be alone in the house, all right? Just come back after your lesson. I'll wait until you come back; maybe we can go and do something."

I was going to say, Why don't you call Mike? I was going to say, Why don't you call Grace? Or Laura? Or Patsy? But I said, "OK, I'll come right back. Wait here for me."

"Are you concentrating?" Mr. Trego asks in a confounded voice. "Warren? Are you distracted by something?" He leans forward in his chair and places his hand on my arm.

"I don't know. No, I'm fine." I look at the music and imagine actually playing what is written on the page. I think of the effort it will take to commit the piece to memory—many hours. "Many moons," as my father used to say to us, quoting from a children's book we'd read when we were young in which an ancient Native American story was retold and time was expressed by how many moons had passed. It was a joke in our family; we were all too sarcastic in the way we viewed the world to actually respect its origins.

My question is this: Once I've learned this new piece of music, once I have committed it to memory, what good will it do there? What use will it have? I think about what other memories it might replace—the details and moral outcome of the ancient Native American story, for instance. Many moons! What more will I lose by learning this new piece of music?

Mr. Trego sits at my side, huffing and shifting uncomfortably in his chair. I can see he's having a hard time reconciling the kind of student I used to be with who I am now.

I am unable to assemble any part of the music. I think to myself, I cannot produce these sounds, I am incapable of expressing this. I simply can no longer do it. It's not worth it.

I look at Mr. Trego, who is scribbling something in my spiral notebook "musician's journal," drawing crude pictures of hands in correct keyboard positions. It doesn't matter, I say to myself. I begin to play, hands separately—the right and then the left—and I don't even attempt to bring them together. They remain separate, unmerged, until Mr. Trego insists I combine them, for the sake of understanding the goddamned tempo.

I think about Joan on the couch, her hand shading her eyes, miserable in her pajamas. I don't know why she gets drunk like that with Mike. But, then, she said that she did it on her own; she was the one who drank her face off. I can't speculate on whether Mike was drunk or not, but he probably wasn't, since he was pulled over and almost arrested for DUI when he was in high school. I don't think he takes risks anymore—she'd said he didn't drink that much last night. Or did he just drink less than she did? What do I know about him? Why do I care if Mike still pounds beers?

Last night he brought Joan home in her drunken state, put her in bed, and left the house after she passed out. I heard him leave her room. I wasn't asleep. I got up and met him in the kitchen, where he was drinking juice and glancing at a magazine.

"What are you doing?" I asked nonchalantly.

"Jesus, Warren, you scared me."

I was pleased. "Sorry." And I was. I realized that for people who don't live in this house—but know what has happened in this house—it might not be the most comforting place to be, especially at night. It's not especially easy for us at any time.

"Why are you up?" he asked. "Did we wake you?"

"No, I was awake."

"Were you waiting up for Joan?"

"I guess."

"Don't worry. She's asleep now."

"Is she passed out? I figured she was."

"She's asleep; she's really tired."

"Is she wasted?"

"She's just tired. I think she pulled two double shifts back to back."

Look at this, I thought, he's protecting her from me. He won't tell me she's drunk. Why would he do that? I thought to myself, Why would he think he had to protect Joan from me?

"Where were you guys?"

"At the River Pub. We met some friends of mine there. It was cool."

"Are you staying over?"

"I don't think so," he said. "I'm heading home."

"What's your plan?" I asked, in a vague way.

"How do you mean? Now?" In the dim kitchen light, he looked taxed and sallow. I imagined that Joan had probably taken him to task, maybe bitched him out for something. I knew what that was like—to deal with Drunk Joan—and I felt bad for him.

"Nothing. I don't know what I mean," I said.

"OK, I'm going to take off. I'm sure I'll see you soon, like probably tomorrow," he said, smiling. "Which is, like, today, so, yeah—later today I'm sure I'll be seeing you." He started for the door in his loping stride.

"You can stay here if you want. If you don't want to drive all the way home." I don't know why I offered; I was surprised at what I was saying. I felt bad for him. He seemed to have lost his normal affable glow; he seemed sort of pathetic. Maybe he was upset about something. Joan might have upset him, I thought.

"Warren, it's OK." He smiled again.

"Really, stay. We can make a place on the couch for you." I don't know why I thought of that. He would have slept with Joan in her bed if he was going to stay over.

He smiled again at me, more warmly because of the idiocy of what I'd offered, no doubt. "Thanks, but I don't live that far away. And I have my jacket on already. It's OK."

"Really?" For some reason I didn't want him to go. I didn't know why, either. I was awake and wanted someone to stay up with. I wanted someone to help me with Joan, in case something might go wrong. What could go wrong?

He rinsed his glass and put it in the drying rack.

"I'll see you tomorrow—er, later, Warren. What are you doing?"

"I have a piano lesson."

"That's cool. I remember you used to play all the time; you were really good. Are you going to play for us sometime soon?"

"I don't know. Maybe."

And he opened the door and left the house.

35

I woke up and looked at the ceiling, out the window, and over the water. I could hear Joan next door, through the wall—she was moving around her room, opening and closing the drawers in her dresser. She had not turned on her clock radio like normal, so I could hear her and picture exactly what she was doing. She was in her closet looking for something warm to wear under her dress. We would be outside for most of the morning, out in the cold. The way the cemetery was situated near the water, the wind came whipping up the hill and between the stones.

The place where she had slept next to me was still warm, though she had smoothed the blankets and tucked them under the pillows, where two long wiry hairs spanned the pillowcase like minute cracks. All night our limbs had collided as we reached out unconsciously for each other, for confirmation that the other was there, that the bed was not empty, that we were not alone in the bed or in the room. Because otherwise, we were alone in the house. Every room was empty.

Two days had passed since the EMTs had come to help me save my mother. I had stopped Joan from going into the house. We stood in the yard and held on to each other. We cried into each other's hair as walkie-talkie mechanical blurts emitted from the paramedics' hips.

They worked on her while she lay on the floor; they pushed the table and chairs up against the wall and down the stairs to the basement. They tried to pump her stomach in the back of the ambulance on the way to the hospital, but she was gone and they could not get her to start breathing. Her heart had stopped before I got home. When I tried to revive her, her heart was limp, soaked like a knotted rag—I couldn't see it, but it had quit its work long before I had put my mouth to hers and breathed inside her again and again.

They came out of the house with her on a stretcher. I saw the pink robe in between the blankets they'd wrapped around her. Oh, God, what a relief, I found myself thinking, when I saw that only blankets surrounded her: no black bag. And then I was horrified for thinking that, since there was no relief in any of this.

Joan ran up to her on the stretcher and started to scream, blocking the progress of the EMTs down the driveway toward the ambulance. Joan vaulted halfway up onto the gurney and screamed "Mom! Mom!" I rushed over and pulled her off. The EMTs looked appreciatively at me and sorrowfully at Joan. One tried to comfort us by telling us to get in the car and follow close behind the ambulance so we could run the lights with them.

When we came home from the hospital, the kitchen was destroyed. It was as if we had been robbed—overturned chairs and mail, newspapers, and catalogs on the floor, dirty dishes in the sink. Dishes. My mother had left her dishes in the sink. I stopped and thought about that. In my state of shock and confusion, at the point when I felt the capabilities of the world were at their most fantastic and cruel, I actually thought that: Look, she left her dishes in the sink before she died.

Joan and I stood in the kitchen and began to straighten up the chairs and table. This, we could accomplish. We got the broom from its hook on the back of the basement door and swept the room. We swept up the paper and plastic wrappings from the useless devices the paramedics had used to try to save her. In the dustpan were wrappings, clumps of hair and dirt and dust, a button, tags from envelopes, inserts from catalogs, the thin pungent paper casings from garlic cloves, many white pills, many capsules and their tiny beads, freed recklessly from their cases.

When we were done we went into the living room. Joan got up and ran to the bathroom, and I could hear her retch into the bowl. I put a cushion against my face, its corner in my mouth, and lay back on the couch and closed my eyes, clenching my teeth, biting down hard on the velvet tasseled trim.

36

The meeting with Mr. Loring, Mrs. Caldwell, and me went well. I was inspired to make it go well after another installment of contention with Joan after I returned home from my piano lesson. I'd told her I'd come right back after the lesson because she'd asked me to so pathetically as she lay hung over on the couch. She said we would do something together when I got back, and even though I was annoyed at her for being obnoxious to me all morning, I was looking forward to it; we hadn't done something together since our last trip to the nursery.

By the time I'd gotten home, she was waiting for me in the kitchen with her coat on. At first, she wouldn't even let me come inside.

"No," she said, barring my entrance into the kitchen. "We have to go now."

"What? I have to go to the bathroom—let me in."

"Warren, I'm going to be late," she complained. "I told Grace I'd meet her downtown ten minutes ago. I thought your lesson was only an hour. Did you go somewhere afterward? Why are you so late coming home?"

"I'm not late coming home." I pushed by her and took off my coat and headed for the bathroom in the hall.

"Don't take off your coat; we have to go!" Joan called after me.

I stood in the bathroom, unable to concentrate. She kept on talking on the other side of the door.

"I need the car for the rest of the day. Grace and I are going into the city because her cousin's in a musical and we're getting free seats. I told her I'd drive because she doesn't have her car today." She rapped on the door with her nails, "What are you doing in there?"

"What do you think? Jesus, Joan." It sounded as if she was pressed up against the door. "Can you get out of here, please?" I asked. "What are you hoping to hear?"

"Warren, gross. Let's just go! I told Grace."

"I thought you were hung over. Why aren't you where I left you, on the couch, moaning and groaning?" I didn't want to mention that she said we'd do something together today. I didn't care. I didn't want to spend time with her when she was acting like this anyway.

"I felt like shit until I threw up," she said factually. "Then I immediately felt better." She sounded proud of herself.

"Why don't you go wait in the car?" I suggested.

"How long are you going to be?"

"I have no idea. But you putting the pressure on is not helping things. There are some things you cannot rush." Our father's words, said at moments exactly like this.

Joan sighed, and I could hear her walk into the kitchen and sit down. "I'm turning on the radio so I don't hear anything," she shouted.

"You do that," I shouted back.

I drove to the library and got out of the car. Joan slid over from her seat into the driver's seat, wrenching the gearshift with her leg as she moved, which produced a terrible grinding sound.

"You couldn't get out and walk around the car?" I asked.

"It's too cold," she said. She settled herself into the driver's seat and put on her seat belt. She changed the station on the radio and gazed at herself in the rearview mirror with disturbing intensity, narrowing her eyes and puckering her lips.

"So, are you coming back tonight or are you staying at Grace's?"

"Oh, I'll be back tonight, but probably late. I assume we'll go out after the show, so I don't know when I'll get home. But I will come home. If Mike comes over or calls, tell him I'll definitely be back tonight. I left him a message, but he might not check it."

I was still astounded by how functional she was compared with her state of misery this morning. That and by the fact that she never once asked me if I wanted to go with her and Grace into the city. And that she didn't ask me what my plans were, and if I needed the car for anything. And if she could wear my black hooded sweater, which she was wearing under her parka and was certain to smell up with perfume and Grace's cigarette smoke.

"Well, have fun," I said unenthusiastically.

"You, too. Love you!" She smiled and drove off.

Walking up the steps to the library, I was intent on making the interview a success, despite the fact that its purpose was still a bit ambiguous to me. I decided I would try my hardest to appeal to Mr. Loring, even though I didn't know what that would take and what results I was ultimately hoping for. The idea that he would pay for tuition at whatever college I got into was one that Mrs. Caldwell put in my head. The idea of him willing his magnificent house to me on the basis of me being interesting, smart, funny, and an orphan was something I had devised on my own. I decided I would focus mainly on funding for school and leave the estate issues for another time, when we were better acquainted.

He looked older than I'd remembered, but in winter no one looks especially vibrant or youthful. Except for Valerie, whom I'd seen a few days ago walking on the sidewalk alone toward the gazebo. Where is your child? I thought. Her face was pink and she was completely bundled, but I could see her eyes beneath her hat, and her slender upturned nose. I honked; she waved cheerfully and smiled. I thought, *I love you.*

Mr. Loring looked pale and skeletal. A million flecks of various sizes, all a sickening butterscotch color, covered his face and neck. His hair had been flattened to his head by the black fur hat he held in his lap with his large white hands. He was wearing his coat, so I figured he'd just arrived, but Mrs. Caldwell was wearing hers too. Evidently, the heat in the third-floor office of the library, where our meeting was to take place, still didn't work. I was sure there were other places to hold our meeting, but I didn't want to say anything. I was here by Mrs. Caldwell's kindness and concern. I didn't want to appear judgmental about the way she attempted to improve my future.

"Right on time!" Mrs. Caldwell announced proudly as I walked in the room. Mr. Loring looked up at me and, like a tent being pulled up into shape, slowly rose from his chair and extended a brittle hand.

"Hello, Warren, it's nice to meet you," he rasped, and smiled. The straight teeth I remembered were still uniform and even, though gray.

"Hello, it's nice to meet you too." Perhaps he didn't remember me at all; it didn't appear that he did. Then it occurred to me that perhaps he knew nothing of the nature of the meeting. Maybe he thinks he's here to talk about the chair he wants to endow and Mrs. Caldwell planned on tagging the idea of him sponsoring me through college to the tail end of the meeting. The entire plan seemed like a mistake—I felt the urge to run out the door.

"You've met before, though, haven't you?" said Mrs. Caldwell, stating what she hoped was the obvious.

I waited for his reply.

"Oh, yes, we have. At my house, right?" He looked at me and lowered himself into his chair.

"At your house, in the yard," I affirmed.

I kept my coat on, but I took my gloves off. I didn't know how things would proceed. I looked over at Mrs. Caldwell, who seemed to be gearing up for something, barely containing her excitement—she looked as if she might burst into song.

She began in a measured way, careful but firm. "Now, Phillip, I told you why I wanted you to come in and speak with us this morning, and I'm glad you could come. We both are."

"It's about the school, yes?" he said, slightly unsure.

My toes curled in my boots. Mrs. Caldwell gave me a look that said, Don't worry.

"Well, right, that's right—something about a school," she said gingerly, more gingerly than the way she generally deals with the elderly people who come into the library, probably because most of them harass her. "More specifically, about Warren and his school," she went on. "Or, rather, his schooling."

He turned and looked at me with a blank expression. I remembered how worried I would get when I'd see him raking the beach by himself. I used to worry that he'd die right in front of me, drop like a curtain on the sand. The same thought occurred to me as we sat in the office of the library. Pale, fragile, and rinsed, Mr. Loring appeared to be just barely holding on to life. I smiled at him and he raised his sparse eyebrows.

"What school is he in?" he asked, as he turned back to Mrs. Caldwell. I felt like an immigrant or an exchange student that no one knew what to do with.

"None right now; he works here. But he's interested in looking into schools, going to college."

I was afraid that he was going to say, Big deal. Who cares? What does that have to do with me? But instead he said nothing, changing his expression from blank to one of mild interest.

"Why don't you tell Phillip what you've been thinking about, Warren?" she said, in a bold voice, as if we were in a commercial.

"OK." I began without any idea of what to say. "I was thinking that going to college might be a good idea." In truth I had never had this thought in my head. Or rather, whether or not it was a good idea was always up for grabs. In any case, as a statement, it sounded stupid or arrogant, privileged, and indifferent. "I mean," I began again, "I'm ready to start thinking about going to college."

Mrs. Caldwell smiled weakly and looked back and forth between us. Mr. Loring stared at me with his one fogged-over eye and said nothing.

"Warren's had to deal with a lot this past year," Mrs. Caldwell began.

I flinched; I couldn't help it. What did I think? It wouldn't come up?

"Sometimes I wonder how he does it." She looked at me with sympathy. I looked at the clock and the calendar on the wall that showed a detail of a tapestry where royal-looking people were eating in a great hall and music was provided by angels.

"Don't embarrass the boy, Dottie," Mr. Loring said. "I am aware of the situation."

"Right!" Mrs. Caldwell said.

Why shouldn't he know? My father knew Milo and Milo hired me and together we worked on Mr. Loring's grounds and Milo probably told him about what happened at some point. It's common knowledge. Why do I forget this?

"I don't mean to embarrass him, I only mean to emphasize that if things had been easier for him, we wouldn't be in this position," said Mrs. Caldwell.

The *we* aspect of her speech made me uncomfortable, as if *we* were a team or a fund-raising pair. It also made me look incapable of advocating for myself, which might bring my character into question in his evaluation of me as a sound financial investment. It doesn't matter, I thought. She has my best interests in mind. It's OK; let her do her thing; she's trying to help me. I have to let her help me.

"Which position is that?" asked Mr. Loring.

"Well—" She paused.

"Asking for help," I said unexpectedly. "I'm asking for help."

Mrs. Caldwell looked astounded, as if she might cry.

"Help of what sort, Warren?" Mr. Loring asked, looking straight at me.

"Of every sort, I think," I stammered. I could feel the tears begin to well up in my eyes. "Sometimes I think I need every sort of help there might be."

We sat in silence, watching, as we each tried to understand what I'd said; we watched each other in hopes of understanding what it might mean.

"Yes," Mr. Loring said quietly, "I think I understand you." He turned toward me and looked me directly in the face. "I'm someone who might be able to offer you some help. And I'd like to help you, Warren. And I will."

"Oh, Warren," Mrs. Caldwell moaned, weeping, her hands clutching her seat as if she might fly up off the ground.

37

The process of getting into college is onerous and uninspiring. I could answer every question with a synopsis of the last year of my life, and any college that didn't at least consider me would probably be breaking some kind of discrimination law. I stare out the window at the islands and the sea; it is a clear day, but nothing about it seems different. I can hear someone knocking on the kitchen door.

Joan is in the living room sewing a patch on her jeans and listening to an excruciatingly bad tape of the musical she and Grace went to last night. She's been playing it all afternoon.

I told her, "Even though playing this tape over and over might remind you of the great experience you had last night when this terrible music was brought to life, I'm going to ask you to turn it off or play something else, because it's making me insane."

"You weren't there, Warren," she said defensively. "It was awesome."

"I just can't believe that."

"Then go upstairs and shut your door."

She came home this morning, having stayed over at Mike's house, even though she explicitly told me yesterday that she was going to come home. There's no point in bringing this up.

I look out the hallway window to see whose car is in the driveway. It's a rare thing for us to have a visitor—or, rather, to have someone knock on the door instead of barge right in, which is what Mike has taken to doing these days. For a second I'm afraid it's going to be

Uncle Steve or Auntie E, coming to seek revenge, or both of them—bitter and betrayed. I look out and see Valerie's car in the driveway.

Downstairs, Valerie and her son Jake are sitting at the kitchen table. Joan is slicing bread at the counter; the kettle is hissing on the flame. Valerie sits upright in her chair and nods and smiles as Joan asks about the rest of her holiday. They are recounting our serendipitous meeting on Christmas Day at Singing Beach; Joan is making it sound like its own little miracle. Jake is quiet but not solemn; he watches his mother and Joan talk and occasionally transfers his small stuffed badger from the crook of one arm to the other.

"Hi, Warren," Valerie says brightly, as I walk in. She is only a year older than Joan is and yet she seems much more poised and mature, probably because she is far more pleasant to be around. Her hair is pulled away from her face and hangs down her back in a thick ropy braid. Her face is bright and so pretty I have to pause for a moment in order to make a response.

"Hi," I say.

"Joan, Warren and I just saw each other the other day. I was walking into town and he drove by." She smiles again at me.

"Warren, you didn't tell me you saw Valerie!" Joan says.

"I'm sorry, Joan!" I say, in a dramatic way. She sneers at me.

"Warren, have you ever met Jake?" Valerie asks. "Jake"—she taps his shoulder and points to me—"this is Warren, Joan's younger brother."

"Oh," he says, looking up at me with Valerie's gray eyes.

"Warren! I can't believe you haven't met Jake!" Joan exclaims.

I shrug.

"You can say hello to him," Valerie encourages.

"Hi," says Jake.

"Hi," I say. "It's nice to meet you."

Valerie gets up. "Joan, are you sure it's not a problem watching Jake while I'm gone? You can back out and I won't be offended." She reaches out and touches Joan's arm.

"Valerie, no, of course not, I mean it. Please, go and do what you have to do. We'll be fine."

I have not heard Joan be so amenable to anyone in years.

"What's happening?" I ask.

"We're going to watch Jake while Valerie goes to the DMV and—where else do you have to go?"

"Bank, post office, dentist. I have such a crazy day; I really appreciate your help." She looks deeply thankful, as if engorged with gratitude.

I say, "Not a problem."

"We'll be fine, we'll have fun," Joan says. "Hey, Jake, what do you want to do this afternoon?"

"I don't know," he says quietly.

Valerie frowns and tilts her head toward him.

"Are you going to be OK here with these guys?" she asks him.

"Don't worry, Val, we'll have fun," Joan insists.

"I'll be back in a few hours, Jake. Don't worry, OK?"

"OK," he says.

She puts on her coat and is out the door. I'm truly sorry to see her go. Joan and I look at Jake, who is looking at the floor.

"Well, what should we do?" Joan asks brightly.

"I don't know," Jake says quietly.

I remember one time eating dinner with my parents and Joan. We were all in the dining room having a normal meal like we usually did. My father sat at the head of the table with my mother to his left. Joan sat across from my mother, and I sat to my mother's left. This was our formation.

My mother was upset. While she was cooking she had been upset. Something my father and she had argued about when he came home made her start crying, though she would not mention it. He just went down in the basement to organize some boxes.

Joan and I were concerned about her but she said she was fine, she was just emotional. This was often true. As a result, by the time we sat down for dinner she was barely able to manage her silverware; she spilled her wine and water glasses, and began to cry openly at the table. As Joan mopped up with a dish towel, I tried to console her, but she was too drunk. My father, who was trying to ignore her, took her upstairs. He came down and finished his meal in a hurried way and told us to clean up, he was going out, back to the nursery.

"Why are you going back? It's almost nine o'clock," Joan said.

"Because there's still work to be done," he said.

"Like what?" I asked.

"Stuff and things," he said.

"Is anyone even there at this hour?" I asked.

My father said nothing.

"Can we come?" Joan asked.

"Not a chance," he said quickly.

"Why not?" Joan demanded.

"Because you have to stay and look after your mother." He put on his coat. "I'll be back in a few hours, OK? Don't worry."

We sit in the living room with Jake, who is drawing on blank sheets of white paper. I had been drawing pictures with him. We were playing this game where he would ask me what to draw and I'd suggest something bizarre.

"Draw a dragonfly wearing a top hat," I'd say.

"OK," he'd say. And he would, and not do a bad job, either.

"OK, draw an elephant paddling a canoe with a fern tied to his head."

"I don't know how to draw an elephant," he'd say, looking at me quizzically.

And I'd say, "Sure you do, just think about what it looks like and draw from the image in your mind."

And he'd say, "No, I can't do it."

And I'd say, "Yes you can, just try."

And he'd say, "No, I don't know how."

"You don't know how to try?" I'd ask.

And he'd say, "No."

And I'd say, "OK, that's interesting. Fine. Make it a cat, a cat in a canoe with a fern tied onto his head."

And he'd say, "OK," and try.

Joan and I watch him draw. We watch him like he is some alien creature capable of anything unexpected and fascinating.

"Do you want a snack?" Joan asks him, when he's finished with what looks like a devil in a peapod with a mass of green frizz hovering above him.

"OK," he says, barely looking up from his paper.

We go into the kitchen and Joan takes cheese out of the refrigerator.

"Get the crackers," she says to me. Ah, yes, our typical snack.

"How is it that we're baby-sitting Jake today?" I ask.

"You don't have to stay if it's an inconvenience for you," she says, in a neutral way, "though I'd like it if you hung around. This is kind of fun. It's cute the way you are with him."

"Really? Anyway, it's fine, I'm just wondering."

"Well, because I have today off and Valerie has all those errands to run."

"But since when are you and Valerie so close?"

"You act like it's wrong to be friends with Valerie," Joan says, her voice beginning to take on her typical whiplash vehemence.

"No, it's not wrong, it's just new, different. I had no idea that you two were close." The phrase *friends with Valerie* strikes me as inexplicably funny, like the name of a sitcom I'd watch during my long passages of boredom alone in the house.

"I see her when she comes into the bakery—I don't know, we're friendly."

Joan rolls her eyes and closes the refrigerator door with a shove of her hip. "Valerie is the kind of person who needs help; she doesn't have the easiest life. Her life actually stinks, so if I can baby-sit Jake, I will. It's not a big deal."

"I think it's great you baby-sit, I just don't know how it came to be. I mean, *beyond* its being a nice thing to do. Do you see what I mean?"

She stops and looks at me. "OK, I know what you mean."

"What do you think I mean?"

"You don't understand why he's here."

"Right. Exactly. *Not* how it's a nice thing to do for someone who has a rough life, and *not* how you're friendly at the bakery. I want you to tell me—"

"How it all came to be. And I suppose you'd like to know the deeper meaning in it all, right?"

"If there is one, of course. I live for that shit."

I look at Joan and wait while she unwraps the block of white cheese and pours the square-shaped wheat crackers out of the box and onto a plate. She looks focused on her task, even though she's only preparing a few cheese and cracker sandwiches for a four-year-old. Or is he three years old? I don't know how old he is. Two?

"Jake, do you want something to drink?" she calls out to him in the living room.

"OK," he says almost inaudibly, "just water." Joan smiles. It is a warm smile that remains on her face as she takes a glass from the drying rack by the sink and fills it from the tap.

"Joan?"

"Warren," she says.

"Are you going to answer me?"

"Warren," she says again, now looking suddenly agitated, "I don't think this is the best time to explain." She focuses on me. "But I'm sure you could figure it out if you thought about it for one second."

"Ugh! Joan! You always do this! Just tell me what's going on. Don't tell me to think about it, tell me what you know!"

"OK, I will," she says. "Why do *you* think he'd be here with us? Think about it."

"No, Joan! I'm not going to think or guess or anything. I'd be wrong—you know it. You always tell me I go too far, that I overthink things. So just tell me! Tell me everything! You obviously know something that I don't, so why not just spill it?" I look at her directly. Is she fucking with me? "All I'm asking is that you tell me what's so important so we can both know, together, what's going on."

She looks at me and closes her eyes.

"Is this something bad?" I ask, suddenly afraid.

"No. Not really."

"Is this something I won't know how to deal with?"

"I don't know," she says. "You've managed OK so far."

"We both have."

"True."

"But is it the kind of thing I should leave for later?" I ask. "At least just for now—for the moment?"

"I can't say." She shrugs.

"But in all your wisdom, knowledge, and experience in these matters, would you suggest that's what I do?" I look at her squarely. "Because you know it's not normally what I would choose to do—forget about something."

"Well, maybe it's not a bad thing to start doing."

"Especially given the fact that I can't quite figure out what you believe should be so obvious to me."

"Yes, that's a big reason."

"And this is something major, right?"

"In some ways, yes. And in some ways, no."

"Well, that's helpful. Thanks for that. Who are you, the sphinx?"

"Warren, I think you should deal with this when you're ready."

"Deal with what? Joan, just tell me!"

"Warren"—she looks at me with kindness—"you're *so* not ready."

"I'm ready! How could I not be ready? I'd say I'm pretty much ready for anything. I mean, at this point, throw anything my way and I'm sure I can figure out some way to fucking deal with it! Jesus!" I suddenly feel desperate and ludicrous, panicked that everything I've been trying so hard to figure out is now—and has always been—far beyond my comprehension.

But I can't believe it. I can't accept that whatever Joan knows is something I haven't already thought of. It seems impossible. And impossible that she would keep something so important from me. It's unfair. We have no secrets. None of this is fair.

"You're driving me insane."

"Warren."

"What?" I say. "What? What? What?"

"Jake is your brother."

"Holy shit."

38

Joan and I had been upstairs in my room searching through my closet for clothes I didn't wear anymore. I had helped her do the same thing. That morning my mother gave us each a green plastic garbage bag to fill, and when we were done we were supposed to take them to the donation bins in back of the Salvation Army. We ended up laughing and joking around, and when we were done our bags were overflowing with outdated, ill-fitting, and embarrassing outfits.

We tied the bags at the top of the stairs and kicked them down, so that they landed with a thud in the living room. This made us laugh too, since we were well in the spirit and would laugh at anything. Downstairs in the living room we heard our mother's shrill voice scream, "What the hell are you doing up there?"

"We're dealing with our clothes!" Joan screamed back.

"You're being obnoxious!" we heard her yell, her voice echoing up the stairway. We looked at each other and laughed.

Downstairs in the living room she was vigorously shaking the ficus tree. She was shaking it high on the trunk right below the canopy, the way a child would angrily shake a doll by the neck. When we reached the bottom of the stairs, our garbage bags at our feet, we saw her by the windows, shaking the tree; leaves, dead and alive, were flying around and falling to the ground.

"Mom!" Joan said, half laughing. "What are you doing?"

"Jesus, Mom, you're going to shake it to death," I added.

Our father had brought home the ficus a few years before because my mother had issued a request: she wanted "an indoor tree." She'd said, in her dreamy, weird way, "I want to feel like I am beneath a bower." His solution was to bring home a four-foot ficus with a clot of tangled roots stuffed into a terra cotta pot. The ficus had grown over the years, full and wide at the top, though never to the point of accomplishing a complete bower. It was irritating because every now and then it shed its many dead yellow leaves, which seemed to turn up in all parts of the house. Once, I found one in my sneaker.

"I'm doing this to rid it of the dead leaves," she said seriously, over the gentle clatter of the leaves and branches.

"Unless you want all the leaves to fall off and die, Mom," Joan said, "I'd let up a bit."

"Yeah, Mom," I said. "It'll just look like a stick in a pot."

"Just let me clean, OK?" She looked at us with a pained expression and she stopped shaking the tree, but her hands were still fiercely gripping the pale, slender trunks. "I hate him," she said softly. "He is a fucking selfish bastard."

What did she say? Who is a fucking selfish bastard?

"The tree?" I asked. I figured I would hazard a guess, even though I suspected that if my mother assigned a gender to the tree, it would certainly be female. Joan laughed and snorted. Then we both laughed at the fact that she snorted. Then we turned our attention to each other's laughter and laughed some more. We thought our mother was just acting strange, which we were used to.

"Mom, what are you talking about?" Joan asked, gaining her composure. My mother's hold on the tree had not let up.

"Nothing, forget it. Where are you kids headed?" she asked, dismayed.

"We're going to take our clothes to the Salvation Army. Do you want us to take yours?"

"Yes, please take mine. Mine are in my room. Do not take your father's. Do not take his bag. Let him do it on his own. He does whatever he pleases anyway."

"Why? We might as well take all of it at once," I said. I didn't realize what was going on. I was too busy trying to imagine how all the bags would fit in our car—if there would even be room for our father's clothes. If he were home we could take his truck, but he was out somewhere. I didn't know where he was.

"Take mine and yours and Joan's and leave that fucking bastard's clothes in bag for him to take himself."

"Come on, Joan," I said.

"No, Warren, you go upstairs and get it. I need Joan here right now."

I went upstairs and got my mother's bag, which was clearly hers, because I recognized a psychedelic-print dress hanging out the side. I figured Joan would yank it out of the bag the minute I went to throw it in the bin—and this is exactly what she did; she kept it for herself. When I went back downstairs to the living room, Joan looked serious and spaced out, slightly green. I could hear my mother in the bathroom, clinking about, coughing and sniffing. Joan looked at me and said, "Come on, let's just go."

"Hold on. I was just laughing about the sweat pants," I began, referring to some painfully tight gym-issued sweats that we found in the back of my underwear drawer.

"Oh, my God, Warren," she said gravely, "we have to get out of here."

39

W e eat our snack of crackers and cheese in the living room. Jake gets tired of drawing, which makes me a bit stressed, because I can't think of what else to do with him. "Are you sure you're tired of drawing?" I ask him. Though in my head I think, *You're my brother. What do I do with you?* He just looks at me with a pained apologetic look.

"Joan," I say helplessly, "he doesn't want to draw anymore."

"Warren," she says gently, "take it easy."

Joan suggests we read a book, and while she's reading Jake falls asleep on the couch. I look at him among the pillows and under the blanket Joan has laid over him. He is peaceful and compact, perfectly tucked into the corner of the couch like a mouse in a pile of wood shavings or an elf in a tree. This makes me think of Mike.

"Where's Mike?" I ask.

"Shhhh!" She motions to me and points emphatically at the kitchen.

I get up from my chair and she rises gingerly so as not to disturb him.

In the kitchen Joan hugs me. "I'm sorry to throw you for such a loop," she says.

"More than a loop," I say. "I have no idea what to do with this information."

"Well, maybe just let it sit."

"You know how good I am at that."

"Just try," she says, and hugs me again.

"I'll try."

"So, to answer your question, I don't know where Mike is. I thought he'd call this morning. Did he?"

The phone rings and she smiles, snatches it off the hook, and thrusts it toward me, insisting in a whisper, "Tell him I'm here, but I'm busy and can't talk."

I take the phone and say into the receiver, "Hello? Joan can't talk."

"Warren! Salutations! It's your Uncle Steve!"

"Wow!" I yell. Joan shushes me again and points emphatically toward the living room.

"Warren, how's it going down there?" Uncle Steve says in a loud voice, loud enough for Joan to guess who it is and freeze up. She looks at me with a blank expression and scrambles around for a pen and some paper.

"OK here, I guess," I say.

"Is that so?" he says cheerfully. "That's not what your aunt seems to think."

"Really?" I say.

Joan writes on the paper IS THAT UNCLE STEVE? Y OR N?

I circle Y. She looks horrified.

"Yes, really, Warren. What's going on with you guys? Yvonne says there's something wrong, you two are up to something weird. So I'm going to get to the point. I need to ask you something and I want you to answer me honestly. Are you two kids into drugs? Have you been using that money your parents left you to buy drugs?"

"What?" I laugh.

Joan scribbles on the paper WHAT DOES HE WANT? And I shake my head and shrug. GET OFF!! GET OFF NOW!!! she writes hurriedly and underlines it a million times. "How?" I gesture. I hold the phone toward her and she jumps away.

"When there is a tragedy that people, young people especially, don't know how to deal with, sometimes they feel the need for escape. And sometimes they turn to bad things, Warren." He pauses. "Because, Warren, they need to get up, get high. They need to feel good, a release from all the bad." Uncle Steve's voice seems more to relish this scenario than deplore it. He continues, "We're worried about you two. We think that something's up."

"What could be up?" I ask almost coyly. I feel insulted by his homily.

Joan writes on the paper I'M GOING TO DISCONNECT THE LINE. I'LL HANG UP FOR YOU. She has a hilarious, threatening look on her face as she grabs the phone cord and pantomimes yanking it from the wall. Like that's going to help, I mouth at her. It all feels like a game suddenly—Uncle Steve being a patronizing buffoon way off in Canada; Joan scrambling about, writing little notes and threatening to tear the phone out; and me on the line, trying to remain calm and composed between them.

"Hold on, Uncle Steve," I say to him with delicacy. I cover the mouthpiece tightly with my hand and say to Joan, "Go get on the other phone. You have to hear this, he's crazy." She runs softly into the living room and returns with the cordless in her hand. I cough as she turns it on so he doesn't hear her line engage.

"What were you saying, Uncle Steve?" I ask.

"Warren, what's going on down there? We know that you and Joan are in trouble; your aunt and I have talked about it. We know something is wrong and we're prepared to help you. It's not easy for you guys, we know, and while your parents provided for you, you can't piss it away with reality-bending substances that are frankly no good."

"Reality *what*? What are you talking about?" Joan suddenly interrupts in an angry voice. I thought the plan was that she was just going to listen.

"Who's that? Joanie?" he asks, startled, as if he's heard a voice at a séance.

"What are you talking about, drugs, Uncle Steve? You're a fine one to talk about that subject!"

"Now, Joan, don't start in like that, honey, you're not well. We know you and your brother have been through some scary times, and we want to help you."

"We don't want any help. We don't need any help. We're doing just fine on our own, thank you very much, Uncle Steve."

I look at Joan standing a few feet from me, spitting venom into the phone.

"Oh, Joanie, you don't know what fine is—you've lost perspective. Your aunt's been telling me that every time she sees you two it breaks her heart. You're killing her."

"Seriously, Uncle Steve"—I try for a reasonable tone—"you don't know what you're talking about. We haven't seen Auntie E in weeks and I can assure you that we weren't drug addicts then and we're not now either. That's a crazy idea."

"And don't start in with that *we're killing her* bullshit," Joan says. "Think about what you're saying. Think about who you're talking to! Jesus!"

"Calm down, Joanie, calm down, I come in peace," Uncle Steve says.

"No, you don't! You don't come in peace at all!" Joan yells. "You're an idiot!"

I almost laugh out loud.

"Joan, there is something seriously wrong, I know it. I can sense this."

This is insane, I mouth at Joan.

"Where are you?" I ask offhandedly.

"Where do you think I am? I'm in Canada but I'm thinking about coming down and fixing you guys straight," he says.

"Don't even try it!" Joan says forcefully. "Don't come down here—we won't let you in!"

"Are you really in Canada?" I ask.

"Look, stay in Canada; stay where you are! And tell Auntie E to stay where she is—we don't want anything to do with you! We want to be left alone. You have to respect that."

"Joan, you don't know what you're talking about. Are you high, girl? Warren! Warren, are you there? Joan, let me talk to your brother."

"Yes. I'm here."

"Is your sister high? What are you two wrapped up in?"

"Jesus Christ! We're not doing drugs, you fucking freak!" Joan says. "Believe it or not, not everyone turns to drugs when they can't deal. We just want to be left alone!"

"Joan, please, let me talk to Warren." Uncle Steve sounds like he's about to explode. "Warren, are you there, my brother?"

"Um, yeah." I had forgotten that Uncle Steve used new-age words like *brother, sister,* and *soul place,* as means of communicating meaningful connections.

"Warren, you both need help, and I'm going to come and help you out. I'm going to do that for you, OK?"

"No! That's not OK!" Joan says. "Jesus, *listen* to us! We don't want you!"

"Joan, I'm not going to talk to you. You're not right. You need to sober up. Warren, I'm trusting that you have your head on straight. I'm looking to you for strength and guidance."

I laugh. I can't help it, I have to laugh. Joan looks at me and cackles victoriously. I can feel Uncle Steve swell with rage on the other side of the phone as we crack up. We are driving him crazy and we are getting off on it.

"No, Uncle Steve, don't come," I say. "Stay where you are. Joan is right. I agree with her. We don't want your help. We don't need it. We're doing fine. You're just going to have to believe that."

"Warren, you don't mean that, I know. You're not going to turn your family away. We're all you have left."

"That's actually not true," I say plainly.

"OK, Uncle Steve?" Joan says. "Warren says so too. We are in agreement at our end."

"You two are not well; you're worse than your aunt said. You need help!"

"No, *you* need help, Uncle Steve!" Joan rants. "You've always needed it!"

"You've turned into a cold little bitch, Joan!" Uncle Steve says. "Your mother would be ashamed!"

"Fuck you!" Joan screams.

"Don't talk to her like that, you fucking stupid fuck!" I scream into the receiver.

All three of us scream into the mouthpieces of our respective phones. Joan's face is red and flushed. I hear Uncle Steve's raspy cigarette-addled voice nearly give out as he yells. I scream along with them, so we're like a chorus of hatred.

"Joan?" a voice chirps quietly from the other room.

I freeze. Joan covers the mouthpiece firmly and says in a grainy voice, "Hold on, Jake, one second, OK?

"Look, we're not going to deal with you anymore—we don't want you around in our lives anymore—ever. Is that clear?" Joan says.

"We're serious, we don't need you, we don't want you," I say.

"Your parents would be ashamed of you for this, you know," Uncle Steve says.

"Don't ever bring them up again," I say.

"Don't even start. We're hanging up, Warren."

"Fine."

"Goodbye, Uncle Steve—don't call us again," Joan says.

"Goodbye, Uncle Steve," I say.

"You two are fucked up! I'm not going to sit here and take this shit from two spoiled fucking brats who don't know how to treat—"

We hang up the phone and look at each other. The kitchen feels like it's a thousand degrees; we're both sweating, totally exhilarated. We go into the living room and find Jake fast asleep again, nestled in the pillows and blanket of the couch.

40

"Who's to say you're not going to give me up too?"

"What are you talking about, Warren?"

We're sitting at the kitchen table, drinking coffee and sorting the mail—a task I asked Joan to help me with since she's been actively neglecting the things I set out for her to deal with.

"You're on a rampage. Who's to say you're not going to oust me next?"

"What's wrong with you? What are you talking about?"

I had been brooding over what happened yesterday. After Valerie came and picked up Jake, Joan called up Mike and asked him to come over. He couldn't, so she took the car and went to where he was. I didn't bother asking any questions as to when she was coming home or if she was going to come home at all. I was upset, thoroughly confused. I wanted to be by myself. In addition to what Joan had told me, which I was still trying to comprehend, I couldn't get rid of the conversation we'd had with Uncle Steve. The entire screaming spectacle was still raw in my mind. We screamed at each other like we were enemies, as if he had done something terrible to us. He hadn't. He hadn't done a thing. He was a strange man who was very irritating, but he hadn't done anything but express concern for us. All night I'd thought about it, how I'd jumped on Joan's vicious bandwagon, how I'd shrieked at him like a youth gone wild. For good reasons, I'd then tried to tell myself—because he insulted her, he called her a bitch, and he threatened us. He thought we were drug addicts. He's trying to conspire with Auntie E to get the money our parents left us. He's psychotic. He's a thief.

Joan got on the phone and went crazy. I just wanted her to listen, to hear how weird and ridiculous he was acting. And then suddenly we were all screaming at one another. And all the while this strange little child slept on our couch. How were we going to protect him? He was ours, I realized, to protect.

Joan said, after we hung up the phone, "If the phone rings and it's him calling back, let me pick it up because I'm telling him that I'll call the police if he doesn't leave us alone."

"Yesterday, when you freaked out on Uncle Steve, it sort of made me wonder if you might do the same to me one day."

"Warren, please! I freaked out on him because he's crazy. We can't be living our lives afraid that he's going to call or show up one day. We had to put an end to it! We shouldn't have to be afraid of him."

"There are still good reasons to be afraid! Do you think he's going to go away now? Do you think our little shouting session has frightened him off? He's going to go mental, more mental than normally. He's going to hunt us down!"

"No, he won't. He won't come down here."

"How do you know?"

"He just won't, Warren. He thinks we're freaks. I'm sure whatever he wants, money or whatever, is not worth dealing with what we gave him yesterday." She leans back in her chair. "Plus, I really don't think he can leave Canada. I don't think he's allowed in this country."

"Because he's a felon?"

"That, and other things too."

"I don't know, though."

"What don't you know, Warren?"

"It was just so vicious. We were so evil to him. Out of nowhere we just went at him."

"Warren, he went after us first. And Mom and Dad. Don't go playing it up like he was innocent—he's up to something, you know he is. The more we don't deal with him, the more we ignore his phone calls, the more likely he is to come down here in the dead of the night and drop in when we least expect it. And we don't have Dad around to kick him out."

"I know. It just seems extreme, what you did."

"Warren, you were screaming at him too! You can't honestly tell me that you want him in our life either."

"I don't know. I felt this way with Auntie E. I don't think we have the right to shut them out."

"What are you talking about? It *is* our right. We don't have to earn it. We are owed it. We get to choose what we want now; it's our life to choose! We've talked about this."

"But why even make this choice? Why not just let it be, let them believe we're still family? We don't have to do anything, we don't have to see them except on holidays or whatever. It doesn't have to be so harsh. We can just ignore them until the holidays."

"Why? Why should we? Like seeing them on holidays is going to be any less torturous than it was before? And why lie to them? Why not just tell them the truth? It's better that way." Joan pauses and calms down, smooths her hair against the back of her neck. She's just washed it so the curls are heavy and damp, staining the back of her T-shirt in a long wet streak. "Warren, we talked about this when we dealt with Auntie E. There's no point to keeping those ties. They're *crazy.*"

"They think *we're* crazy."

"Fine! Who cares? Let them! It makes it easier: We get left alone and they feel they've done everything in their power to help us. Soon enough—to them—we'll just be lost unrecoverable souls."

"That's a cheery thought."

"It is, when you think about not having to see and deal with them ever again."

"I just can't believe you feel no remorse for doing it."

"Do you feel remorse?"

"I do. I feel bad. Uncle Steve had no idea what hit him and neither did Auntie E; we just blindsided them."

"That's just the way it happened. But who says anyone should be prepared? We weren't prepared for what happened to *us.*"

"I know. But does that mean we have to do this to our relatives?"

"Warren, you can't tell me you actually feel close to these people?"

"Only because they're our family. They're Mom's brother and sister; they're related to us."

"But since Mom is not around anymore, since she didn't feel reason enough to stick around, I don't exactly feel all that inviting toward Uncle Steve and Auntie E."

"They're not responsible for what she did! And neither are we. It doesn't really make sense."

"It doesn't have to. The point is, Mom is gone, she left us, so why should we be keeping up any kind of relationship with people we never really cared for in the first place? Now that she's not around anymore, there's no real reason for us to associate with them. In a way, the thing that bound us in relation to them no longer exists. She's gone. She didn't think about us at all. Why should we think of her? Why should we have think of her anymore?" Joan starts to cry.

"No! I mean, I don't mean to make this more confusing. I just don't understand. I'm having trouble understanding what happened yesterday—*everything* that happened. I feel like I've been clueless my entire life." I reach across the table for Joan's arm. "And I just don't know if it's worth destroying whatever bonds we do have with our remaining family, however fucked up they might be, because Mom and Dad didn't care enough about themselves or us to stay alive."

"I don't know either, Warren." She starts to sob. "I just don't need any more reminders, OK? The same goes for the fucking nursery and fucking Richard. Let him have the fucking place and sell it or burn it down. I don't care. I'm glad he turned out to be such an asshole. It doesn't matter." She starts crying as hard and as wholly as she had screamed yesterday at Uncle Steve.

"I don't know what to say! I don't want to fight with you. I want us to agree and be on the same side."

"We are. We're on the same side." She is holding my hands tightly in hers and we're both crying.

"I'm just afraid," I say to her. "I'm afraid that you'll look at me one day and see me as another totally fucked-up relative. The one who's just going to remind you of Mom and Dad and all that shit that you hate. And you'll kick me out too. I'm afraid that's what's going to happen."

"Warren, no!" she shouts, her face wrenched in anguish. "No! Shut up! You're all I have, Warren. Listen to me, you're all I have!"

"But you have Mike. And now with everything else—"

"No, Warren!" she says, in horror. "Shut up! I don't have Mike. I don't have him at all. Don't say that! It's totally different; it's two totally different things! You're my brother; you're my best friend; I love you. He's just some stupid fucking guy. And what I told you yesterday—that doesn't matter. I mean, we can decide what we want. That's what's important, OK? Listen to me. Listen. I love you. You're the only one I love. "

"I'm sorry." I cry.

"Please don't worry about that, Warren. God, I'm not ever going to leave you, and you can't leave me. Warren, don't. The whole reason I did this to Uncle Steve and Auntie E was for us. I'm doing it to protect us from them, to keep us separate and safe. You know that, right?"

"Yes, I know. I understand."

"You have to understand it because it makes sense. It will make more sense as we get older. We start with us and we build from there."

"I understand."

"This is our choice," she cries.

"We've chosen this," I say.

41

It's New Year's Eve day. I'm walking back home from my piano lesson. The sky is clear; from the highest point of Granite Street I can look out over the water and see a bank of clouds crammed against the horizon, the bright ocean stretched out in front of me like a glossy tiled floor. I feel relieved. Our conversation with Uncle Steve happened three days ago, but because we have not heard from him or Auntie E, the entire terrible scene seems to have almost evaporated. When I think about it, it is distant and unreal, like a scene on TV or a story someone told me about something that had happened to someone they know.

I am relieved to be out of Mr. Trego's music room. Today's lesson was no less frustrating than the last few; it was also awkward and almost unpleasant. After I'd made the same tempo error three times he got visibly angry with me and accused me of not practicing. I hadn't, so I sat there and kept quiet; I just stared at the woman on the wall and wondered how old she was when the painting was done, whether she's alive or dead now.

I was fed up with him being disappointed in me. I stared out the windows of the music room while he lectured me. The sun burned against the snow in the yard, and beyond the stone wall I could see the edge of the quarry. We were trapped inside, and all I wanted was to be free, outside in the open air and bright winter sunlight. But I was sitting at the piano, playing badly and disgusting my teacher.

"We should stop here for today, Warren," Mr. Trego said in defeat.

"All right," I said, and I began to put my books in my backpack.

He got up and stretched, toyed with the thermostat on the wall, waiting to walk me to the door, the way he did every week.

"Warren, let me ask you something," he said, as I sat down on the red bench in the mudroom to put on my boots.

"OK."

"Is this something you want to do? Are you sure these lessons are helping you in some way?" He looked confused, as if, when speaking to me, he were looking into a machine whose gears and parts had no coherence to him.

"I don't know—but I like them," I said, not altogether convincingly. What I wanted to say was, No, I don't think they're helping. They're not helping me get better at the piano and they're certainly not helping me feel good about myself, considering how badly I play.

"Really?"

"Yes. That's why I started them up again." This didn't really make sense, but I was hoping Mr. Trego would not pursue the topic any further. I didn't want him to feel bad that I was miserable in my lessons, and I didn't want him to think he was the cause of it. Even though, in the short version of things, he was to blame.

"You really don't seem to be enjoying yourself, Warren. You don't practice and you don't concentrate. And frankly that doesn't make it enjoyable for me as your teacher. I think if you're going to continue, you're going to have to figure out what it is about these lessons that matters to you."

In my head I was thinking, The last thing in the world that matters to me are these fucking lessons. Do you realize how much shit is going on in my life? Do you have any idea? How can you think that these fucking piano lessons mean anything to me?

But how could he know?

"I'm sorry," I said, looking up at his kind, fleshy face. "You're right. But, and I know that this is no excuse"—I paused—"I'm just a bit confused these days."

"I know you are—there's no excuse necessary. I can't imagine how you wouldn't be."

I sat quietly lacing my boots and wishing I were out the door, heading home.

"But, Warren," he said wistfully, with increasing hope in his voice, "what I'd imagined was that these lessons and our playing would take you away from those distractions, free you from those things that keep you so serious and glum."

That he used the word "glum" to describe me was irritating. I thought about Joan and how she reacts to things like that—with rage—and resolved to let it go.

"Well, I don't know," I said.

"I thought these lessons would help in that way, help you become less burdened." The look on his face was so authentic and beseeching I couldn't help feeling sorry for him. He was very kind. He must have been a very loving and emotionally progressive father. What he didn't know, however, was that his aspirations for our lessons could never be true. No amount of piano lessons, I imagined, could free me from these burdens.

"Mr. Trego, I appreciate how nice you are to me. I really do." I stood up and looked him in the face, which was difficult, given its unwavering expression of concern. "But I think you might be right— maybe I should take a break. Maybe just to settle myself."

"No! That's not what I was suggesting at all, Warren! I don't want you to stop. This is exactly the time, in my opinion, when you should be playing and practicing; playing more and more." He grabbed my hands in his, which struck me as both comforting and invasive. "I'm just bringing this up to suggest that perhaps we should meet more often, maybe twice a week, once at the beginning and once at the end. I was thinking that perhaps one of the reasons why you're not developing at the rate you used to is that you aren't able to really focus—because your lessons are spaced too far apart. There's no continuity with the work we do here and the practicing and playing you do on your own."

Which is almost none, I wanted to say.

"I don't know," I said, though I did know. There was nothing I wanted less than to have double sessions with Mr. Trego.

"Think it over, Warren. We can talk about it next week."

I thought about Joan and what she might do in this situation. She would probably turn to him and say, No, we won't talk about it next week. I never want to take lessons from you, much less see you ever again. And if you call me or try to make me play another fucking Bartók sonata I'll call the fucking police!

"I've been very distracted lately," I said.

"I know, Warren, and you have every right to be."

"No, I mean for other reasons too." I was looking all around the room, searching for something to focus on: Mrs. Trego's plaid wool coat, an umbrella whose handle was carved into the shape of a duck's head, a small framed etching of a rabbit in a briar. "You see, I'm applying to college," I said distantly, "and I think I'll be going soon."

"What? You are? When? You didn't tell me that you were even applying! Warren, when did this happen?" He looked genuinely surprised, which made me glad.

"It's been in the works for a while now," I lied.

"It has?" He gasped. "Well! Where have you applied?"

"Just different schools, mostly around here, within driving distance," I said.

"When do you suppose you'll hear?"

"Any day, I guess," I said, "or in a few weeks."

"So, you'll be leaving? You'll be leaving town and your sister?"

"Oh, but I definitely think I'll start lessons up again, once I'm settled in school and everything. I'll definitely make time in my schedule for the piano."

I reach the bottom of Mr. Trego's hill. Granite Street is empty of traffic, and I think of how Joan and I had walked this way to town last fall to see the fall parade. It feels like it was years ago, but it was only a few months, three months. That was the day she saw Mike; we watched as his name was pulled from a hat for a raffle. And that's when they started up again. What a pit in my stomach I had on that day, when I saw his long body lope through the crowd to the gazebo to collect his prize. I remember Joan digging her nails into my arm, in shock, in awe. And soon he was calling the house, his voice garbled on the answering machine's failing tape. And then she was going out to meet him. Or he was coming into the bakery early, just when they opened, before he'd go to work. And then he'd come over, I'd hear them come in, clanking around in the kitchen, tromping up the stairs late at night. And I'd be there, ashamed and poised, listening to them next door in Joan's room, my ear pressed to the wall.

On that day, when we walked downtown to see the fall parade, I was asking Joan if she remembered something and she was giving me all kinds of horseshit about how she didn't remember it, or that her brain wasn't capable of retrieving such remote memories. What was I asking her? What was the memory I was trying to remember? It seemed so important that she remember it too, that we could assemble the memory between us. She'd told me it didn't matter. I remember I was pissed because she wouldn't even try. It had something to do with us, with Mom and Dad and us when we were children. I can't think of what it was.

Valerie's car comes over the crest of the bridge that passes over the train tracks.

"Hey, Warren," she says as she pulls over, rolling down the window on the passenger side.

"Hey," I say, not able to meet her eyes. "Where's Jake?"

"He's with my grandmother. I was at work," she says. "He had such a fun time with you guys the other day."

"Yeah, we had fun too," I say.

"I'm glad. He seems to have taken a real liking to you."

"Seriously?"

"Warren"—she grins—"it's not surprising."

I have no response.

"So, what are you doing out here?" she asks, with a blend of curiosity and concern, still smiling up at me. "Just out for a walk?"

"Sort of," I say. "It's nice out."

"A little cold."

"A little," I say. "But I don't really mind the cold."

"Really?"

"Well, you know. I don't like to freeze."

"Do you want a ride home? I could just turn around up there and drive you back."

"It's not exactly on your way. I don't want to trouble you."

"Warren." She laughs. "It's no trouble."

"Then, sure, OK," I say.

She unlocks the door and moves some books—library books—off the seat. Her car smells like incense and coffee. There are cracker crumbs in the crevices of the upholstery and random bits of cereal scattered around the floor. Between the dashboard and the windshield are a variety of broken shells and sand dollars. A chain of ivy hangs from the rearview mirror—Joan has one just like it, hanging from the mirror in her room; Helen gave it to her when she left the nursery for her job at the bakery.

"Sorry for the mess," says Valerie.

"Don't worry about it. I'm used to it."

"What?"

"Our house," I say. "It's always a mess."

"Oh," she says. "Should I take you home, then?"

I think for a minute. What do I have to do at home? What awaits me there?

"Or we could just drive around a bit," I say. "Or no, you probably have to go and pick Jake up. I don't want to make you late."

"No, you're not making me late," she says.

We're sitting side by side in the car. For a split second I wonder if my father had ever sat here with her, looking at her the way I am now. I decide to let it go.

"Let's pick up Jake and maybe drive around for a bit. Maybe go to the beach?" She looks at her watch. "But I don't want to make you late for anything. Do you have things to do today? Is Joan expecting you?"

I think about Joan. I think about how it might have been hard for her—painful, even—to tell me what she did. And I think about the other night, how we stood in the cemetery looking at our parents' stones—their names in script, the flowers we had brought them lying in the snow.

"No, she's not expecting me," I say. "I'll see her later on for dinner."

"So, should we go then?" she asks.

"We should go," I say.

42

Joan and I had steeled ourselves for the trip to the nursery. We hadn't been back since our fight with Richard, when he told us he was selling the place and had swindled us out of our money.

When we arrived, the nursery was almost empty; most of the employees were lethargic, as if everyone had just woken up. We went into the flower shop, where Helen was talking on the phone in Chinese. The conversation seemed angry and harsh, her voice firing off a flurry of quick verbal blasts. She looked up at us and smiled, blurted something terse into the receiver, and hung up.

"Roan! Wowren!" she said, and sprang up from her chair, hugging us both warmly, disappearing into the billows of our coats.

"Hi, Helen," Joan said. "Who were you talking to?"

"My ma!" she said and put her finger to her lips. "Don't tell that I called her." And then she laughed. "I ony call her when Richuwd is out 'cause it's long distance!"

"That's the right time to do it," I said supportively.

"Drain him dry," Joan said cheerfully.

Helen laughed for a good minute, and we stood and smiled at her until she was done. It was warm in the flower shop, and yet she was wearing a knit hat and leather-soled wool slippers. The hat was in the shape of a cylinder, a knit column of blue and green yarn, poised on her head like a chef's hat. She scuffed around the long marble-topped table; she pulled up some stools for us. We sat down and she gradually rose off the floor, ascending the stairs of a stepstool that was hidden from our view.

"I wan to talk to you guys but I have to finish this," she said, gesturing to an arrangement that had large slender leaves arching out of a simple square-shaped clay pot. "This is for the boss, he needs it to take to a party," she said, with a sour look that made us both laugh, "so sit and talk to me while I finish this, OK? It will be easier to finish with you here with me."

"Of course," Joan said.

We watched her put in and take out flowers one by one. She would put one in and turn the pot around and contemplate all sides and angles; the pot was on a turntable, so it was easy for her to do. We sat and watched as she added more leaves, taking out and putting in vines and thin, delicately knuckled bamboo poles. The arrangement consisted mostly of green leaves and ferns, a few light-colored flowers. There were no flashy blooms or bright ribbons; it looked like something that might grow in the shallow waters of a bog.

"Helen, I miss working with you and watching you work," Joan said, with a sigh.

"Oh, Roan, I miss you here!" she shouted, and she smiled deeply at Joan. I watched Joan look at her with admiration, asking her questions about plants she didn't recognize. And when Helen responded, she spoke to us both, looking back and forth between us.

"This is jewelweed," she said and held up a delicate stalk with pale yellow flowers.

"Isn't that an herb?" Joan asked.

"It is!" she said happily. "And a weed!"

"This is fennel. This is columbine." Gradually the pot was filled; around its edge fell the many shapes of leaves and stalks and petals. The arrangement rose high off the tabletop and poured down over itself like a fountain frozen in its own cascade. It looked amazing, lush and alive; I was mad that Richard was going to have it. I wanted it.

"It's beautiful," I said to her.

"Aw, Wowren, it's not. It's all green weeds. Like compost, but prettied up!"

"Perfect for Richard," I said.

"Yes, exac'ly," she said.

We admired her arrangement as she spun it slowly on the turntable.

"Helen, I'm afraid we have to go," Joan finally said.

"No!" Helen gasped.

"We're going to visit our parents," Joan continued, "and the cemetery closes soon."

"At sundown," I added needlessly.

Helen frowned. She stepped down from her ladder and left the room. She came back a minute later with two paper cones of flowers. She held them out and pointed to each of the flowers in the arrangements. "This is rue. These are violets. These are daisies." She smiled up at us, her black eyes glittering. "Each flower has a meaning."

"Thank you so much. These are beautiful," Joan said, and she bent down and hugged her.

"Thank you," I said, and then I hugged her too. "I like your hat, by the way."

"Aw, yes, it was a present. Walerie made it for me. It keeps me warm all the time. She gave it to me because I look after Jake some afternoons. Do you two know Walerie?" She asked this with a curious expression.

"Yes, we both know her," Joan said.

"We do," I said.

"She's our friend," Joan said.

"Good." Helen smiled.

As we were driving out of the nursery, we saw Richard. His truck was turning into the parking lot. As he passed by us, he looked right into the windshield of our car and then recognized who we were. We stared at his tired-looking face, his sunken eyes, sullen and dumb beneath the cuff of his watch cap. He was caught off guard. He looked shocked to see us. We just stared at him until he could do nothing more than give us a useless little wave. Then we drove away.

We got to the cemetery just as the custodian was preparing to lock the gates.

We said, "Please, we'll only be a few minutes."

We said, "We were caught up on our way here."

We said, "No, this can't wait until morning; we've brought flowers."

He let us in, locked the gate behind us, said he'd wait in the guardhouse to let us out when we were through. "Take your time," he said. "I'm just going to sit here and watch the game."

We drove through the snowy place to find them. The light was disappearing from the sky, and dusk began to set in until Joan cleaved the washy twilight with the headlights' beams. All around, the statues of children and their animals, the saints and crosses and angels, were coated in snow, perfectly fitted in white, like slipcovers. There was silence and stillness among everything around us as we drove along the roads, which had been plowed with immaculate precision. I felt no fear and no anticipation. Joan drove smoothly and steadily, with intent but without her normal anxious directive. Our car seemed to move toward our parents as if pushed by an invisible current, which we allowed, which we invited and were grateful for. The banks of snow and the white field that dissolved into the thick stands of trees at the cemetery's perimeter absorbed the sounds our car made and gave us entrance, invisibly; and we went in farther, undetected.

We parked the car and trudged our path through the snow to where our parents lay—the small plot beside a dogwood tree, a spindly wintry hand. We tamped down the snow to make a place for the flowers. We propped the cones against the stones and waited as they settled against the granite, their stems bowed but upright. We stood side by side, holding hands, the light from the headlights illuminating our parents' names, their dates, as our breath clouded around us.

We looked around, beyond the plot and the trees that surrounded us, into the sky, which was almost pink, crammed full of flurries. We looked down the hill and beyond the tree line out at the water, the black cloth of ocean and the red lights blinking high and distant on boats and, farther away, the muted flash of the lighthouse's beam. We could see the islands. Some of them we recognized and could name, while the shadows of others overlapped, forming new islands with shapes and names we could not know. Behind us, in the forests, I pictured the quarries, silenced by ice, the cold granite walls austere and abused, spray painted with words and hearts for which they had no use. And beneath the quarries, beneath the ice and clot of roots and trash and rock, there was water moving, filling, draining, and refilling the gulch; there is a spring somewhere below us, I thought.

Joan and I stood before their stones; our feet were cold in our boots. The car's headlights pulsed in a pitiful way, pleading with us to turn them off or start the engine to charge the battery. I ran and turned them off and joined Joan again, now in the darkness, standing where I had left her. In the sudden lack of headlights, everything around us began to realign, reorder, seek a new balance in the absence of light. Somewhere inside the snow, a flicker like a bulb spread its lambent glow evenly across the fields. And the stones sank in farther, pinned more steadily into place. All the saints and angels, everything carved from stone and set on columns to watch over this place, became alive or, if not alive, transformed, imbued, newly animated in the darkness. In this new light, the entire place seemed to be living by its own accord. And Joan and I, imperceptible, remained among them.

Our idea was that we'd leave the flowers by the graves. We'd meant to leave the paper cones leaning against the stones or resting on the curved crown of each granite block, poised above the carved names.

But we changed our minds. We peered down at the flowers leaning against the stones, freezing in the same air that we breathed. We knew they would die. We agreed that the image of them frozen and brittle in the morning was too sad to bear. It was not right to leave them here to die in the snow.

Joan looked at me, then crouched down and took her paper cone in her hands. The pale petals of the daisies glowed dimly against her coat. I could see her face; the shadow of her hair concealed her eyes and expression. Her skin was blue, luminous.

I imagined she was looking at me in the way I knew best, the way I had known since I was born, with her entire range of ire and disabled joy, with willfulness and patience. Her face showed concern for me. It showed annoyance. I saw her face in tears and confusion; it was enlightened, amorous. It was a child's face, a woman's. I looked at her through the scrim of evening, the flowers pressed against her jacket. I saw her completely. She was looking at me. The light was failing us. We didn't say a thing. There was no need. We were in agreement. I bent down and took the other flowers up from where they lay in the snow.

Acknowledgments

I would like to thank my family and friends for their patience and support. Thank you: Daniel Menaker, Deirdre Faughey, David McCormick, and Deborah Treisman.